"You're an incredibly sexy woman. Men want you. Men have always wanted you. Doctors, construction workers, chefs, waiters and pretty much everyone who knows you sees you're a wonderful woman. Don't let one jerk spoil it for every guy out there who wants a shot with you."

Was that what she had been doing? Jackson had hurt her, and to date, he was the one significant romantic relationship in her life. "What about you? Do you want a shot with me?"

Rafe leaned away. "Getting involved with each other won't be simple and safe. If that kiss was any indication, it would be hot and wild and absolutely consuming. I don't deserve a shot with you. I am leaving. And your brother carries a weapon."

A joke at the end of a harsh truth. Disappointment and sadness streamed through her. Future together or not, Gemma wanted Rafe. "I know that you can't offer me a future. But I want you to know that we would be good together. While you're trapped in Dead River, don't you think you should make the most of your time?" She lifted her lips to his.

Dear Reader,

Welcome back to Dead River, Wyoming! If you're new to the series, welcome. If you've read *A Secret Colton Baby* and *Her Colton Lawman*, you know that the residents of Dead River are under quarantine because of a deadly virus that threatens their lives.

The task of finding a cure for the virus falls to the staff of the Dead River Clinic. The people in Dead River are feeling their worst, and the doctors and nurses at the clinic are expected to perform at their best. For nurse Gemma Colton, she's everything a nurse should be: strong yet compassionate, determined yet gentle.

But Gemma needs someone to lean on, too. She turns to Rafe Granger, a doctor at the clinic. Dr. Rafe Granger is a driven man with something to prove. Being stuck in Dead River is his worst nightmare come to life, but he'll do everything he can for his patients. He's a good doctor, and the sooner he cures them, the sooner he can leave town. Except Gemma Colton is making him reconsider how he feels about Dead River and how he feels about her.

I had a great time working with Karen Whiddon, Carla Cassidy and Allison Carroll, our editor, on these books, and I hope you enjoy the final installment of this continuity.

Happy holidays,

C.J. Miller

COLTON HOLIDAY LOCKDOWN

—

C.J. Miller

HARLEQUIN® ROMANTIC SUSPENSE

Special thanks and acknowledgment to
C.J. Miller for her contribution to
The Coltons: Return to Wyoming miniseries.

ISBN-13: 978-0-373-27898-5

Colton Holiday Lockdown

Copyright © 2014 by Harlequin Books S.A.

Recycling programs
for this product may
not exist in your area.

Printed in U.S.A.

www.Harlequin.com

C.J. Miller loves to hear from her readers and can be contacted through her website, www.cj-miller.com. She lives in Maryland with her husband, son and daughter. C.J. believes in first loves, second chances and happily-ever-after.

Books by C.J. Miller

HARLEQUIN ROMANTIC SUSPENSE

This book is dedicated with love and gratitude to the Medstar Franklin Square Medical Center Pediatric Emergency Department and Inpatient Unit, especially Kim B., nurse extraordinaire. You all are amazing!

Chapter 1

Dr. Rafe Granger would never escape this rotting purgatory. The small, cramped town where he had grown up had sucked him back inside, barring and locking the gates behind him. If being trapped behind a perimeter monitored around the clock by armed guards wasn't bad enough, Rafe's return had brought with it a terrible series of events: an unidentified virus was claiming victims by the dozens, the virus research lab had been trashed and a murderer had escaped the local prison and was adding to the terror and paranoia of every person in town.

Unless he foolishly attempted to brave the Laramie Mountains and climb his way to freedom, there was no way to escape Dead River. For Rafe. For the killer. For anyone.

Rafe strode to his childhood friend and current Dead River Chief of Police, Flint Colton. "You know what we're trying to do here, don't you?" He knew he sounded like a perfect jerk, but he was beyond caring what anyone thought of him. He was angry and he didn't care who knew it.

Flint nodded, touching the brim of his cowboy hat. "I do." He sounded calm, which only frustrated Rafe more. Did no one in this town understand?

"This can't happen again." Rafe could feel the ends of his temper burning, but he couldn't help himself. Knowing two months of research into a cure for the Dead River virus, the virus that was responsible for quarantining the entire town, had been destroyed was enough to push him over the edge. "I'm going in there." He pointed to the clinic and pushed past Flint.

His old friend grabbed his arm. "Wait for Stan to clear the scene," Flint said, referring to Fire Chief Stan Burrell.

Rafe tugged his arm away. "Forget that. I need to see the damage." The clinic wasn't on fire. The fire had been contained. If it hadn't, they would have been evacuating the patients inside.

Flint didn't try to stop him again. Rafe entered the clinic through the single metal entry door. The smell of smoke hung in the air. Behind the reception area, the clinic's patient files had been pulled from the shelves and littered the floor, the rainbow of folder colors mocking him. The path of destruction led to the tiny, closet-sized offices he, Dr. Abigail Moore and Dr. Lucas Rand occupied. Rafe suspected they were once intended to be just that: closets. Dr. Rand's office had been broken into and searched a few days before by an unknown culprit. Rand had reported that some of his notes had been stolen. The culprit had returned to do much worse to Rafe's office and the lab.

The metal trash can in Rafe's office was charred, whatever had been inside unrecoverable. His computer was missing from its location on top of his desk and the two-drawer file cabinet tucked under the desk was overturned, papers spread on the floor and into the hallway. Dread pooled low in his stomach. What had been taken? What had the thief been looking for?

Rafe had not much of importance in his office. The most critical work had been stored in the lab. The mobile lab had been brought in to Dead River by the Centers for Disease Control and Prevention. State of the art, it was attached to the clinic via the backdoor. The lab had a biosafety level of four, the level reserved for research centers that worked with the world's most deadly viruses: Lassa, Ebola, Marbug and in this case, the unknown virus rampaging through Dead River. The lab had a closed venting system, complex HEPA filters for the air and epoxy surfaces for cleaning and sterilization. Though they were missing the proper security, like a round-the-clock guard and iris scanners to enter the lab, it was the best the CDC could do under the current conditions.

Given the events of late, skimping on security in lieu of expediency was a mistake.

Rafe checked and pulled on his protective gear and entered the lab, noting the lock was broken on the door. He connected his suit to the hoses that hung from the ceiling and then signed in, noting the last authorized person inside the room had been Dr. Rand, the doctor who had been on shift when the break-in had occurred. The staff at the clinic was working every spare hour they had to find a cure for the virus spreading through Dead River.

Only Dr. Moore hadn't been cleared to work in the lab due to her asthma.

Anger and frustration shook Rafe to his core. The inside of the lab was a disaster, tables overturned and petri dishes and beakers smashed to the ground. Equipment was thrown to the floor but the most alarming thing was what had been done to the samples. The small refrigerator they'd been using to store the carefully labeled Vacutainer tubes was open and emptied.

Rafe let loose a curse he almost never used. But this situation was beyond all repair.

He felt a hand on his back and whirled around, coming face-to-face with Gemma Colton, one of the clinic's registered nurses. He was ashamed of what he'd said when she most likely had overheard him, but her face spoke of the same anger he felt.

"Where are our samples?" Gemma asked, sounding shocked and panicked. Her green eyes were filled with concern. As many times as he had looked into those green eyes, the vibrancy and beauty of them struck him every time. She was the one pleasant surprise he'd found when he'd returned to Dead River. Young Gemma Colton was grown up and she was worth a long look.

Her voice sounded deeper through the microphone and speaker equipment built into the gear, making it possible to hear over the roar of the vents. Deeper and sexier, though some of it could be more related to her exhaustion than the speakers.

"Stolen," he said.

Gemma turned to scan the room.

Rafe and the clinicians had been collecting blood samples from every victim of the virus they could and looking for a common sequence. The process had taken thousands of man-hours and now, those samples were gone. Starting from ground zero would have a devastating impact on their research.

"Who would do this?" she asked.

Someone who didn't mind taking their life in their hands. Handling the blood samples that contained the virus was dangerous for the trained professionals at the clinic. The CDC expert, Dr. Colleen Goodhue, reminded them daily to exercise precaution whenever coming into contact with patients or working in the lab. She was understandably strict about following every security procedure. "That virus on the street is deadly," Rafe said.

"We already have an epidemic and now we have to worry about someone running around with vials containing the virus," Gemma said, her voice shaking.

Rafe heard shouts and banging from the clinic. He and Gemma exchanged looks. What else could go wrong? They exited the lab, stood in the chemical shower, removed their protective gear in the suit room, and hurried to find Anand Gupta, the clinic's other registered nurse, his normally calm demeanor vanished. He was standing in the clinic's storage room among shelves of ravaged supplies. Their drug locker had been forced open and bottles of life-saving medicines spilled on the ground.

The culprit had been bent on destruction. Rafe knew of no other explanation for this level of ruin. He had no understanding of why someone would do this. Who in Dead River didn't want a cure found?

"It will be days, if not weeks, before we receive another shipment to restock these supplies," Anand said.

Shipping products into Dead River was difficult and slow.

Gemma slipped her arm around the large man and hugged him. Rafe ignored the sense he was intruding on a private moment. Anand and Gemma were good friends and Rafe hadn't worked at the clinic as long as they had. Rafe didn't have the same connection with the staff Gemma and Anand did with each other and the rest of the doctors and nurses.

"Why don't you head home, Anand? Your shift is over and I'll clean up what I can," Gemma said.

Anand shook his head. "I'll stay a few more hours and help with this mess."

The staff was working twelve-hour shifts and far too many of them per week since the virus had started spreading.

Gemma and Anand bent to the floor to pick up supplies and organize the salvageable ones on the shelves. The small room didn't have enough space for the three of them, so Rafe excused himself. "I need to speak with Flint," Rafe said. He left the clinic via the front entrance and tried to put a lid on his anger. He was only wearing scrubs and the cold December air felt good, almost a welcome contrast to the heat of his fury.

Rafe needed answers. He needed a plan to put them back on track to finding a cure.

Flint was directing another officer who was taking pictures of the scene. He stepped away as Rafe approached.

"Is it as bad as you thought?" Flint asked.

"Worse. They took samples of the virus."

He didn't need to explain to Flint how devastating that was. Many residents of the town who had contracted the virus were remaining in their homes. The clinic didn't have enough beds or staff for every patient, though Dr. Goodhue was checking in with every known victim of the virus and tracking symptoms and changes.

"What are you doing about this?" Rafe asked.

Flint tipped his hat back on his head and in the sunlight, Rafe saw the dark circles of exhaustion around the chief's eyes. "Everything I can. I'm trying to keep this quiet and out of the media to avoid more panicking, but the virus is big news, maybe the only news anyone in this town wants to read about. I suppose the media would be distracted if we recaptured Hank Bittard, our resident killer-at-large, but we haven't managed that yet. I'll have some uniforms drive by the clinic more often, but we're stretched thin as is."

The clinic was stretched thin, too, and somehow, they were expected to do more with less. More patients, more problems, limited time and dwindling supplies. "Can't you ask the National Guard to help with security at the clinic? They have enough soldiers patrolling the border. They can spare a few men," Rafe said.

Flint shook his head. "No one in and no one out."

"We won't find an antidote if every time we take a step in the right direction, we're tossed back two," Rafe said. It took all his willpower to keep the edge off his words and not lash out at Flint.

"I'm sorry, Rafe. No one wanted this. Everyone is pulling for you to find a cure."

"Not everyone. Whoever did this doesn't want a cure found," Rafe said.

Flint folded his arms across his chest. "You have a theory on why?"

Rafe couldn't imagine anyone who wanted to stay in Dead River longer than they had to. "I have no clue why anyone would want this to drag on longer than it has to. The virus will keep spreading and claiming more lives."

Rafe, for one, couldn't wait to beat feet out of Dead River and not solely on account of the virus. He was honoring a promise he'd given his late father by working at the clinic. But that was as far as his commitment to Dead River extended. He wasn't getting entangled in small-town life again. He could almost hear his mother's raspy laughter knowing that he'd planned to stay a short time and now couldn't leave. She'd warned him about getting sucked into this tiny town. She used to say Dead River had wrapped its tentacles around her, one by one, until it was impossible to leave.

His mother's big dreams had died when she'd become a young mother. Rafe felt lucky he'd had an opportunity for an education outside the small Wyoming town and had used his career trajectory to escape.

Only now, he was back and he was stuck. He refused to let any of the town's charms keep him here. Not even his friendship with Flint or his attraction to Flint's sister, Gemma, would trap him. The job and the life he had worked hard for was waiting for him in New York City.

After a few minutes, feeling nervous about Rafe's irritation and what he might do, Gemma left Anand in the storage room with an apology and a promise to return. She followed Rafe outside. Her brother Flint was on the scene and she was worried about him and Rafe. Flint had been working too hard and while his new relationship with the Dead River Diner owner Nina grounded him, the pressure was wearing on him.

It was wearing on everyone.

Rafe, on the other hand, didn't have someone to confide in. From what she could see, he was married to his job and without an outlet for his stress, he was a time bomb. He behaved as if the patients at the clinic and finding the cure for the virus were his responsibility, and that was too much pressure for anyone. Rafe seemed to believe that the health and welfare of every single patient rested solely on his shoulders. Though Dr. Goodhue was leading the effort in finding a cure and lending her considerable expertise and experience, Rafe was driving them hard and closer to a breakthrough.

Gemma had tried to be a friend, but Rafe was a hard man to get close to. He was standoffish and prickly, bullheaded at times, and a strange combination of self-centered and completely selfless. Self-centered in that he thought he had control and selfless because he did it for his patients.

The most difficult trait for Gemma to deal with was how intensely handsome she still found Rafe Granger. Bad-boy-turned-doctor, wild-teenager-turned-disciplined-man and, oh, what a man he was. Sexy and brooding and someone she should stay far away from. Her brothers had warned her in high school about Rafe and her instincts warned her now. He was a twelve out of ten on the scale of her top temptations. Better than wine. Better than chocolate.

If she let him, he would burn her. He would break her heart. She knew it, but even that didn't stop her from thinking he was the single most fascinating man she'd ever met.

She was closer to her brother and Rafe now and she wished she had minded her own business and stayed inside to help Anand. She had often stood between her brothers Theo and Flint when they argued, but this was different.

She didn't know Rafe as well and he didn't have a soft spot for her the way her brothers did.

The tension between Flint and Rafe was palpable.

"Everything okay?" she asked, knowing it wasn't, but looking to tamp down their mutual frustrations.

"We've lost hundreds of hours of research," Rafe said.

"I know," Gemma said. "But we'll get it back." She didn't know how they could do more, but they would. Too many people were relying on the clinic to succeed.

Rafe stared at her incredulously. "How is that, Nurse Colton? Do you have the test data and the lab results and additional samples we can work with?"

His sharp tone stung. He was mad and having trouble controlling his temper.

"You know that I don't," Gemma said, countering his anger with a cool tone.

"Then how can we make this right?" he asked.

"We have the data we uploaded to the CDC. We have what we've learned. We won't make the same mistakes and we already know what doesn't work," Gemma said, thinking of the time they had lost because they'd stored earlier samples at the wrong temperature and killed the virus.

"Mistakes?" Rafe asked.

He and Dr. Rand insisted the temperature issue hadn't been a mistake. It was research. Gemma preferred to call a spade a spade. "I'll give you that if we could lower our patient's temperature to zero degrees Celsius for a time, the virus would die." A concession.

He scowled. "We learned from that same failure

that the virus can't live off a live host for more than a couple of hours."

"See? We have dozens of those observations that we can start with. We're not starting from a blank slate this time," Gemma said. "We're past the initial confusion. We know better what we're doing."

Rafe looked away, though his shoulders relaxed a fraction of an inch. She was calming him and she took it as a win. Every little forward step with Rafe was progress.

"Hey, easy," Flint said, patting Rafe's shoulder. "She didn't do this. She's trying to help."

Rafe rubbed his eyes, perhaps trying to shake off his exhaustion. "Let me tell you what I don't get. How did someone break into the clinic, trash my office, destroy the storage room and then decimate the lab without anyone hearing it? It took a flaming fire to set off the alarms and summon help."

Gemma agreed the timing was strange. "Dr. Rand, Anand and Felicia were in the virus wing. You know it's hard to hear inside the suits," she said. At least, it was her understanding that Felicia, Anand and Dr. Rand had been alone. The overnight shift was bare bones. Dead River wasn't big enough to support a hospital, so the clinic provided the town's medical services. Before the outbreak, complex and inpatient cases were referred to nearby Cheyenne Memorial. Now, they were short staffed, trying to run the clinic twenty-four hours a day.

"I'll look into it, Rafe," Flint said carefully. "Maybe someone saw or heard something that will help."

Rafe looked at the sky and then nodded at Flint. "Let me know if I can help. In the meantime, I have more samples to collect. We're starting over and I don't have time to waste."

He turned on his heel and stalked away.

Gemma stared after him for a few seconds, deciding if she should tag along to help or give him time to cool off.

"Careful, Gemma," Flint said.

Gemma inclined her head at her brother. "Careful about what?"

"He's not sticking around. I know that look in your eyes. You can't save him. Rafe is a man with too many demons."

Gemma straightened. She wasn't thinking about saving Rafe, but she could be a friend, one he sorely needed. If he could stop seeing her as his friend's annoying kid sister, they could have a real relationship. "The look in my eyes is a look of concern. I am worried about you. I am worried about everyone on staff here. I am worried about my patients." She threw up her hands and gestured around them. "I am worried about everyone in this town if we don't find a cure."

Flint slid his arm around her shoulders. "I know you are. You have the warmest heart I've ever met, except for maybe Gram Dottie."

At the mention of their grandmother, Gemma's heart fell. "I'm worried about her," Gemma said. Their grandmother had contracted the virus and had been admitted to the virus wing because her case was severe. Gram Dottie was tough, but the virus was proving tougher. As yet, not a single person had recovered.

"Me too," Flint said. He kissed the top of his sister's head. "Go help Rafe. He's always been rough around the edges, but he's smart. I've got my money on you and him to find the cure."

Gemma was doing everything she could, but virology and epidemiology weren't her fields of expertise. "We'll find the cure. You find who did this," Gemma said. She hugged her brother goodbye, smiling when she smelled Nina's perfume on him. She was happy to know her brother finally had someone special in his life.

Gemma returned to the clinic and put on her protective suit. She entered the virus wing, where she knew she'd find Rafe. She didn't hear him over their comm system. He must have shut off his microphone.

He was in one of their patients' rooms. From his demeanor, if she hadn't witnessed it herself, she wouldn't have known he'd been upset. With his patients, he was warm and concerned. He joked with them, laughed with them and didn't rush them, taking time to answer questions at length. With the influx of critical cases, they were short on time, but Rafe didn't make anyone feel that way. He had an easy way about him that was disarming.

Rafe was the only doctor on staff who drew patients' blood samples. Dr. Goodhue, Dr. Rand and Dr. Moore always called for a nurse to take care of the task. It was another way in which Rafe was different. From the time Gemma had started working at the clinic, she was an assistant to the doctors. Rafe didn't make her feel like she was helping him. When they worked together, she felt she was pulling her weight and making important contributions.

Gemma entered the room and Rafe glanced over his

shoulder at her. "How can I help?" She had to speak loudly for Rafe to hear her over the venting in his suit.

"We need samples from each of our patients," Rafe said.

He was accustomed to giving orders. His tone was mellow, but Gemma heard the edge and the command.

Carter Saunders, a wrangler in his midforties, struggled to sit up. "Have you made any progress on a cure?"

Rafe hadn't told Carter about the break-in and fire at the clinic. They needed to keep their patients' spirits high. Rafe had undertaken the project to make their patients more comfortable, setting up video streaming on-demand via the small televisions in the rooms and providing e-readers for patients. He'd also configured video conferencing software on laptops so patients could see and talk with their families during their extended time in isolation. His kindness touched her and his savvy with technology impressed her.

"Every day, we're getting closer," Rafe said.

"Can I bring you anything while I'm here?" Gemma asked Carter. Since the outbreak, the clinic had taken to serving food around the clock to their patients. The Dead River Café and the Blue Bear Restaurant were dropping off soup and meals for the patients and staff daily. It was an unexpected and welcome convenience. The clinic hadn't been constructed to provide food service, and without an on-site kitchen, Gemma guessed she and the other nurses would be heating canned soups over Bunsen burners for their patients.

"Some more water," Carter said.

"I'll be right back," Gemma said. She retrieved water from the small sink in Carter's room. Though the patients had confirmed cases of the Dead River virus, they were confined to their rooms to prevent the spread of symptoms.

Gemma sat with Carter for a few minutes, and as he dozed off to sleep, she and Rafe slipped from the room. The Dead River virus was exhausting for patients to fight. Some slept fifteen to sixteen hours a day. Keeping them hydrated and eating enough nutrients was a challenge.

Rafe typed notes on Carter's chart and Gemma moved to the next room.

Tammy Flynn, their youngest patient, a six-year-old girl, was watching television in her room when Gemma entered. Her parents video-conferenced with her several times a day, but the separation was taking its toll. Tammy had grown close to Gemma and Gemma had "adopted" her as her temporary daughter.

Thinking about what the virus was doing to families broke her heart. Gemma didn't allow her patients to see her break down, but some nights, she returned home and did just that. The Dead River virus had brought so much heartache to this town.

"Hey, Tammy," Gemma said, coming to the girl's bedside.

"I have a gift for you," Rafe said, entering the room behind Gemma.

He handed Tammy a shiny pink gift bag. Tammy's eyes grew wide and she opened it, pulling out plastic beakers and tongs and a pair of goggles.

"This is awesome!" The little girl held up a plastic beaker with the tongs.

"That's really cool," Gemma said, surprised at Rafe's thoughtfulness. When had he had time to acquire such a gift and how?

"I told you I would bring some lab equipment so you could help me," Rafe said.

Was she hearing the conversation properly? As distant and cool as Rafe was with everyone in Dead River, he had certainly allowed Tammy into his heart. It was touching and Gemma wondered how detached Rafe was able to stay.

"Please show me what to do," Tammy said, sounding excited.

"We'll set it up," Rafe said.

With a couple pitchers of water and some food coloring, Tammy was conducting her own study. She fell asleep with her beakers lined up on the slim table next to her bed.

After they left the room, Rafe took notes on the laptop in the hallway to update Tammy's case. The notes would be sent electronically to their record system in the main clinic and uploaded to the CDC at the end of the week.

"That was really nice of you," Gemma said. It wasn't the first gift Rafe had brought Tammy or the other patients. The staff tried to think of activities to keep boredom and cabin fever at bay. Rafe had a knack for coming up with games for Tammy to play.

"Danny helped me put it together," Rafe said. "I told him about Tammy and he thought of it."

Danny was Rafe's foster son. Rafe mentioned him often, though he didn't delve into much detail about him. The few times Gemma had tried to draw him out, Rafe hadn't taken the bait.

"I'll take Jessica's blood sample," Gemma said.

Rafe's hand on her arm stopped her. Even with layers of plastic between them, her skin prickled with desire. Rafe dripped charisma and a raw sensuality she couldn't ignore.

"Are you planning to tell her what happened?" Rafe asked.

Jessica was Gemma's best friend. They told each other almost everything. But Jessica was pinning her hopes on the staff at the Dead River Clinic finding a cure and if she knew how much they had lost that night, she'd be devastated. A blow to her morale was bad for her health.

"No, not today," Gemma said.

Rafe nodded his approval. Gemma collected the supplies she needed.

Jessica had lost ten pounds since being admitted. She was a tall, slender woman and didn't have the weight to spare. Jessica smiled when Gemma entered the room. She put the television on mute. "Tell me you have some good news."

Gemma double-checked that her microphone was off so Rafe wouldn't hear their conversation. "I dropped off Annabelle with Molly before I came to work. Molly was planning to meet Ellie and Amelia at the library for story time."

"She'll love that." Jessica closed her eyes. Like most of their patients, she'd been chronically tired, sleeping the majority of the day. It was difficult to see Jessica, who was normally active, being so listless. "How is Tom holding up?" she asked.

Jessica's husband Tom was struggling under the weight of his responsibilities of being a single parent while Jessica was in isolation. Gemma and her cousin Molly had stepped in to lend a hand, but he wouldn't feel better until Jessica was home. "He's doing the best he can."

Jessica smiled a weak half smile. "That bad?"

Tom had confided how scared he was for Jessica and for their daughter Annabelle. He worried about his little girl becoming another of the virus's victims. His worry wasn't unique. Some parents had stopped sending their children to school because of that fear. "He loves you and he wants you to feel better," Gemma said.

"I know. I love him and Annabelle too. I'm trying. But this virus is like a flu that won't quit."

Many of the virus's symptoms were similar to the flu, which was how they had missed the severity with their first case. The flu wasn't an emergency, not for someone otherwise healthy, as their first virus patient had been. This virus was new territory for them. "I uploaded new pictures for you to look at and a video of Annabelle reading a new book from school."

"Thank you for everything that you're doing. Talking to my family and you is getting me through this." At Gemma's prompting, Jessica took a sip of the drink at her bedside. "Tell me what's new with you. You tell me about my family, but you have a lot going on too."

Gemma rolled her eyes. "It's a regular revolving door of men at my place. Everyone's looking to score a date with the plague nurse who works all the time. When I can, I've been visiting Theo, Ellie and baby Amelia. She's getting big so fast and I love spending time with her."

"They do that. One minute, you're cradling them in your arms, the next, they're grown and rolling their eyes at you. What about that new doctor? He's worth a second look."

"Rafe? He's not new exactly," Gemma said, feeling the heat rush to her cheeks.

Jessica hadn't attended high school with Gemma. Tom had moved to town to work on Theo's ranch, bringing his pregnant wife with him and Gemma had hit it off with Jessica immediately. They'd been fast friends ever since. "Oh, come on, you said you thought he was cute in high school. What about now?"

Still cute, although seeing him now brought entirely different feelings. She didn't feel like giggling and blushing when she saw him. She felt like seeing if he was as incredible a kisser as he was a doctor. "He is. I'm not blind. But I'm also not interested in an affair. He's only here until we find a cure for the virus, then he's heading back to New York City. His dream job awaits him."

"His dream job, but maybe his dream girl is right here."

Gemma laughed. "No way. I dated a doctor once and you know how that went down. Badly. Like a ten-mile-long-train-wreck badly."

Jessica sighed. "I do. But that was one person, one time. You can't judge the whole lot of doctors over one jerk."

Gemma waved her hand. "I'm too busy, anyway. I'll worry about finding a boyfriend when men can come and go freely in this town."

"Valentine's Day is right around the corner."

A day Gemma didn't like much. Being single for the majority of Valentine's Days in her life gave her a different perspective. The perspective that she didn't need another excuse to drink wine and eat chocolates—

that she bought herself—in her home alone. "Not right around the corner. It's not even Christmas yet."

"You know as soon as those Christmas decorations are put away, the red hearts and boxes of chocolates come out," Jessica said.

Gemma nodded, but she thought of the bare shelves at the grocery store and shops along Main Street. If the quarantine wasn't lifted, nonessentials like seasonal items wouldn't make it on the shipments into town.

She couldn't imagine this dragging on for that many months more, but what if it did? What if every person in Dead River succumbed to the virus?

Dr. Colleen Goodhue said she had only seen rare cases where a virus obliterated an entire town, usually in third world countries. The Dead River virus was proving to have staying power. It was stronger and stealthier because it kept its human host alive long enough to infect many others.

With her grandmother and best friend sick, Gemma had plenty of reasons to devote everything she had to finding a cure. Knowing so much was on the line only drove her harder.

Chapter 2

At the end of her shift, Gemma found Dr. Goodhue and Rafe in the lab. Dr. Goodhue seemed shell-shocked as she looked through some notebooks, but as usual, Rafe worked like a man on a mission.

"It's hard to believe someone would do this," Dr. Goodhue said. "I called the home office and they said they'd send more supplies, but it will take time. How will our research continue without a proper lab?"

Gemma didn't like to hear Dr. Goodhue sounding distraught. She was the most experienced in this type of work and while the break-in and fire were upsetting, they didn't have the option to quit.

"We'll work with what we have left," Rafe said.

Rafe wouldn't let time pass while they waited for a shipment and forgo possible progress. From the beginning, he had been driving them hard, urging them to work more and longer. He had good reasons, but sometimes Gemma thought breaks and time away could give them a fresh perspective.

What did Rafe do with his free time? Did he have free time? Gemma didn't go out often, and rarely now that she worked so much. What would it be like to have a social life again and how would she feel if Rafe was part of it? Her conversation with Jessica had given her something to think about.

"What is left?" Dr. Goodhue asked, slamming closed the notebook she was reading.

Gemma had spaced out. Was Dr. Goodhue speaking to her?

"Rafe and I collected blood samples from our current patients. Those are places to start," Gemma said.

"What about patient zero? We can't obtain more blood from her!" Dr. Goodhue said.

Until they had evidence to prove otherwise, they believed Mimi Rand was patient zero. Mimi Rand, the ex-wife of Dr. Lucas Rand, had died in the clinic, but not before she had infected several other people in town.

"We don't know that blood from patient zero will help," Rafe said.

Rafe had mentioned the possibility of the virus morphing over time. Their patient information indicated that patients who had contracted the virus early on seemed to be faring better than those who had been admitted more recently.

Mimi Rand was dead. Dozens of others had died. These were facts not far from Gemma's thoughts.

"We'll salvage what we can and we'll reproduce the results we need," Gemma said. "Rafe? Our shift ended an hour ago. I've been waiting to speak with you." She had decided she would reach out again, offer her friendship and see if he needed to talk.

Rafe turned in his chair. He looked at her as if he expected her to speak to him now. At least he'd faced her.

"Alone. Please," Gemma said. Talking in their protective suits was uncomfortable and no way would Rafe open up in front of Dr. Goodhue. He might not open up at all, but the chances were better if they were alone.

Rafe stood. He looked at the clock on the wall. "All right. Let's scrub out."

Twenty minutes later, changed into street clothes, Gemma searched for the right words to explain what was on her mind. The latest interference in their research was a good reason to take a step back and regroup. If they were tired and run-down, they'd be ineffective and inefficient. Maybe if Dr. Rand, Anand and Felicia hadn't been so drained, they would have heard the break-in and prevented someone from getting into the lab.

"I'm hungry. Mind grabbing a bite with me at the diner?" Gemma asked. A friendly environment would make it easier to talk. In the clinic, despite his treating her as a colleague, Gemma still felt strict professional boundaries.

"I have dinner with Danny," he said.

She didn't want to give up so easily. "You can grab some carry-out. This won't take long."

"You can't tell me what you need now?" he asked. He used that irritated tone he sometimes had with the rest of the staff. Gemma ignored it. Some doctors thought they could strong-arm others into bending to their will.

Gemma was not one of those people. Even though she didn't enjoy confrontation, someone needed to talk to Rafe and have him blow off some steam before his head exploded.

"No." Gemma folded her arms across her chest.

Rafe jammed a hand through his hair. "You are persistent. You win. Let's go."

He'd agreed if only because he knew she wouldn't back down. That was fine with her. When she had a problem on her mind, she needed to say it. Then she would smooth things over.

The Dead River Diner was crowded. As they searched for a free booth, Rafe felt eyes on him. He was accustomed to stares in this town. From the time he had been a young boy, he'd been given looks that made it plain he was not welcome.

Whether it was because he was now an outsider or his medical degree hadn't covered the stench of being from the worst part of town, he wasn't welcome in Dead River. He had never felt it more than now.

He ignored the looks, like he always had. He slid into a booth across from Gemma. Why did she need to talk here? It had been a long, bad day. He wanted to go home, have dinner with Danny and catch up on some virology articles that were waiting for him. One might spark an idea that could lead to a cure.

"Dr. Granger—"

Too formal. "When we're not working, call me Rafe."

He almost surprised himself, but the words had come naturally.

"Rafe," Gemma started again, sounding unsure. "How can I help your stress level?"

Rafe inclined his head. "My stress level?"

Gemma shifted in her seat. "We're under a tremendous amount of stress, but you most of all. You drive us hard and yourself harder—"

He felt a criticism coming from her pink mouth. "Are you saying you need a break?" Losing a member of their staff would be hard, but he wouldn't work someone into the ground. If she needed to step back from her duties, he understood.

Green eyes narrowed. "I don't need a break. I'm concerned about you."

Why? He hadn't come apart. "No reason to be. I know my limits."

The waitress took their order. Rafe asked for his food to go and a coffee. He couldn't feed Danny cereal or a sandwich again as a meal. They were guys, but Rafe had hit his limit on crap food and Danny was a growing teenager.

The waitress lingered at the table. "Any news?" she asked.

About the cure? The break-in? "About what?" Rafe asked. He'd been in the clinic and didn't know if news of the break-in had hit the gossip mill. It was Dead River, so most likely it had.

The waitress looked around. "About the virus. I heard you found a cure, but it ended up making everyone sicker. Is that true?"

If they'd had a cure that made people sicker, it wouldn't be a cure. Luckily, Gemma answered before Rafe could make any more enemies with his sarcastic response.

"We're doing our best, but we're still working on it," Gemma said.

The waitress frowned. "It's been months. Have you tried asking for outside help?"

Rafe kept his temper. It was difficult for people of the town to believe that finding a cure wasn't a straightforward task. It wasn't as if the clinic had a computer that would take the virus, find the antidote and print it out on paper like a recipe for them to mix. "There are a number of factors at play. We're closing in on it," Rafe said. He curbed the urge to say more.

The waitress nodded. "Okay, thanks. Everyone is so worried." She bit her lip. "I'll put your order in."

Gemma reached across the table, and then drew her hands back into her lap. "Dr. Granger, she didn't mean to be insulting."

The people of Dead River wanted a cure found and they were putting their faith in the clinic to deliver. "It's hard to explain to someone why we don't have a cure."

"Everyone knows you're an exceptional doctor," Gemma said.

He didn't need his ego stroked. "But what?"

Gemma smiled. "But I am worried you'll burn out. You can't keep going at the pace you're going and not break down."

She had no idea what he could and could not do. Since he had gotten out of Dead River, he had worked as if the devil was chasing him and would catch him if he slowed. College, medical school, a fellowship with the CDC and his residency had led to the pinnacle of his success: a position as an ER doctor at Presbyterian University Hospital in New York.

"I will not have a breakdown. Is this about getting upset with Flint earlier today?" The Coltons had always stuck together. Rafe understood if she was sticking up for her brother.

"This isn't about Flint. He's a big boy and he can take it. This is about you. You're the only doctor who works additional shifts." Gemma pointed to the coffee the waitress had slid in front of him. "Is that the majority of your meals?"

Rafe glanced at the coffee. He wasn't keeping track of his food. "Worried I'll have shaky hands during a procedure?"

Gemma shook her head. "Please hear me. I am not concerned about how you treat others. I am not concerned about your patients. I am concerned about you and how you will drive us crazy if you don't ease off."

Gemma had struck a nerve. Ease off. Slack off. Sit around and wait for someone else to do the work. He would set Gemma straight now. "I do not expect you or anyone else to help." The cold in his voice hit its mark. Gemma drew away and her face dropped.

"I can do this entirely on my own if that's what it takes. I don't need to rest. I need to find a cure to help the people of this town get better. I will not put my personal needs ahead of someone's life."

Gemma seemed shocked and then gathered herself. "That's not really true is it, Dr. Granger? You want to help our patients, but you have another motive."

He'd made no secret of his desire to escape this town. "Like everyone else here, I can't wait to leave."

Gemma drew back. "I don't want to leave."

She wouldn't. She had a great family, people who cared about her and she'd gone with the flow and seemed happy doing what was expected of her. Even in high school, she'd been the school's sweetheart, not popular exactly, but few had a bad word to say about her. "Then I guess that's one reason we don't get along. I don't want to be here a minute longer than I have to."

Gemma leaned in and glared at him. "You can try that bad-boy routine on me, but I see through you. You're here because you want to be."

He snorted. "You know nothing about me. I am here because of a promise I foolishly gave."

"Why not break the promise if you hate it here?"

"Because breaking a promise to a dead person would make me the tyrannical, self-serving shithead you're implying I am."

Gemma's mouth dropped open. "I said no such thing."

Rafe threw several twenties on the table. "See you at work."

He fled the diner and ignored the looks from the people around him. He didn't need their condescension and he didn't need this town.

Rafe opened the door to his rental, a two-story, three-bedroom colonial. It was too big for him, though somehow he thought it was too small for him and Danny. The teenager seemed to have a lot of stuff, or maybe it seemed that way because nothing was ever put away.

"Danny! Are you home?" Rafe asked.

Rafe was accustomed to some signs that Danny was inside. Muddy shoes by the door, winter jacket thrown over the chair in the living room or the sound of music pulsing from the boy's bedroom.

It was quiet.

"Danny!"

Was he wearing headphones?

Rafe took the oak stairs to Danny's room and found it empty. No backpack slung on the floor. Rafe picked up an empty box of cookies and tossed it in the trash. He called the cell phone he'd given to Danny, but the call went directly to voice mail.

Worry knotted in his stomach. He gave Danny his freedom and his privacy, as Danny's grandfather had, but Rafe and Danny had an agreement. Danny would let Rafe know where he was and when he would be home and Rafe did the same for him. That morning, Danny had told him he'd come home directly after football practice. After the fire at the clinic, Rafe had texted him that he would be late tonight. Danny was usually good to his word.

Rafe called the Dead River Youth Center. It was a safe place for students to hang out after school and Danny had friends there. Maybe he'd forgotten to tell Rafe he'd changed his plans. A quick call to the director of the youth center and Rafe was again at square one. Danny wasn't there.

His worry increased. Dead River was usually quiet, but with the virus outbreak and a murderer hiding somewhere in town, Rafe didn't like the idea of Danny anywhere alone. He could be sick and unable to call for help. His cell phone battery could have died.

Danny wasn't naïve or helpless, but Rafe cared about the boy. His anxiety ticked up a notch. Returning to his car, he drove the short distance Danny walked to school, checking the sidewalks.

No sign of him.

Football practice was over. The field was clear. Rafe's phone rang and he fumbled to answer it. It wasn't Danny. Worse still, it was Flint. If he was calling because Danny had been hurt, Rafe wouldn't forgive himself. He should have called Danny after school or told him to text when he was home safe. He hated to place restrictions on Danny, but how else did a parent keep a son safe?

Rafe stuttered on the thought. Not that he was Danny's father. Foster father was a big stretch from real father. Still, he'd taken Danny in without any parenting experience and he'd had no idea how hard it would be.

"Flint, what's going on? Is it Danny?" Rafe rarely felt this panicked. Panic was an emotion he had learned to lock away in emergencies.

"No. Why? Isn't he with you?"

At least Danny hadn't been found hurt. "He's late from practice," Rafe said.

"Sounds like this is a bad time, but I need you back at the clinic."

Another outbreak? "What's happened?"

"Someone's attacked Dr. Rand."

Dr. Rand wasn't a small man. He could handle himself. It would be ballsy for someone to openly attack him. "Is he okay?"

"Shaken, but okay."

"What about Gemma?" Rafe asked. He had second thoughts about leaving her at the diner. Had she returned home safely? Recent events gave Rafe plenty of reasons to worry.

"I talked to her a few minutes ago. Gemma's fine, why?" Flint asked.

"I was curious." More than curious. Though Gemma was intrusive and pushy and seemed too eager to talk about how everyone felt, he liked her. She was good at her job and he enjoyed working with her.

If she had wanted, she could have her pick of hospitals to work in.

Rafe changed directions and drove to the clinic. He called Danny several more times on his cell phone.

He even tried calling a couple of Danny's friends.

They hadn't seen him since football practice. He tried Danny's brother, Matt, who hadn't spoken to Danny recently. When Rafe arrived at the clinic, he parked in the lot. Half the spots were piled with snow and the ice underfoot was slick. In this part of Wyoming, snow and ice would stick around until the spring melt.

Rafe strode directly to Flint. It was the second incident at the clinic in twenty-four hours. "Did you find the person who did this?" Rafe asked. They had to have a lead to find and stop the person hindering the clinic's research and attacking the staff.

Flint shook his head and pointed to the ambulance where Dr. Rand was being examined by a paramedic. "That's what I need to speak with everyone about. Whoever is targeting the clinic is now targeting the staff. I need everyone to be careful."

Rafe should ask the paramedic if he needed a consult. It wasn't like Kit could take Dr. Rand to the nearest hospital in Cheyenne. Rafe approached and waited for Kit to acknowledge him. Nothing was more irritating than another medical provider intruding during an exam.

"Hey, Dr. Granger, good to see you. Wish it was under better circumstances," Kit said. Rafe had known Kit in high school. Even after so many years, she still had a splash of freckles across her nose and a warm smile.

Josh Hadaway, the EMT, climbed out of the back of the medic. "Crazy times around here, huh?"

Rafe was familiar with Josh from drop-offs at the clinic from time to time.

Dr. Rand was looking sad. Or was he embarrassed? Angry? Rafe wasn't a huge fan of Dr. Rand's. Lucas was arrogant, even more arrogant than most doctors. He'd claimed he had a cure for the virus, but it had proven to be ineffective with their patients. Rafe wasn't sure why the man had thought his "cure" would do anything. Their lab tests were nowhere near ready to make such a claim.

"Dr. Rand, I'm sorry to ask you to tell your story again, but maybe you've remembered additional details," Flint said, joining them.

Dr. Rand sighed and rubbed his face. "We have enough problems in this town. I don't want anyone in trouble."

Flint arched a brow and Rafe tamped down his irritation. They didn't have time for this! If they could find the attacker, maybe they could recover their lab results or samples. Could Dr. Rand identify his assailant?

"The faster we find the person who stole our samples and destroyed our lab, the better off we'll be. We can't have these endless setbacks," Rafe said, using the voice he usually reserved for speaking to his patients. Calm and relaxed. Rand wouldn't respond well to irritation and threats.

Out of the corner of his eye, Rafe saw Gemma approach. She was wearing the same clothes she'd had on at the diner, but she'd done her hair differently. It was braided over her shoulder. He liked it. Too much.

Gemma stood between her brother and Rafe. Gemma shivered as the wind blew stronger. Rafe removed his jacket and draped it over her shoulders and Gemma looked at him in surprise. "Thank you," she said.

"Dr. Rand, please tell us what you know," Flint said.

Rafe took his eyes off Gemma, though he could see her watching the exchange intently.

"We don't need to stand in the cold debating this," Dr. Rand said.

They weren't debating anything. They were waiting for Dr. Rand to tell them what he knew. Did everything with Dr. Rand need to be a production? The man's eyes welled with tears and if he hadn't recently lost his ex-wife and wasn't struggling with his grief, Rafe would have punched him. He wanted to tell him to stop crying and focus on what was important. Like finding the vandal and finding a cure.

"I was attacked as I was leaving the virus wing. I only caught a glimpse of him."

A disgruntled patient? A dissatisfied woman Dr. Rand had had a one-night stand with? Rafe kept his thoughts to himself. He was in a bad mood and he didn't need to share his mood with everyone.

"That boy who's living with Dr. Granger. Danny. He attacked me," Dr. Rand said.

Flint and Gemma turned to Rafe. His denial was immediate. "You're mistaken. Danny had football practice after school."

"Where is Danny now, Rafe?" Flint asked.

Rafe had already told Flint that Danny hadn't been home. Rafe felt Gemma's hand on his back, her touch the only factor keeping him from going off the rails. Typical for the poor kid to be blamed, the kid from the wrong side of the tracks. The kid who'd had a rougher childhood than most of these elitists could imagine. "He wasn't home when I got there tonight. I don't know where he is."

He wouldn't feed Flint any more details to use against Danny.

"I didn't want to say anything. I know he's had a hard time, with his grandfather dying and his brother taking off and leaving him," Dr. Rand said.

Quiet rage hummed inside him. Danny's brother, Matt, hadn't taken off. Matt hadn't been prepared to care for a fourteen-year-old boy and had let Danny enter the foster care system. Rafe understood where Matt was coming from. Rafe was years older and had access to more resources, and still he had trouble keeping track of Danny at times. Hence, his lack of knowledge about where the boy was. "Danny wouldn't hurt someone. It isn't in his nature."

"You just said he plays football. Aggressive sport," Dr. Rand said.

What did Dr. Rand play in high school? The flute? "Danny has no reason to attack you," Rafe said. Danny and Dr. Rand had met once or twice when Rafe had brought him to the clinic, but Danny wouldn't lash out at Dr. Rand. They'd barely spoken.

"If a cure isn't found, then the quarantine remains in place and you have to stay in town," Dr. Rand said. "That could be worth a lot to a boy who's lost everything else."

Guilt tripled in Rafe's stomach. He'd agreed to take Danny into his home because Danny needed a place to live and Rafe thought he could help him. Help him through some of his grief, show him a life outside of Dead River was possible and put him on track to build a good future. Had he been wrong to take the boy into his home knowing he'd be around only a short time?

"I'll try to reach him again," Rafe said. He took a

few steps away and dialed Danny. Speed dial number two. Why wasn't Danny answering?

The call went to his voice mail again.

Rafe's emotions were a combination of anger with Rand and worry and fear for Danny. He returned to the group. Gemma was watching him, worry plain on her face.

"It will be his word against mine, and it's more trouble than it's worth. I won't press charges, but I want that punk to stay away from me."

Rafe ignored the name calling and addressed Flint. "I'll find him. I've been worried." But now, he was deeply concerned.

"When you find him, I want to talk to him," Flint said. His words seemed to please Dr. Rand, which may have been his intention.

"I'll go with you," Gemma said.

"I can handle it. You don't have to take care of everyone," Rafe said.

Gemma flinched, but then lifted her chin. "You are in no condition to drive and search. You tell me where you want to look and I'll take you."

She was right. It was dark and while he had a short list of places where Danny might be, what would he do if Danny wasn't there? He'd need to search the town and two people working the problem were better than one.

"Come on," Rafe said. He tossed her his keys.

Gemma slid into the driver's seat and adjusted it so she could reach the pedals. "We'll find him, Rafe. I'm here for you."

It wasn't the first time she had spoken those words to him. Did she remember the last time? Years before, when they'd been in high school together, Rafe had been desperate to leave Dead River. Even then, he'd hated this tiny, small-minded town. He'd gotten fired from his job at the record store because he'd been late for work again. His reasons for being tardy hadn't mattered to the store owner, but then again, Rafe hadn't explained that his father was on a bender and he'd stayed with his mom until his father had shown up because she had been worried. Gemma had tried to console him with those same words while he had waited for his father to show.

Drunkard fathers were something he had in common with Gemma, though his had eventually gotten sober. It wasn't anything they discussed. Rafe's father had been inconsistent, unreliable and more bent on getting drunk than moving his family out of the trailer park where they'd lived. Rafe had hated that trailer park. Hated it and everything it had stood for. Gemma's father was destructive on a whole other level. Showing up now and then, causing problems, embarrassing his family and leaving her grandmother to raise her and her brothers.

"I know you and Mr. Sergeant were close," Gemma said.

Rafe made a sound of acknowledgment. He and Danny's grandfather, a guidance counselor at the high school, had gotten along. Rafe credited Danny's grandfather for getting him into Harvard University, which had changed the course of Rafe's life. "He knew I wanted out of Dead River and he gave me a study guide for the SATs. I read that book cover to cover." Multiple times. He'd practically memorized it. Donald "Donny" Sergeant had told Rafe if he wanted a ticket out of Dead River, he'd have to earn it. Rafe'd had decent grades, but his SAT score had been the clincher to a full ride at Harvard.

"Now you can't wait to leave again," Gemma said.

Her voice held the slightest censure. "Can you blame me?"

"For wanting to leave? No. For not seeing how much you have here, yes."

Her words struck a chord in him, but he didn't want to talk about the reasons he could not stay. "Can you drive by the graveyard?"

Gemma turned his car in that direction.

"You can say it, Gemma." He could practically hear her thoughts.

"You say mean things to me because you want to keep me at arm's length. Me and everyone. Why?" Gemma asked.

He did no such thing. He didn't sink time into his relationships because he didn't have time. Danny was an exception and he felt guilty that he couldn't do more for him. "I am doing everything I can." He was working at the clinic. He was working for a cure. Why wasn't that enough?

"Danny adores you," Gemma said.

"I know. He's a great kid."

Another pause. "What will happen to him if you leave?" Gemma asked.

As if he hadn't asked himself that question before and struggled with the answer. On a good day, he told himself he'd bought the foster care system another three months to find Danny a suitable, permanent place, one with experienced parents who could give Danny a family. He'd been honest with the social worker about his limitations. The social worker knew Rafe planned to return to New York City. Rafe was listed in their system as "temporary."

On a bad day, Rafe couldn't think about Danny being passed from family to family trying to find a fit. He couldn't stand the idea of someone taking Danny in who cared more about the stipend than Danny. "The same thing that would have happened if I hadn't returned to Dead River."

"I am glad that you did," Gemma said. "Even if it's for a short time."

Rafe wouldn't read into her words. Why was she glad? Why did she care? Gemma was nice to everyone it seemed. But she wasn't an easy woman to get to know. She hated being in the spotlight and she didn't speak her mind as often as she should. Whenever she spoke, he felt like she was carefully choosing her words. He wondered what it would be like if she let loose and let her emotions run wild.

The thought triggered an entirely inappropriate image of Gemma he hadn't had since high school. Gemma used to have a short black-and-red plaid skirt that she wore with a white collared shirt and a black sweater. He had fantasized about getting her on the back of his motorcycle and then getting under that sweater, and under her skirt. Gemma on a motorcycle. His motorcycle. He shook loose the thought before it escalated and he was forced to hide a raging hardon in his jeans.

He didn't have a motorcycle anymore. It was impractical in Wyoming weather. Gemma was off-limits, then and now.

Gemma turned onto the unpaved road leading to the graveyard.

The graveyard was surrounded by tall, bare trees. It was a peaceful place, the groundskeeper putting time into clearing the snow from the path leading to the headstones. Rafe had been there more times in the past several months than he had all his life. He'd visited his mother and father and sat with Danny at his grandfather's grave.

Danny had told Rafe that the quiet of the field made him feel better and closer to his grandfather. It was a place where he could cry or think without anyone judging him. A tough admission for a teenage boy and Rafe gave him credit for finding an outlet for his grief.

The metal gate around the graveyard was locked.

"He can't be in there. It's closed," Gemma said. She drew the car to a stop.

Two angels holding harps looked over the entrance.

"The groundskeeper might not have checked that it was empty before closing it. Or maybe Danny did what I'm going to do."

Rafe climbed out of the car and scaled the fence. Though it was dark, he knew the way to where Danny might be.

"Rafe, be careful," Gemma said.

When he was on the other side of the fence, he looked over at her. Underneath the sole light, she was beautiful. It was impossible to miss.

"I will," Rafe said. He jogged through the snow. When he reached the back of the graveyard, he saw a dark figure hunched over.

Relief tore through him. "Danny, I've been calling you."

Danny's head was lowered, his hands jammed in his pocket and his shoulders tucked forward as if he could close into himself. He stood in front of his grandfather's grave, his body shaking and not just from the cold. His eyes were red-rimmed. "I'm sorry. It was a bad day."

Rafe drew the boy into his arms. He didn't like treating Danny like a child, knowing he wasn't. And given what he'd been through, Danny was more mature than most boys. But Rafe couldn't stop himself now. He hugged the boy and wanted him to know he was a friend.

"What happened?" he asked.

"I asked a girl to the winter dance," Danny said.

Rafe had been in his shoes enough to know this could be going many painful places. "Didn't go well?"

"She said she wouldn't go out with someone like me," Danny said.

Someone like him? That could mean anything. "Like someone smart, strong and brave?" Rafe asked.

Danny let out a short bark of laughter. "Right. I'm none of those things."

Rafe's heart squeezed. He took Danny by the shoulders. "Look at me. You are all of those things. Every single one. If she's too clueless to see it, then forget her. You don't need that dragging you down."

Danny shrugged him off and looked away. "No one wants me. Everyone rejects me. My mom died, my grandfather died, my dad didn't want me. Matt says he wants me, but he rarely comes by. And you…"

Danny didn't need to finish the thought. Rafe's guilt did that for him. He was leaving. He was another person in the long line of people who had let Danny down. It felt terrible.

"Danny, I think you're amazing. I think you're an incredible person with a bright future. You know I have to return to my job in New York. I signed a contract. I gave them my word."

"You have a job here," Danny said. "The clinic needs you."

It was a job he liked, but a town he didn't. "Before I leave, we will find you a good family."

"Yeah, right," Danny said. "I wish you would stay. Forever."

Rafe put his arm over Danny's shoulder. "Let's talk more about this at dinner."

"Are you pissed I was late?" Danny asked.

"Not really. I was worried," Rafe said. "Maybe we need a better check-in policy."

"Okay," Danny said.

Rafe was surprised he was agreeable to it. He expected resistance. He would have resisted if his parents had tried it with him.

"Danny, I need to talk to you about something that happened tonight."

Danny sighed. "Here it comes. Am I grounded?"

Was he copping to the attack on Dr. Rand? Rafe sensed this was still about going missing. "You're not grounded. This isn't about coming here instead of being home. There was an incident at the clinic and Chief Colton needs to speak with us about it."

Danny shook his head. "I'm not talking to the police. I didn't do anything."

"I know you didn't. But we've had some problems at the clinic and Chief Colton wants to speak with us to make sure we're safe and that we're not doing anything wrong," Rafe said.

Rafe read anger in Danny's face. "I'm always doing something wrong. Everyone expects me to screw up."

"I don't," Rafe said. "I don't think you've done anything wrong."

Danny looked at the ground. "I want to go home."

Rafe hated forcing Danny to speak with the police, but drawing it out meant the real attacker was at large and Danny would remain under suspicion. "We have to talk to Chief Colton. He's a friend. Trust me on this, Danny."

Danny let Rafe lead him to the car. Once they were closer, Danny stopped when he saw Gemma. "Is she your girlfriend?"

"I don't have a girlfriend. I would tell you first if I did." He wanted Danny to feel safe in his home and not worried about random women passing through. Random flings weren't Rafe's style, anyway. "You know Gemma. We work together at the clinic."

Danny tossed Rafe a half smile. "I know her. Maybe she'll go to the dance with me."

Rafe gave Danny points for courage. "She's a little old for school dances."

Danny mumbled under his breath, but he climbed into the backseat of the car.

"We were so worried about you, Danny. Are you cold?" Gemma turned up the heat in the car.

"I'm good," he said.

"You look upset," Gemma said.

"Girl stuff," Danny said.

"Can I help? My brothers used to tell me about their girl problems when they were in high school," Gemma said.

"Nah, I'm okay," Danny said.

Gemma made small talk, mostly with Danny.

"We're going directly to the police station," Rafe said. "To talk to Flint."

Rafe glanced in the rearview mirror. Danny appeared scared.

"Chief Colton is my brother. He's a good guy. Trust me. He's just trying to figure out what's happening at the clinic," Gemma said.

Hearing her words, Danny seemed to relax. Gemma drove them to the police station and parked.

"Gemma, could you give me a minute alone with Danny?" Rafe asked.

Gemma nodded as she exited the vehicle. "See you inside." She closed the door and hurried to the station.

Rafe faced Danny. "I will only ask you this once and I will believe anything you tell me, okay?"

Danny nodded. "Something bad happened. I knew it. You're blaming me."

"I told you we had trouble at the clinic. Were you near the clinic today?" Rafe asked. He realized he was holding his breath and he let it out.

"No."

"Did you go to football practice today?" Rafe asked.

Danny shook his head. "I skipped it. I didn't feel like it."

No alibi then. "Have you seen Dr. Rand today?" Rafe asked.

Danny shook his head again. "No."

It was all Rafe needed to hear. Though he wouldn't say why he believed Danny was telling the truth, he did. Wasn't that what a good parent was supposed to do?

Chapter 3

Gemma waited in the Dead River police station while Flint was speaking to Danny and Rafe. Rafe and Flint would butt heads over the issue surrounding Dr. Rand's accusations against Danny. Rafe would back Danny and Flint would press for the truth. He would press hard.

It was a volatile cocktail. Someone would leave furious.

Gemma had witnessed her brothers fighting with Rafe at school, on the football field and when they were hanging out. Rafe had an edge. He always had. As much as he seemed to want to polish those edges with his medical degree and a prestigious fellowship and coveted job, deep down, he was still a bad boy.

A bad boy her brothers had kept her away from and warned her to keep her distance from. He had been fun and free and wild enough for them, but he was off limits to her. She had once fantasized about Rafe asking her to his prom. Ridiculous. He had gone to the prom with the wildest, prettiest girl in school and Gemma had cried when she'd found out.

Rafe had skipped school, smoked cigarettes in the parking lot and wore jeans and a leather jacket, a flannel shirt often tied around his waist. When he'd started coming to school on a motorcycle, one that every single girl had wanted to ride, Gemma had thought she would absolutely die. Flint had told her Rafe had bought the junker and fixed it himself.

It had been so thrilling and exciting and forbidden.

Rafe was different now. He'd outgrown his rebellious tendencies, he wasn't late for his shifts, he worked hard and yet he still had an air of strength and power and excitement around him. She couldn't get enough of it and she couldn't stay away. Not that she would ever tell anyone how she felt about Rafe. She'd been hiding it for so long it wasn't hard to keep doing so. It was futile anyway. He couldn't wait to flee Dead River for his new job and no way would she leave her family. The one time in her life that she had, she had made colossal mistakes, enough that she realized she was better off with family around.

The door to the interview room banged open and Rafe strode out, his hand on Danny's shoulder.

"Rafe, just a minute. I have more questions. Danny might know something important," Flint said.

Rafe whirled and glared at Flint. It was a meeting of titans. "If you have more questions, you'll ask them when we have a lawyer present. Danny did nothing wrong and I won't have him interrogated like a criminal. Go find an actual criminal. Like whoever trashed my lab, or the rat who stole Molly Colton's savings or the escaped killer."

Gemma knew her brother could keep his temper, but Rafe was pressing his buttons, like he did with everyone. She rushed to intervene before it escalated into fists being thrown. "I called in an order for pizza.

Let's go pick it up together. I think we're hungry and cranky and we can talk after we've eaten." Hot pizza had to appeal more than the now cold carryout Rafe had ordered from the diner.

Gemma set her hand on her brother's shoulder and smiled at Danny, hoping to show him she was a friend. This didn't have to be a knock-down, drag-out fight. Nothing ever did.

"Fine. Pizza and a conversation," Rafe said.

Flint seemed relieved that he wouldn't have to force answers out of them.

Ten minutes later, they were sitting in Rafe's kitchen. He was playing host remarkably well. She wouldn't have expected him to set out plates or napkins or serve drinks.

"Danny, I'm not trying to get you into trouble," Flint said.

Rafe tensed.

"But Dr. Rand accused you of attacking him," Flint said.

Rafe sat next to Danny and put his hand on Danny's chair. They might be on Rafe's turf, but he was as defensive of Danny as he had been at the station.

"I didn't attack anyone," Danny said, looking at the floor and sounding miserable.

"I've spoken to your teachers, and I know you were in school when the clinic was burglarized and vandalized, but Dr. Rand was clear it was you who attacked him," Flint said.

"He's crazy," Danny said. "He doesn't like me."

Gemma wished he had better answers. Dr. Rand certainly wasn't the Colton family's biggest fan after what had happened with her brother Theo and Rand's ex-wife Mimi, but Dr. Rand was a good doctor and he had no reason to lie about what had happened to him.

Fifteen more minutes and they were getting nowhere, even though Rafe was encouraging Danny to tell Flint where he had been after leaving school. Flint believed Danny had seen or knew something that could help them.

Flint seemed frustrated.

"You just want to leave," Danny said to his plate.

The comment was obviously directed at Rafe.

It was Rafe's turn to look frustrated. "Danny, we've known from the first day you came to live with me that this was temporary."

"Does it have to be?" Danny asked.

He sounded so hopeful and sincere Gemma turned her head to hide the tears that came to her eyes. Danny reminded her of herself and her brothers when they had asked their father to stay. He never had. It was better that he hadn't.

Rafe seemed flummoxed. "Yes, it's temporary."

Danny appeared crushed.

"Danny, it's late and you have school tomorrow. You agreed you would let Rafe know where you are and what you're doing. You'll have to stick to that plan really closely," Gemma said. It had been one of Gram Dottie's rules and it had worked for the most part. At least if they knew were Danny was, it would avoid panic and confusion.

"He doesn't always answer his phone when I call," Danny said, pointing at Rafe.

"If I'm with a patient and I can't, leave me a voice mail or call Gemma," Rafe said.

Gemma hid her surprise. He was giving her some

responsibility with Danny? Rafe looked at her as if to question if it was okay and she nodded.

"Hit the shower, Danny. I'll be up to say good-night, okay?" Rafe asked.

Danny and Rafe clapped each other on the shoulder before Danny did as Rafe asked.

"I need to head home," Flint said. "Nina is waiting for me. You want a ride, Gemma?"

"I'll finish my pizza and then I can walk back to the clinic to pick up my car," Gemma said.

Flint looked between Gemma and Rafe, but Gemma ignored the silent question. Nothing was going on between her and Rafe. They were coworkers. She wasn't a high school girl with unchecked hormones. She was a grown woman and she could make her own decisions.

"You are not walking anywhere alone," Flint said. "The last time you went for a walk you were almost killed."

She hadn't been almost killed. An exaggeration.

Gemma touched her throat where the bruises had mostly healed. She'd been walking alone, trying to clear her head, needing time to think and someone had pulled her in to an abandoned alleyway along Main Street. "I defended myself."

"You were lucky," Flint said.

Rafe eyed her. "There's a killer loose, Gemma. It's a bad idea to walk alone."

"At least we agree on that," Flint said.

Gemma wasn't foolish. She knew to be careful. "I won't let these problems make me paranoid."

"I'll give her a ride to the clinic to pick up her car," Rafe said, as if it settled the matter.

Gemma wouldn't decline. Thinking of the night she

was attacked was enough to make her feel afraid, despite her brave words to the contrary.

"Night, Flint," Gemma said, wanting to make it clear that she wouldn't stand for an argument about it, especially not in front of Rafe. She was safe with Rafe. She was even safe with Danny. She couldn't picture the young man hurting her or anyone. There had to be an explanation for Dr. Rand's accusation. Maybe the attacker looked like Danny or maybe Dr. Rand had been shaken up and had been mistaken.

They said their goodbyes and Gemma took another slice of pizza from the box.

"You're really good with him," Rafe said.

"Flint or Danny?" Gemma asked.

Rafe laughed, a deep male laughter that sounded good to her ears. "Both, but I was referring to Danny."

"He's a good kid and he's scared," Gemma said.

Rafe furrowed his brows. "Of going to jail?"

Gemma shook her head. "Of you leaving. Of something bad happening to you. People in his life who he's loved have let him down. It's a hard place to be."

"It's a hard lesson to learn, but isn't that life? People who love us let us down. It's what happens."

His negativity surprised her. "I don't believe that. My grandmother and my brothers don't let me down."

Rafe shrugged. "Consider yourself lucky."

Rafe hadn't had an idyllic childhood, but at least his parents had been around for him, and after his father got sober, it seemed their relationship had improved, at least from an outsider's perspective. When Rafe was out of state, his parents had spoken of him often as if they were a close-knit family. "I'm sorry you feel like everyone disappoints you."

"I wasn't talking about myself," Rafe said.

"Weren't you?" Gemma asked.

"Has anyone ever told you that you pry too much?" Rafe asked. He leaned closer to her and seemed to study her face.

Gemma touched a napkin to her lips, wondering if she had smeared pizza sauce. "I am not prying. I care about people."

Rafe looked from her lips back to her eyes. A scorching look and she felt the intensity from her mouth to her toes.

"That will be your downfall," Rafe said.

He stayed close. Was he thinking about kissing her? Gemma wasn't sure what to say or do. If she closed the distance between them, would Rafe characteristically pull away?

She waited. Rafe called uncle first. He stood. "It's late. When you finish eating, I'll take you to your car."

After telling Danny he'd be out for a few minutes, Gemma followed him to his car.

This time, Rafe drove. "Coming back was a mistake," Rafe said.

Gone was his characteristic confidence.

"It wasn't," Gemma said. "You've done good here."

"Danny is angry at me for needing to leave," Rafe said.

"I know," Gemma said. Now wasn't the time to tell him again that she thought he should stay, that passing through wasn't fair to anyone who'd grown to care about him. "Maybe you can tell him you'll visit." Was she putting the thought out for Danny or herself? Would Rafe visit Dead River? Rafe hadn't been back to Dead River except for after his parents had passed. His return in October had been a surprise.

"I don't like to make promises I can't keep and I don't think staying in Danny's life is fair to his new family. He has to give them a chance and I don't know if he can do that with me showing up every few months."

The chances of someone adopting Danny were slim. He was looking at a few years of being shuffled around between foster homes. Maybe he'd strike it lucky and someone would keep him for the next four years, but at least having Rafe in his life would provide some consistency.

"Say it, Gemma," Rafe said.

"Aren't I allowed private thoughts?" she asked, not wanting to rock the boat with him. He'd been clear at the diner he didn't want her two cents' worth on matters pertaining to his life.

"You are, but you need to speak up for yourself more often. You champion everyone else's cause, but never your own."

"I like to be careful what I say, since I can't get the words back."

"Sometimes, you just need to spit it out and not worry about the consequences."

"Why do I have the feeling you're the one who has something to say?" Gemma asked.

The clinic was ahead on the right. Would Rafe finish this conversation with her or use the time as an excuse to end it?

"I know you had a crush on me in high school. You didn't say anything. Was that because admitting it was embarrassing for you?" Rafe asked.

Gemma sputtered. "What? You knew?" Why was that so humiliating? Had she been obvious and blatant about it?

"Flint told me."

"When?" she asked.

"At some point in high school," Rafe said.

Gemma silently promised Flint she would get him back for that. "Every girl in school had a crush on you."

"That's incorrect," Rafe said.

"It seemed true enough to me," Gemma said.

"You could have told me," Rafe said.

Gemma rolled her eyes. "Right. I didn't have that confidence and even if I did, what would come of it? You shooting me down? Telling me 'no' in front of my brothers so they could tease me about it mercilessly?"

Rafe appeared taken aback. "I wouldn't have done that."

Said no or humiliated her? "If you wanted me to ask you out, why didn't you ask me?"

Rafe shifted and Gemma sensed a rejection. She felt foolish for asking. That's what happened when she spoke plainly.

"Forget it," Gemma said.

"Let me answer. I didn't ask you on a date because I didn't date much back then. I didn't have enough money to take you anywhere worthy of you. I thought being out with me would have embarrassed you. Theo would have pounded me and then Flint would have killed me. I knew I wanted to leave Dead River and I didn't want any additional reasons to stay.

"You would have been a good reason to stay."

Wow. Even if he was implying she would have and could have ruined his life by tying him to Dead

River, knowing he had thought about asking her out boosted her teenaged self-confidence. "I wouldn't have guessed."

Rafe pulled into the clinic's parking lot.

"I wasn't big on talking about things back then," Rafe said.

"You aren't big about talking about them now. But I do need to correct you. I wouldn't have been embarrassed to be seen with you. I wasn't then and I'm not now."

Buoyed by the knowledge she had caught Rafe's eye all those years ago, she leaned across the seat and kissed his cheek. "Thanks for the ride."

She hurried out of the car before he could respond. Cowardly, yes, but absolutely critical if she wanted to keep distance from a man who she knew could easily break her heart.

Gemma was running five minutes late for work, having dragged this morning getting ready. The long, frequent shifts were wearing on her, but she was determined to find a cure.

Then life would go back to normal. At least, as far normal as it would be after Rafe left Dead River.

It was silly to have feelings for Rafe. He had left before and she'd suffered the heartbreak of losing her crush. He was closed off and Gemma had made the mistake before of getting involved with a man who wasn't available. It wouldn't end well for anyone. She had to keep her distance.

Dr. Colleen Goodhue had worked overnight to set up the lab, test their equipment and take inventory of what supplies they had remaining. Though they had some test results they'd uploaded to the CDC for review, the stolen samples were the most devastating loss to their work. They'd kept notes on the samples in the lab including the optimum growth conditions and reactions with possible antidotes.

Suited in her protective gear, Gemma entered the lab through the air-stop chamber.

Rafe was already working and didn't look up when she entered. What time had he arrived? Had he slept at all? Their conversation from the night before reran piecemeal through her thoughts. He was devastatingly sexy, alluringly honest and frustratingly distant. The combination was playing with fire and she wasn't looking to be burned again. She could tell herself she could handle a fling, and she could, but not with a man like Rafe.

"How can I help?" Gemma asked.

Rafe lifted his head from the microscope. "You're late."

Gemma fell back a step. Gone was the sweetness she had encountered in his car the night before. She hadn't had enough sleep, and irritation sharpened her tongue. "That is what I was trying to talk to you about at the diner. No one is resting on their laurels. I am doing my best. You don't need to tell me I'm late. I know it. It's not like I'm being paid overtime and even if I was, don't I get some credit for giving up every spare moment I have to work on this?"

Rafe blinked at her. She couldn't read his face under his mask, the glare from the overhead lights not making his eyes clear.

"Say something," she said. Dr. Goodhue would not

approve of violence in the lab, but Gemma would shake him out of his emotional stupor.

"I'm glad you took my advice to heart," Rafe said.

"What advice was that?" Gemma asked.

"Sticking up for yourself," Rafe said. He returned to his work and Gemma checked her temper. She would get nowhere by pressing him and they had much to do.

"Just tell me where we are," Gemma said, taking a seat next to Rafe.

"I'm taking pictures of every step. It's faster than writing everything down. Dr. Goodhue couldn't salvage our computer and we hadn't uploaded our last batch of data to the CDC. She's ordered another one, but in the meantime, this will have to be enough."

When they had labeled each of the samples they'd taken and recorded their observations, Gemma lifted the tray to return it to the refrigerator.

"Careful, don't drop them."

Gemma set the tray on the counter and whirled on him. "You do not have to tell me to be careful. You do not have to instruct me like I am about to screw up at every turn. I am always careful when I am in here. My grandmother and my best friend's lives are at stake!" Gemma felt tears coming to her eyes and she blinked at them, unable to wipe at them from under her suit.

"I think we need a break," Rafe said.

Gemma glared at him. "Is it so hard for you to apologize for being an ogre?"

"I've always been this way. What's changed? Why are you upset about it now?" he asked.

What had changed? For him, nothing. Everything was still right as rain in Rafe's world. He was the center of it and she was in orbit somewhere around him.

Her irritation with him was based somewhat on his frank admission to her last night before shutting her out today.

High school and her crush on him—former and current—should be nothing to her. Feelings for Rafe should roll off her like water on a duck. But confronting those untested emotions was troubling.

Rafe carried the samples to the refrigerator.

Gemma exited the lab, standing under the chemical shower before stripping off her protective gear and hanging it to dry in the cubby.

Standing in the clinic in her scrubs, she waited for Rafe to join her.

When he stepped out of the air-stop chamber, her breath caught in her throat. It was wrong for a man who was this big of a jerk to look this good to her. She'd always had a thing for a man in scrubs and now that it was Rafe, she was absolutely beside herself. Her breasts tightened and she felt drawn to him, desperate to slake the sensations moving like a storm through her.

She eyed his broad shoulders, his lean length, and arms and hands she knew were strong and capable. She wanted those hands on her.

"Will you take a walk with me? I think we need to talk," he said.

What she had in mind wasn't talking. Jessica said she was sexually repressed because in Dead River, she had her brothers and her grandmother swarming around her. Gemma had laughed, thinking she had plenty of fun with the men she had dated. But Jessica's words came back to her now and Gemma felt like she needed Rafe to give her something that no other man could. Had she ever felt this attracted to a man? This taken with him? Gemma's every sexual experience to this point had been deliberate and she had liked being in control of herself and that part of her life. She had the feeling if she was alone with Rafe, she would willingly turn herself over to him and let him do whatever he wanted to her. She would love every single moment.

Putting on their jackets they stepped outside. The air was dry and cold and Gemma pulled her hands into the sleeves of her coat.

"Gemma, I know I come across like a tyrant sometimes. I am doing my best."

She wasn't in the mood to talk about work. Rafe had turned her on and those emotions persisted. Couldn't they talk about that? "You can do your best without being rude to the people around you."

"I don't mean to be rude." He appeared ashamed. Or was the pink in his cheeks the cold?

"Then what do you mean?" she asked.

"I mean to keep you safe. I hate that you're working in that lab with that virus, one that we know could kill you if you were exposed."

Just her? The entire staff was at risk. "Same goes for you."

Rafe shook his head. "With the exception of Danny, I don't have people counting on me. You have your brothers and this town. They need you."

He sounded disgusted when he said "this town."

She wanted to refute his words and tell him that she needed him. But speaking the words would have cost her too much. She wasn't ready to let him know how badly she wanted him. Even if it was an attraction-only thing, a one-time experience, she wanted Rafe in her bed. She wanted him to look at her like he had looked at other girls in high school, a look that promised pure pleasure.

"Now you're cold," Rafe said. He put his arms around her and pulled her against his jacket.

"I needed to cool down," Gemma said. She slipped her arm around his waist, feeling the tightness of his back. He was in good shape.

A laugh rumbled in his chest and then Rafe did the most unexpected thing. He tipped her mouth up to his and kissed her.

Softly, gently on her mouth. No feverish, frantic, desperate hunger, but the impact was thoroughly arousing. A shower of sparks ignited around them and her surrender was immediate. She let her body sink against his and his arms went around her waist.

Gemma wanted this to go on forever. His mouth explored hers and this kiss was more potent than she had imagined. She was his in every sense of the word, and all from a kiss.

Having their coats between them frustrated her. She wanted bare skin and his big body over hers, sinking into her. Her insides clenched with longing, and heat pooled between her legs.

He could have pushed her up against the wall of the clinic and stripped her naked, and she wouldn't have stopped him.

He pulled away first and stared at her. It was the look she had dreamed about being on the receiving end of a hundred times before and it was so much better. She read possessiveness, heat and desire in his expression.

"Why did you stop?"

Rafe ran his thumb across her lip. "I needed to do

that. I've been thinking about doing that for far too long."

"It wasn't enough," she said, not embarrassed by her words. If she'd learned one thing in a relationship, it was that she had to ask for what she needed.

"Not enough?" Brown eyes met hers in question.

"If that was a sample of what this could be, more will be better."

Rafe's eyes lit with excitement. "I never imagined I would hear those words from your mouth."

"You went away from this town and came back a changed man. I might not be the woman you knew either," Gemma said, feeling bold.

"Flint will kick my butt for kissing his little sister and I think I just made a colossal mistake. Kissing you is one thing. Not doing it again is another."

"Then let's go inside and finish our shift. Then come home with me."

Rafe jammed a hand through his hair. "I didn't bring you out here to kiss you. I thought we needed to calm down."

"It didn't work."

"Clearly," Rafe said. "But this can't happen again, Gemma. You're Flint and Theo's sister."

"That means I can't have sex?" For the first time in a long time, Gemma wished her small town innocent reputation would disappear.

Rafe seemed flustered. "I'm sure you've had sex. Plenty of it. Look at you. How could you not have men pounding down your door? But even as I'm saying this to you, I'm realizing I shouldn't be included in that. I'm not good for you, Gemma. You deserve better."

* * *

Kissing Gemma had driven home the idea of having sex with her and unless he was misreading her, she was offering it to him on a silver platter.

Go home with her? Hell yes, he wanted to. Rafe wanted to strip her out of her loose scrubs and touch her everywhere. He wanted to use his hands and his mouth on her and make her come until she screamed his name. He wanted her on her back, on her knees and on top of him. The Gemma Wish List was long and getting dirtier by the minute.

But how could he think of her that way? She was Gemma. Resident good girl. Sweet.

She indicated she wasn't a virgin and of course he didn't expect her to be, but thinking of her in another man's arms was driving him insane.

After their rounds, which had a sobering effect on his libido, they returned to his trashed office to review their notes. His replacement computer was working, although it was old and slow. They hadn't recovered his other one after the break-in.

He waited for the patient records application to load.

"Who was it? Josh Hadaway?" The EMT was handsome and single, as far as Rafe knew.

"Who was what?" Gemma asked.

Was he having this conversation with her? "You dated men in the past. Men I know?"

Gemma shrugged. "Maybe."

"Are you trying to make me jealous?"

Gemma straightened. "Not at all. I pointed out to you that I am a woman and I have had boyfriends. You seemed confused by the idea that I would…" She blushed and looked away.

Her behavior now was more what he had expected. Her boldness outside the clinic, while surprising, had utterly aroused him. "That you would have sex?"

"Yes, that," Gemma said.

Rafe rubbed his eyes. "You're a surprise, Gemma. I knew you were smart and sweet, but you're stronger and sexier than I realized."

She smiled. "It's taken me awhile to move out from my brothers' shadows. They're larger than life. It's hard to grow up with them hovering."

"They still hover," Rafe said. Maybe their hovering would keep him from doing something monumentally stupid, like sleeping with her.

"Not as much," Gemma said.

The software loaded and Rafe turned his attention to the computer. Gemma circled the desk to look over his shoulder. She leaned on his chair and her hip brushed his arm.

He closed his eyes against the assault of sensations. Her scent, light like jasmine, her ponytail swinging off her shoulder and brushing his neck.

"Are you doing that on purpose?" he asked, not sure he could resist. From the time they had started working together, they'd had an unspoken, understated chemistry. Now that they had brought it out in the open, it seemed to sharpen and strengthen.

"Doing what?" she asked. Her green eyes danced with amusement.

He would teach her to play with fire. If he showed her the man he was, she would back away. Gemma was too innocent, despite her assertions she'd dated.

Rafe stood and pushed her against the wall. He

watched her face for a sign of fear. She didn't look afraid. She looked turned on.

He pushed her feet apart and positioned his hips between hers. "Don't toy with me, Gemma."

Gemma set her hands on his shirt and he anticipated she would shove him away. Instead, she held him close. "I am not toying with you. You don't seem to know what you want."

"I am not interested in a girlfriend."

Gemma blinked, but she didn't look away. "I don't need a boyfriend."

"Are you suggesting colleagues with benefits?" he asked.

She pressed her hips into his and rocked slowly. "I am suggesting that we see where this goes before telling ourselves it won't work."

Now that she was calling his bluff, he didn't know what to do. He didn't like backing down. "This will interfere with our work."

"Stop making excuses," Gemma said.

Rafe bought his mouth to hers and kissed her in shameless abandon. He slid his hands to her waist and then under her shirt, his hands lingering at the bare skin of her taut midriff. He lifted her, to better align his body with hers.

She wrapped her legs around his waist and he had a preview of exactly how he planned to have sex with her the first time.

"You're holding back," Gemma said.

He was keeping his emotions in check. He wouldn't strip her naked in his office and have sex with her here. "We're in my office." If they had sex now, it would be off the table and out of their system.

The phone rang and stopped Rafe from taking this further.

Rafe set Gemma down and answered the phone. It was food delivery from the Blue Bear. Since the break-in, they'd started keeping the clinic doors locked. All patients, visitors and deliveries had to be buzzed inside.

"I'll meet you out front," Rafe said to the delivery person.

After gathering the food, he and Gemma sorted it and loaded it onto the food cart to be delivered to their patients.

Once Gemma had left to complete the task, Rafe was alone. Mercifully alone. He had to stop thinking about the feel of Gemma pressed against him.

He opened the spreadsheet he was using to track their patients' symptoms. He needed to determine which observations were relevant to the virus and which were unrelated.

Gram Dottie, Gemma's grandmother, was sick with the Dead River virus, but she also had arthritis in her knees and hands. The arthritis, as far as he knew, was not related to the virus, but he was looking for complications that could arise so he could head them off.

He was relying on his instincts, observations and experience. The likelihood of missing a warning sign was high and Rafe didn't want any more patients to die.

He had books that Dr. Goodhue had brought with her and he had access to the CDC databases. He was doing some cross-checking, hoping that somewhere else in the world, another clinician was dealing with the same virus and had found a cure.

Rafe had complicated matters by kissing Gemma.

Twice. Blaming the pressure or the stress was non-sense. He lived with pressure and stress every day of his life. He had no one to blame for the decision to kiss her but himself.

Now, it occupied far too much of his thoughts. Her responses to him tonight had been like nothing he would have expected from Gemma. She was beautiful and intelligent, but had never been so overtly sensual. Her words, her body language and her tone had given him a glimpse into how hot it would be to sleep with her.

He didn't need another reason to consider it.

Gemma Colton had always appealed to him on some deep, primal level, but she'd always been too good for him. Too beautiful. Too smart. Too pure. Too everything. He'd been the boy from the trailer park without a future and nothing to offer a woman.

He'd run into people from high school who hadn't aged well. Women and men who had been beaten by life and seemed haggard, tired and used. Not Gemma. She was as fresh-faced as she was in high school and the traits she'd added to her list of good qualities—supportive, independent and honest—appealed to him.

This wasn't a school-boy crush. When he looked at her, he saw a vibrant and remarkable woman.

Gemma returned with two brown bags. She set one on his desk. "It's a gourmet hamburger. Eat. Please."

She opened another across from him.

"Thanks, Gemma." He was hungry and maybe food would take the edge off.

Gemma wiped her mouth and took a drink. "Before the lab was trashed, we were thinking the virus could be some mutation of the flu, stronger, more lethal. Any more thoughts on that?" She seemed to be directing the conversation away from what had happened before the phone call and Rafe let her.

"I'm not ruling it out," Rafe said. "If we can classify the virus, we can look at similar ones and how a cure was manufactured."

"We haven't found an exact match, but why don't we review the viruses that are close and see if anything else jumps out at us?" Gemma asked.

It was as good a technique as any. The more they studied this virus, the more likely they'd find ones similar and close in on a cure.

Dr. Lucas Rand appeared in his doorway and Rafe's appetite flattened. Dr. Rand's accusations of Danny rubbed Rafe the wrong way. "Chief Colton doesn't seem to be making any progress on apprehending the person responsible for the problems we've had."

"Flint is doing everything he can," Gemma said, sounding defensive.

Dr. Rand sniffed. "Maybe his best isn't good enough."

Rafe sensed Dr. Rand would push Gemma too far. "Have you reviewed our lab notes?" Rafe asked.

Dr. Rand shook his head. "I haven't had time. Since my attack, my head is throbbing."

"Take an ibuprofen," Rafe said.

Dr. Rand chuckled. "I am a doctor. I know how to treat a headache."

"Some headaches go beyond medical treatment," Rafe said. He looked at Rand for an extra beat. Not to put too fine a point on it, but Rafe considered him an enemy.

Gemma lowered her head to cover her smile.

Rafe knew he was being hostile with Dr. Rand, but he was angry at his false accusation and his inability to admit that he could have been mistaken about Danny being his attacker. How much could he have seen in a few brief seconds?

Dr. Rand stood taller. "I'll review your notes after my meeting with Dr. Goodhue. We're meeting for a late dinner at the diner." He left and Rafe closed the door.

"That guy gets under my skin," Rafe said.

Gemma set down her hamburger. "This is a tough situation for everyone. I know you're feeling protective of Danny and we're tired and stressed out—"

"Gemma, stop. You don't have to play peacemaker."

"I wasn't playing anything."

"It's okay not to get along with everyone."

Gemma inclined her head. "I want everyone working together to find a cure. There are no leaders or followers here. Just everyone doing everything we can. You think it doesn't bother me that he blames Theo for what happened with Mimi?"

"I'm sure it does." Rafe had heard bits and pieces from rumors, Theo and Flint. After Dr. Rand and Mimi had divorced, Theo had slept with Mimi, and their one-night affair had resulted in a baby. From what Theo had said, he hadn't known Mimi was pregnant until she'd shown up with baby Amelia.

"It doesn't matter if it bothers me. I have to get over it. If we let problems fester between us, it will be that much harder."

She'd made the point he'd been thinking about. "Problems. Like sleeping with a colleague?"

Gemma gave him a long look. She picked up her hamburger and strode to the doorway. "You're good at that, Rafe. Pushing people away. Just be careful. You push everyone away and you'll end up a lonely, old and bitter man."

Chapter 4

Gemma would rather eat alone while she sorted files and folders behind the reception desk than eat with Rafe. He said he knew what he wanted and maybe in his career he did.

When it came to her, he was sending mixed signals. She hated the confusion that came along with it.

Had she been too forward with Rafe? He had told her to speak her mind and she had. Ever since she had left Dead River for nursing school and had a taste of freedom, she had learned she liked kissing men. She liked sex, most forms of it. She was willing to try things with a trusted partner and she didn't need to be ashamed of it.

That persona seemed to be at odds with the person she had been in high school, when Gemma hadn't even kissed a boy. She hadn't been asked to a school dance. She hadn't gone to prom. Her grandmother had told her that her brothers had frightened away possible suitors, but the more likely reason was that she just hadn't known how to talk to boys, how to flirt, and with her father abandoning her family, she carried an inherent distrust of men.

While that distrust was often present at the start of

a relationship, she wouldn't lose her ability to trust because of the men who had disappointed her.

She could trust Rafe, couldn't she? He had always made her feel safe.

Rafe hadn't wanted her to play peacemaker between him and Dr. Rand. Was that what she had been doing? Theo and Flint had often accused her of taking on that same role between them. They'd fight and she'd jump in the middle of it. Her grandmother and her father—when he bothered to show up—would fight and Gemma would try to smooth the problems over.

It was who she was. It was better when everyone got along. Doctors were competitive. Nurses were sometimes, too. Doctors, in the struggle to be placed in the right job at the right hospital, needed the conflict and the competition to propel them.

An alarm blared, the shrill sound of a problem in the virus wing. They had practiced drills for a patient going into distress, for a breach in the ventilation system and for other emergencies. Which was it?

Gemma met Rafe in the suit room and they hurried to pull on their protective gear. As she zipped her suit, she imagined what they would face on the other side of those doors.

Before they opened the doors, Rafe grabbed her hand. He wanted to hold hands now?

"Your glove," he said.

Gemma looked down at her hand. In her hurry, the seam of her glove had torn. His attention to detail might have saved her life. "Thank you. Go on without me. I'll fix it and be with you in a minute."

She hurried to put on another pair of gloves and reseal her suit. She entered the double enclosure and then when the second doors released, she entered the virus wing.

The alarm was still blaring, making it hard to think.

Rafe was in the small control room to the right of the entry door.

"The heat and ventilation systems are down," Rafe said.

Without heat, the temperature in the virus wing would drop quickly. The ventilation system used a complex series of HEPA filters in the ceiling above them to clean the air. They would run out of oxygen quickly, and opening the emergency doors of the virus wing would expose the town to the worst cases of the Dead River virus.

"What should we do?" Gemma asked. With so many hours to cover, she and Rafe were the only two scheduled tonight.

"We fix it or we risk contaminating the entire town," Rafe said.

Rafe lifted the metal housing enclosing the unit.

Gemma stared at the complex cords, hoses and circuits. She had no experience with HVAC repair. Touching anything was akin to guessing.

"Any thoughts?" Gemma asked.

Rafe was moving around the unit, inspecting it. He lifted a set of wires that were lying along the side of the unit connected to nothing. "These have been cut."

"One of the patients?" Gemma asked. Every room in the ward was locked to prevent cross contamination. Had someone broken out of their room? Been disoriented? She couldn't imagine anyone in the ward sabotaging the ventilation system.

Rafe shook his head. "Our vandal is at it again."

"If someone entered without a suit, they've been exposed," Gemma said. If they'd been unprotected and were walking around the general population, they could be spreading the virus to others.

"Someone has the blood samples from our patients and has been inside this wing. That makes them a walking time bomb."

Rafe located electrical tape in the tool box on the shelf above the unit. He and Gemma pieced together the wires, securing them with the tape. The oxygen sensor beeped incessantly, alerting them the air was low on oxygen.

Once the wires were connected, Rafe restarted the system. Nothing happened.

Rafe swore and they started again, looking at the cut wires and trying to match them. More tape. They shut down the system and then pressed the button to power it on.

Nothing.

"We need to evacuate our patients from their rooms. They'll suffocate," Gemma said.

Rafe seemed calm. Gemma was thinking of her grandmother and Jessica and young Tammy. They needed fresh air!

Rafe arranged the wires again and then restarted the system. This time, it engaged. The pump began moving the air.

Gemma silenced the oxygen alarm and watched the sensor climb from dangerously low levels to the safe zone.

The vandal had almost killed everyone in the virus wing. Why? Who in town had a reason to do this?

* * *

Reassuring the patients that everything was fine took hours. Some of the patients were demanding to know what was happening and continuing to lie to them was becoming difficult.

Their patients were questioning why they were in isolation when others in the town who were sick were living in their homes, keeping themselves in isolation. No ventilation system, no around-the-clock care, but they were with their families and the comforts of their homes.

The best answer Gemma had was that while infected residents were walking around, the virus was spreading. Staying isolated would help contain the virus and protect loved ones.

Gemma and Rafe were in his office sorting through the paperwork that had been thrown to the floor when the vandal had trashed Rafe's office, the clinic and the lab.

"We need a safe place to keep copies of our lab results," Rafe said, more to himself than to her. He had said "we" but she wasn't sure if she was included in that sentiment.

"I can take them home," Gemma said.

"No," Rafe said firmly. "If anyone learns you have data in your home it makes you a target. Besides, you can't take anything from the lab."

"Then what's your plan?" Gemma asked.

"Our plan needs to stay between us. We don't know who we can trust."

"Agreed," Gemma said.

"Our scanner and copier are broken. We'll need to transcribe whatever we can remember after we're finished in the lab and take our notes to the Dead River library. They have a section in the basement where they store old newspapers. We can collect our papers there," Rafe said.

"We can't do that!" Gemma said.

"Why not?"

"That's stealing," Gemma said.

"It's not stealing. We're not taking anything."

"What if someone finds out?" Gemma asked.

"We need to make sure no one does," Rafe said.

"Do you have an in at the library?" Gemma asked. She didn't like breaking the rules.

"I don't, but you do," Rafe said.

Gemma groaned. She and Anand were members of the book club at the library and while they hadn't met in months, not since the virus had broken out, Gemma was friendly with the head librarian. "I'll get in trouble."

"You won't. You have to do this, Gemma."

Gemma jammed her fingers through her hair. If they were caught, she could lose her license for taking patient data to an unsecured location. She could lose the trust of the town. With Rafe asking her and the importance of what they were doing weighing on her, she felt she had no choice but to agree. "Okay, I'll do it."

Rafe smiled at her and she melted a little. "I like it when you're willing to bend the rules."

"You would," Gemma said. "As the number one rule breaker in high school you started enough trouble."

"I didn't start trouble because I liked it. I started trouble because I don't believe in following the status quo," Rafe said. "When I don't like something, I won't go along with it."

"Sometimes, you have to compromise." Every discussion they'd had today felt like a dual conversation, about Rafe and about their relationship.

"I do compromise. We're working together. Normally, I prefer to work alone."

Gemma rolled her eyes. "I'll need to teach you to make an actual compromise."

She picked a few more papers off the ground and found a photograph of Rafe and his parents. She held it up. "You'll be happy to know this survived the vandal."

She gave the picture another long look and then handed it to him. "Do you miss them?"

Rafe swallowed. "They were my parents."

Not a direct answer. Gemma was treading on a difficult topic. "You didn't say much when you came back for your mom's funeral."

"What was there to say?" Rafe asked.

"Why did it take you so long to come home?" Gemma asked.

Rafe lifted his head from the photograph. "Are you asking why I didn't come back to Dead River while my mom was dying? Are you asking me why I waited until she was dead to return?"

The anguish was thick in his voice. "No, I just meant—"

"Don't do that. Don't speak the truth and ask the hard questions and then back away. Always give me the truth. Give me honesty and I'll meet you with some of my own. I didn't come to Dead River when my mom was sick because I didn't know. My parents didn't know my mom had cancer until it was too late. She ignored the signs and by the time she was sick enough to need help, her doctors couldn't do anything to save her. My dad said they didn't want me to come home and blow my fellowship over it." He snorted. "Like a fellowship mattered."

A fellowship was an important milestone in a doctor's career. Hearing him make it clear that his family came before his career touched her. "They were so proud of you. Your fellowship meant a great deal to them, just like your medical degree did."

Rafe set the picture frame on his desk. "How do you know that?"

Rafe's parents talked about him all the time. Every chance they had, they bragged about their son, the marvelous, life-saving emergency room doctor. "Your dad and mom talked about you every time I saw them. Good things. Great things. I half expected when you came home, you'd learned how to heal someone by laying your hands on them."

Rafe closed his eyes and lowered his head into his hands. "My dad wanted me to come back and work at the clinic."

"Because he wanted to show you off."

Rafe's eyes were damp and she sensed his grief and loss. "He was proud of me. Every time we talked on the phone, he told me that. I was proud of him too. He got sober while I was away at school and he never went back. My mom said those were some of the best years they had together. Whenever they visited me, they seemed so much happier than I remember them being when I was young."

She crossed the room to him and pulled him against her. "I'm so sorry, Rafe. I know this must be hard for you."

Rafe shifted her into his lap and sat in his chair in

one swift motion. He banded his arms around her and held her.

"I hated growing up in that trailer park. I hated being poor. I hated how people looked at me and dismissed me because of it. But as soon as I had the chance, I did the same to my parents. I turned away from them. I refused to visit them in Dead River. I made excuses about work and I always flew them out to stay with me."

Surprise and sympathy warred with her emotions. Rafe was confiding in her. This was a day of firsts. "I am sure they didn't see it that way. They knew you were trying to make something of your life. They were happy for you and proud of you."

He seemed to collect himself. "Does it get easier?"

"Does what get easier?"

"Losing your parents?"

"I don't know." Gemma hardly remembered her mother and what she knew of her father left nothing to be desired in having him in her life. "I know that if Gram Dottie doesn't get well, I'll be destroyed."

Rafe straightened. "Then we need to get her well. I won't accept any other outcome."

"You expect too much of yourself," Gemma said. "You have to remember we're in this together."

Would Rafe ever believe that? Or would he continue to draw her to him and push her away?

Rafe had never asked a colleague to spend time with him outside of work. Gemma was the first. Rafe tried to attend Danny's football practices a couple of times per week and this week, he wanted Gemma with him.

Gemma was therapy. She was a nurse and a healer

by trade, but being with her did something to him that was deeper than that. When he was with her, Rafe could be himself. She'd known him in high school and she seemed to know him now, better than most.

Patients were nice to him because he could help them. Nurses were nice to him because he was a doctor and a source of income. But Gemma saw through that facade, beyond the title he wore like a mask and into who he was as a man.

She awakened a part of him that was different than who he'd trained to be. With Gemma, he felt simultaneously out of control and totally enraptured. What he wouldn't give to have his old motorcycle and have Gemma on the back. To take her out to the mountains for a ride. To find a quiet place and lay her down and make slow, thrilling love to her.

He'd have to settle for keeping her as his friend and colleague. When he left Dead River after a cure was found, he didn't want to hurt Gemma or ruin his friendship with Flint and Theo.

Gemma was sitting next to him on the aluminum bleachers surrounding the football field on one side, a shared blanket over their laps, watching Danny's practice.

Rafe liked to watch Danny play when he could, even if the season had been put on hold. Without the ability to leave the town, games had been cancelled, but practice kept up the players' spirits. Some of the other students' parents were watching the practice as well. One of the parents had brought a large thermos filled with hot chocolate for the boys and the parents.

Gemma took a sip of the hot chocolate. It was already cooling. "Danny's good."

Rafe agreed. Danny worked hard and he had unresolved emotions. The time on the field, the exercise and the practice seemed to have taken the edge off his anger. Except for the incident with Dr. Rand, which Rafe didn't believe Danny had anything to do with, Danny had been great. He experienced the ups and downs of anyone coping with losing someone they loved while going through puberty, a confusing time in everyone's life.

"You really care about him," Gemma said.

"Of course I do," Rafe said.

"He looks up to you," Gemma said.

"Better me than someone without direction. He doesn't have role models in his life. His brother's not a bad guy, but he's as lost as Danny is," Rafe said.

One of the parents crossed over the benches and sat next to Gemma. She held out her hand. "Betsy Morris."

Gemma's face lit with recognition. "So glad to finally meet you in person." Gemma leaned back so Betsy could shake Rafe's hand. "Betsy is organizing the creation and delivery of the care baskets for those who are too sick to leave their houses."

Rafe had heard of Betsy and her volunteers. Betsy was also the local holistic healer. Though the scientist in him was wary of anyone claiming to have a medicinal cure without any hard evidence behind it, Betsy was a good person. They'd been in the same class in high school and even then, Betsy had been interested in healing. "I know you have your hands full at the clinic. We're trying to help people however we can."

"I hope you're being cautious," Rafe said. They still didn't know how the virus was spreading, but visiting the homes of those afflicted could easily make Betsy a victim of the virus.

Betsy nodded solemnly. "I've been instructing volunteers to be cautious. Have you made any progress with a cure?"

Gemma shook her head.

Rafe interjected. "We're doing everything we can." How many times had he said those same words in the last several weeks? It was the most he could say without giving false hope, but it wasn't inspirational or comforting to anyone.

"I guess you heard that Principal Lewis called out sick today," Betsy said, lowering her voice.

Gemma shook her head. "We hadn't heard."

Betsy looked across the field. "I stopped by with a care basket when I heard. He has the symptoms. He said it came on fast. Fever. Headache. Sore throat."

A mild panic shook Rafe. Maybe it wasn't the Dead River virus. Maybe it was the flu. If it was the Dead River virus, then the entire student population could have been exposed. The clinic didn't have the resources to care for dozens of additional people, especially children. The CDC was planning to ship additional trailers, but who would take care of the patients? Doctor and nurse volunteers weren't lining up to enter Dead River and be quarantined until a cure was found.

Rafe's anxiety rose. If the exposure had occurred at school, Danny could be at risk. He had told Danny to wash his hands often, not shake hands with anyone, not drink from anyone's cup or bottle and to avoid anyone who was coughing or sneezing. A cold or the seasonal flu was one thing. Catching the Dead River virus when they had no cure was another, much more deadly, problem.

"Maybe it's not the Dead River virus," Gemma said, echoing Rafe's thoughts. "Flu symptoms are similar."

"I hope so. The flu is bad enough," Betsy said. "Principal Lewis put himself in isolation. He hung a black flag from his window."

Rafe had seen the black flags waving from house windows. It was the Dead River community's way of alerting others that someone inside was sick. The number of flags increased daily, making for a disturbing view of the town.

Betsy nodded and pulled a card from her pocket. "Please call me if you need another set of hands. I am willing to answer phones or organize supplies or visit with the sick. Whatever you believe will help."

"Thanks, Betsy. That's sweet of you," Gemma said, taking her card.

They said their goodbyes and returned to watching the practice.

"Maybe he should stop going to school," Rafe said, thinking again of Danny.

"I'm not sure what I would do in your shoes," Gemma said. "It's scary to think about the kids being exposed, but stopping life while under quarantine will make everyone crazy. What can people do? Sit around their houses? Wait to die?"

If he knew they'd find a cure in a week or even a month, he would pull Danny from school and have him make up the work later. But what if this went on for months? Questions he didn't want the answers to flew through his mind. "What will the CDC do if we can't find a cure? Keep us trapped here indefinitely?"

Gemma leaned away, appearing surprised. "We will find a cure."

Sometimes no cure was found and entire towns were wiped out. Sometimes a virus would disappear as mysteriously as it had arrived, only to rear its head when least expected years down the line. "If someone would get better, we could study them to find a cure. But no one gets better. Some people die and some people get worse and worse."

Gemma touched his arm. "I know it seems bleak right now, but I have faith in you. I have faith in the people of this town. Look what Betsy is accomplishing with her volunteers. Look at everyone who is lending a hand to their neighbors so we can push through this."

"I don't want to let everyone down. I don't want to let you down." Rafe cupped the back of her neck and brought his forehead to rest on hers. Being close to her made him feel at ease. The shouts of fear and his own voice demanding he work harder and longer quieted.

"Shouldn't you be working?"

A hostile tone from a voice Rafe didn't recognize. Rafe turned slowly, ready for a confrontation. Tensions were running high and everyone was living with added stress.

"Trevor, we are doing everything we can," Gemma said, rising to her feet.

They needed to put those words on the clinic's voice mail and website. They were trying. They were working on it.

"It's getting scary," Trevor said. "I have a little girl and one on the way. I can't leave this town and I am not bringing Gabriella to the clinic to have her baby."

Rafe saw the man for who he was: a scared father.

Not a jerk. "I'll come to you when the time comes for your wife to have her baby."

Trevor looked between Gemma and Rafe. "You're the new doc."

"New to the clinic. I grew up in Dead River," Rafe said.

Trevor's shoulders relaxed. "Gabriella hasn't been seen by her obstetrician in too long. She said she knows everything is fine. I don't agree. A phone conversation doesn't cut it."

Rafe's schedule was jammed, but people needed routine medical care. That part of the clinic's services were lacking with so much time and resources going toward the effort to find a cure for the virus. "Why don't you call the clinic tomorrow and I'll set up a time to see your wife somewhere that you're comfortable?"

"Are you an obstetrician?" Trevor asked, setting his hands on his hips.

Rafe had some experience in obstetrics, but it wasn't his field of expertise. "I work in emergency medicine. I've delivered enough babies to know what I'm doing." Most of the deliveries he'd performed were when the mother couldn't make it to the labor and delivery room. He'd been trained to help people and perform whatever tasks were needed. If he needed to reassure a pregnant woman she and her baby were healthy, he would.

"Thanks, Doc. I'd appreciate that." Trevor almost seemed embarrassed now.

"We're doing everything we can. I've spoken to the fire chief to see if we can't rent a space at the fire station to schedule drop-in hours. I know people are reluctant to come to the clinic." Though they had assured everyone that the virus was being isolated and the chances of coming into contact with the virus was higher in town, most patients wouldn't take the risk.

Rafe and Trevor shook hands and Trevor walked away, almost looking lighter on his feet.

"That was nice of you," Gemma said.

He was a doctor in a small town. It was part of the role his father had asked him to play. "You sound surprised."

"You're busy enough. You keep adding things to your to-do list."

Rafe shrugged. "How do you know Trevor?"

"He's a distant relative," Gemma said.

"Then I'm glad I offered to help him," Rafe said.

"I didn't realize you'd spoken to Stan about opening a clinic at the fire station," Gemma said, referring to the Dead River fire chief.

"We need a place to meet with other patients and some of the firefighters have EMT training as well. It's not a bad place to set up a temporary clinic," Rafe said.

Gemma sighed. "I hate to sound like a broken record, but there's only one real way to fix this."

She didn't have to say it. He knew. They had to find a cure.

"You'll come too, won't you, Gemma?" Gabriella asked her on the phone the next morning.

Gemma hadn't planned on it. She hadn't seen Gabriella in years and Gemma had so much to do that she was hesitant to spend her limited free time driving to Trevor and Gabriella's ranch when Rafe could handle the checkup alone. Granted, being with Rafe did have a certain appeal.

Gemma couldn't say no to family. "I'll come with him."

A quick call to Rafe and he seemed unenthusiastic about her joining him. "It's a long drive for a routine check."

"I'll keep you company. It will make Gabriella feel better." The truth, and Gemma knew Rafe put his patients and their happiness first.

As she'd expected, Rafe agreed and twenty minutes later, his car pulled up in front of the clinic. She said goodbye to Anand and Dr. Moore and grabbed the clinic's OB kit. Though Trevor hadn't mentioned that Gabriella was in distress, it was best to be prepared. The clinic wasn't equipped to deal with critical cases. Those were referred to Cheyenne Memorial Hospital where they had newer equipment, a larger staff and a hundred times the resources. Gemma tried not to think about her cousin having a troubled pregnancy.

They started down the road and Gemma was shocked at the number of black flags hanging from bannisters, doors and windows. The virus was taking a toll on the town.

"You aren't close with your cousin?" Rafe asked, breaking into her morose thoughts.

"Not really. We don't have much in common." That part of the family was significantly wealthier than she was and they lived a different life.

"It sounds like she has a life I thought you'd have," Rafe said.

Rich wife of a rancher? "In what way?"

"Husband and kids and ranch life," Rafe said.

Was that a compliment? "Me too. Didn't work out that way. I planned to leave Dead River, get educated and start my life." A life that included a husband and children. But a husband and children weren't goals she could work for. She hadn't figured out how to have them. In part, she blamed her broken family. As wonderful as her grandmother had been to her and her brothers, losing her mother at a young age and then dealing with her father's drunken behavior had warped her sense of home and family.

"I thought you loved it here," he said, almost sounding sarcastic.

"I do. My family is here. But I thought I would have a life away from here." She had loved her time away, but in the end, she'd returned to Dead River.

"What went wrong?" Rafe asked.

"I went to college nearby and then I applied to the clinic for my first nursing job," Gemma said. She bit her tongue over the urge to defend her decision. She didn't need to defend it. She hadn't done anything wrong. Her first taste of freedom had led to a few mistakes, but also learning about herself.

"Didn't you want to see the rest of the world?" Rafe asked.

Based on what Gemma had experienced, life in Dead River was better. At least in Dead River, she knew people, the residents cared about each other and she had a safe place to land. "I like it here."

"What was that pause?" Rafe asked. "Part of you is curious."

She wasn't eager to tell him about her misadventures in love and life. She'd discovered parts of herself, but she'd also had her heart broken. "I've always wanted to visit London and Paris and Dublin."

"Why haven't you?" Rafe asked.

"No interest in traveling alone."

"Who was he?" Rafe asked.

"Who was who?"

"The man who broke your heart."

How did he know? "Did Flint or Theo tell you, because I swear, I will kill them." She hadn't told her brothers much about the man who had broken her heart, but they'd known a little about him.

Rafe shook his head. "Your brothers have said nothing to me about you since I came back to Dead River. You know how protective they are. They wouldn't tell me a Gemma secret. I've known for a while there's something going on with you."

"How?" she asked.

"You kissed me like you wanted it to go further. You said it was fine for us to sleep together."

Gemma laughed. "I am not sure if I said those exact words, but how does that mean there's something going on with me?"

"The Gemma I know wouldn't sleep with a man who wasn't her boyfriend."

"Are you calling me trampy?"

"Never. I would never think that about you. I was thinking something must have happened to make you okay with having an affair without commitment."

"My brothers and the people of this town like to think of me in a certain way. That's fine. Of course, everyone else does what they want without being judged. Case in point, Theo sleeping with Mimi Rand and having a baby with her."

"I think people judged that a little," Rafe said.

"Small minded people and Dr. Rand, sure. He still

holds what happened between Theo and Mimi against me. But I don't have to tell you that two single, consenting adults don't need to provide explanations to other people for their behavior. The reality is I'm a single woman who likes sex and I don't date doctors. That's my prerogative."

"You won't date doctors, but you'll sleep with them?" he asked.

Why the scrutiny? "I like you. I was open to something happening between us." She had been for a long time. Rafe had always been able to turn her head and turn her on.

"Has that changed?" Rafe asked.

She still wanted Rafe. Her desire for him wasn't the problem. "It's not me that's closed off and confused," Gemma said.

"Tell me what he did to you."

Again with the scrutiny. Why did it matter what had happened in the past? The past was over and she had moved on. It had been embarrassing and she had been a world-class chump. Was she over it enough to discuss it? "I met a surgeon while I was in nursing school."

Rafe winced. "Surgeons. Tough crowd."

When it came to their jobs, surgeons had a reputation for being hardworking, driven and logical, but also egocentric. Jackson fit those qualities and had more unwelcome characteristics, like being selfish, rude and a liar. "We dated. I thought it was serious. He thought we were just having fun. Unfortunately, he was also having fun with several of the other nurses in my program, and women at the hospital and my friend, who he got pregnant."

"Wow. No happy ending there for you," Rafe said.

It wasn't a happy ending for anyone. "He told my friend he had no interest in being a parent and applied for a job across the country. He agreed to send child support payments, but he doesn't speak to her or his son."

"He sounds like a piece of work," Rafe said.

Gemma couldn't believe she hadn't seen it. Jackson had been the exact opposite of everything she wanted. "He was wrong for me and yet I picked him. I was head over heels, absolutely blind about his faults." Part of what had completely captured her attention was how good Jackson was in the bedroom. Toe-curling, mind-blowing sex, lots of it, over and over all night long; he was insatiable and did things to her body she hadn't known were possible. He was all technique and no emotion.

Thinking of it, heat flooded her body. Jackson had awakened her sensuality and Gemma hadn't had sex that good or that hot since. Was it the lack of emotional connection that was great? Or had she tricked herself into believing the connection was there?

Enter Rafe. He was as emotionally unavailable as Jackson had been, but at least he was up front about it. He would be amazing in bed. The few moments she had been in his arms, she had known sex with him would be incomparable. Maybe she would finally have someone to say to herself, "See, Jackson? Other men know how to have great sex too and they don't have to lie about it." She hated that she was still making comparisons, but that was natural, wasn't it?

"You made a bad judgment call. I've been there. You shouldn't be so hard on yourself," Rafe said.

"At least I learned. I won't lose my heart to a doctor. Not again."

Rafe said nothing and stared ahead down the long road leading to Trevor and Gabriella's ranch on the outskirts of town. Then he turned on the radio. Loudly.

Gemma turned it off. "That was rude. We were talking."

"I'm rude sometimes. You know that."

"I do, but tell me why."

"I don't have anything else to say on the matter. I'm no better than this douche. I don't commit to people in my personal life. I commit to my job. So what can I say to you that wouldn't make me a hypocrite? I'd like you to know that not every doctor would be so cavalier with your feelings, but those words from my mouth are two-faced."

He almost sounded angry. "I wasn't making a personal attack on you by telling you this story."

"All my life, people have stereotyped me. I wasn't good enough for you when I was the poor trailer trash living on the wrong side of town and I'm not good enough for you now when I'm a doctor."

"You've always been good enough for me," Gemma said. "Being good enough isn't what this is about." They were talking about commitment, knowing what she wanted and not being afraid to go after it.

A muscle flexed in his jaw. "What is it about?"

"It's about not making another mistake. I won't fall for a man who wants different things than I do. I want a family, Rafe. A family I didn't have. I want someone who sticks around for me. The opposite of my lazy, piece-of-crap father. I don't see how that has anything to do with you because you want to leave Dead River.

You don't want me and you don't want me in your life. You don't want anyone in your life."

Rafe pulled the car to the side of the road so abruptly Gemma was afraid he would skid out of control on the open highway. He jammed the car into park and faced her. "I don't want you? Gemma, you might be sweet, but you are not that naïve. You know when I look at you, I want to peel off every piece of clothing on your body and make love with you until you are delirious with pleasure and satisfaction. I've thought of having you in my office. In my bed. I want to kiss that pretty little mouth and I want to put my hands everywhere. I want to know where you like to be touched best. Tell me, Gemma, where would you want me to touch you first?"

Gemma felt her mouth go slack-jawed. Did he expect her to answer? Or was the question meant to throw her off? "Rafe, we have an appointment."

"Stop it. Stop avoiding. You were plain enough about what you wanted in my office. Don't be shy now."

Her mouth felt dry. "I don't know." She was overwhelmed by sensations and was almost dizzy with desire.

"Do you want to find out?"

It was either shock or curiosity, but she felt her head nodding, her hair brushing the window.

Then his mouth came down on hers in a kiss that was endlessly passionate and absolutely dominating.

This was what she had been missing and this was what she knew would happen if she let her relationship progress with Rafe. Being his friends' kid sister, then his colleague, then his partner in their quest for a cure had blended into a shaky friendship.

What was happening now wasn't friendship. Even if she wasn't the most experienced woman in Dead River, she knew what Rafe wanted.

Her.

She pushed on his shoulders and he immediately leaned away, breaking the kiss.

"I'm sorry, Gemma."

Sorry? "I'm not sorry. I'm just confused."

Rafe jammed a hand through his hair. "About what?"

"Why did you kiss me?"

"To prove a point."

"Which was what?"

"You're an incredibly sexy woman. Men want you. Men have always wanted you. Doctors, construction workers, chefs, waiters and pretty much everyone who knows you sees you're a wonderful woman. Don't let one jerk spoil it for every guy out there who wants a shot with you."

Was that what she had been doing? Jackson had hurt her and to date, he was the one significant romantic relationship in her life. "What about you? Do you want a shot with me?"

Rafe increased the distance between them. "Getting involved with each other won't be simple and safe. If that kiss was any indication, it would be hot and wild and absolutely consuming. I don't deserve a shot with you. I am leaving and your brother carries a weapon."

A joke at the end of a harsh truth. Disappointment and sadness streamed through her. Future together or not, Gemma wanted Rafe. "I know that you can't offer me a future. But I want you to know that we would be good together. While you're trapped in Dead River, don't you think you should make the most of your time?" She let her eyes drift down his body.

Rafe's eyes blazed sex. She knew he was thinking of lowering the seat of the car and having sex with her on the abandoned highway.

Maybe it was her love of a man's body or maybe it was her feelings for Rafe, but she ran her hands over his shoulders and down his arms, encouraging him to move closer.

When he did, she let a moan escape her lips. "Yes."

"Gemma." A warning.

Could she push him past the point of control? Why did it make her even more excited to think about seducing Rafe? She'd always been the one seduced. Could she convince Dead River's most notorious bad boy to sleep with her?

She kissed the underside of his jaw, then his chin. She ran a finger down his throat and then replaced her finger with her mouth.

She unlatched her seatbelt so she could maneuver better in the small space. Grabbing the handle of the seat, she lowered the driver's side and pushed Rafe onto his back. Then she climbed on top of him.

As a petite woman, being astride a man and getting leverage was sometimes hard. But with her feet braced on the dash of the car, she rocked her body over Rafe's.

She unzipped his jacket and pushed the heavy fabric to the sides. Grabbing the hem of his shirt, she lifted it and he shivered.

"Are you cold?" she asked.

"Turned on," Rafe said. He slid the seat farther back

until she had room to kneel in front of the steering wheel.

She scraped her nails lightly against his bare skin and alternated her mouth and her hand until she reached the waistband of his pants. The evidence of his lust was in front of her. Was she bold enough? Rafe wasn't stopping her.

She set her hand over him and squeezed gently, then rubbed up and down. He grew larger and she drew his pants down to have better access.

Gemma flicked her tongue out and licked the head of his arousal. Rafe bucked in his seat.

When her mouth closed over him, he let out a groan. Using her hand and her mouth, she stroked and sucked, alternating her touch between feather light and just shy of rough.

He stroked his hand down her cheek and she lifted her face to meet his gaze.

When their eyes connected, he went off in her mouth.

She didn't release him until every drop was spent. Then she crawled up his body and kissed his closed eyes.

"Gemma, that was awesome."

She hadn't enjoyed pleasuring a man that much before. She had felt powerful and excited too. "Thank you."

"Tell me what you like. Let me make you feel good." His hand moved down her body to her rear end. He gave it a light slap.

She liked that. But she wanted more than a quick orgasm in Rafe's car. She wanted him to think about her mouth on him and what else she could do and come to her, night after night. Gemma craved the power.

"Later."

He lifted his head. "Later?"

"I'll let you know when and how I want it."

Chapter 5

Since the explosive incident in his car two days ago, Rafe had kept his distance from her. Had she spooked him with how easily they had gone from driving in the car to Gemma's mouth on him in the most intimate way? She couldn't stop thinking about it.

They hadn't so much as brushed by each other in the lab. The shift they had worked together had been tense, all business with no mention of what had happened. Was he waiting for her to bring it up? Initiate another encounter?

Gemma gathered up their notes. She and Rafe had been diligently writing about their progress. Other members of the clinic were assisting in the lab, but only she and Rafe knew about their backup plan. She would do everything she could to keep their notes safe.

She pulled on her coat and gloves, tucking the folder into her handbag and zipping it. Wyoming in winter could be brutally cold. She didn't need papers about the virus blowing down Main Street.

Gemma walked at a quick clip toward the library. It wasn't far from the clinic and it wasn't worth driving the short distance.

She had been alone on Main Street the time she'd

been attacked and since then, she had harbored a strange, fear-fuelled response every time she walked unaccompanied from the clinic. Her brother had tried to find her attacker, but since she couldn't identify him or give any clues to his identity, he had no leads.

Gemma didn't have many enemies in Dead River. She worked hard to make that the case. The quarantine had created a peculiar reaction in some of the residents, propelling people to act in a manner they wouldn't have otherwise. The wind was blowing hard and Gemma kept her head down and pulled her hood up, tightening the straps under her chin.

Her bag grew heavier and she reached for it, whirling when she felt it being pulled away.

She came face-to-face with a masked man. The last time she had been attacked, she had fought back. This time would be no different. After a brief impulse to hold onto the bag, she released it. Their notes weren't anything to lose her life over.

The man—or woman—it was difficult to tell under the winter coat, scarf and ski mask, held her bag and circled her. Gemma stood in the self-protective stance she had learned in her defense class. "Leave me alone!" she screamed. "Get away from me."

The attacker lunged at her, punching her in the shoulder. Gemma tried to turn and run, but the attacker grabbed her by her jacket and flung her to the ground. He was strong. The sensation of the cold ground was second to the pain of her knees and hands hitting the concrete. She rolled, putting distance between herself and the attacker. She had to flee. She climbed to her feet and ran, expecting the attacker would give chase.

When she turned around, she was again alone on the street. Was he lying in wait to attack her again?

Gemma raced for the nearest business, Dead River Hardware. Gemma ran inside, the heat of the store stinging her face. She collected herself. She was shaking and scared and dizzy with panic.

The salesclerk came from behind her cash register. "You all right, honey?"

She wasn't all right. "Please call the police. Call Flint. Someone attacked me."

"You need to come with me to the clinic so I can assess your injuries," Rafe said. When he finally found the man who had attacked Gemma, he would kill him. Without hesitation. The idea of someone laying their hands on Gemma in a rage infuriated Rafe. He wasn't a violent man, but when someone he cared about was under attack, his sense of civility and calm disappeared.

Gemma shook her head. "Someone stole my bag and my notes. That's the most important thing."

Rafe didn't care about the notes or the bag. "Why are you so stubborn about this? You need a medical assessment."

Gemma blew out her breath. "Me? I am talking to Mr. Stubborn."

Flint stepped between them. "Okay, you two. Take it easy. Let me get some details from Gemma and then I want her to go with you to the clinic. Please make sure she's okay."

Rafe took a step away so Flint could talk to his sister.

Rafe should have followed Gemma when she left

the clinic. He had seen her putting on her coat and he had suspected she was carrying through their plan to conceal their notes safely at the Dead River library. Why hadn't he accompanied her?

He'd been working with their virus samples, but it could have waited an hour.

Rafe was feeling uneasy about what had happened between them in the car on the way to Trevor and Gabriella's ranch. Why had he let the heat escalate to the point that Gemma had him in the palm of her hand? Gemma had been like a siren. He couldn't stop her and he couldn't tell her no. Not that he'd wanted to. The warnings from her brothers to stay away from Gemma and his short time in Dead River had drifted away when her petite hands had touched him.

After that incident between them, awkward or not, he should have followed his protective instinct and made sure she was safe. Someone was attacking the staff at the clinic, and Hank Bittard, the escaped killer, was still free and could be responsible. While Rafe didn't know why Hank would target the clinic, it was a terrifying thought.

If Flint couldn't provide around-the-clock security, then Rafe would step in. When he'd heard and seen the ambulance and Flint's police car race past the clinic, he had known something was wrong.

Feeling agitated with himself, he returned to where Gemma was speaking to Flint.

"There's good news from this," Flint said.

Good news was welcome. Rafe waited.

"Gemma doesn't believe her attacker was Danny."

Rafe could have kissed her. Again. Of course the

attacker wasn't Danny and if the person who had attacked Dr. Rand and Gemma were one in the same, then that supported his conviction that Danny wasn't involved.

"Did you see who attacked you?" Rafe asked.

Gemma nodded. "He or she was wearing a ski mask. I think it was a man based on the build and the height, but it could have been a woman. He was wearing sunglasses, but it definitely wasn't Danny."

"Will you let me take you to the clinic now?" Rafe asked.

"It's a waste of time. I'm fine."

She needed to be assessed and she should speak with a nurse about the incident. "If you were in my shoes, would you let that fly?" he asked.

The corner of Gemma's mouth lifted. "Not a chance. I would demand an assessment."

"Then don't argue," Rafe said gently. "Tonight, you're coming to stay with me, at least until we catch this guy."

"What?" Gemma asked, shaking her head. She looked at her brother and jerked her thumb in Rafe's direction. "He's crazy."

He wasn't crazy. He was trying to ensure she was safe. "Living alone isn't safe."

Gemma narrowed her eyes at him. "I'm safe in my home."

Flint seemed unsure. "Maybe you should stay with him. Or with me."

"You need privacy with Nina. I'd feel like I was in the way."

Flint folded his arms across his chest. "Don't make me pull Theo into this. We'll gang up on you."

"Not that staying with my niece and Ellie is any cross to bear, but I like my space and my privacy. Besides, driving from the clinic to the ranch every day is too far."

It was the second time she'd been attacked. Rafe wouldn't let her dig in her heels about this.

Rafe was accustomed to getting what he wanted. He would find a way to convince Gemma she was safer staying with him. Was it the attraction between them giving her pause? "I have three bedrooms. I have an office on the main floor if you'd prefer that. I will give you space."

Gemma inclined her head and Rafe almost thought he could hear what she was thinking. Staying in the same house with him was removing a number of barriers between them. When they were alone, something might happen.

"No. That's my final answer. I have some say over my life. I am staying at my place."

"We can talk about it later," Rafe said, willing to let the conversation end now. Let her have a few hours to think about what had happened and what could have happened. He didn't feel good about her being alone. Being attacked twice and being on staff at the clinic were dangers enough.

Back at the clinic, Gemma allowed him to lead her to an examination room. He handed her a cloth gown and Gemma folded her arms over her chest. "I do not need that detailed of an exam."

Rafe took a deep breath. He'd worked enough years in the ER to anticipate the worst when a woman reported she'd been attacked. He was trying to be professional about this and treat Gemma as if she were any other patient. Ignoring his rage for her attacker and focusing on her health was hard enough. "Would you like a female staff member to examine you?"

Gemma took his arm. "Listen to me. You're worse than Theo and Flint. I fell. My knees hurt. I didn't even break the skin."

"You were attacked. I need you to tell me if it was worse than you told your brother. I know it can be hard for people to relive the experience, especially this close to the incident. And to tell your brother..." Rafe swallowed the unexpected emotion. He touched the side of Gemma's face gently, as softly as he could. "I can't bear to think about something happening to you."

Gemma put her hands around his wrist. "I am fine. I will show you myself. I'll have a nasty bruise on my shoulder and knees and I know what you're worried about because I would too. Believe me when I tell you it wasn't a vicious attack."

Rafe let his forehead fall against hers. "I shouldn't have let you leave alone."

"I'm a grown woman. You don't let me do anything. I make my own decisions."

Why did that turn him on? He shouldn't be thinking about sex with her. He should be worried about conducting an examination and writing a detailed report for the police with any findings. Being alone with Gemma did crazy things to his head and his pulse. "Let me look you over and then I'll take you home to rest."

Gemma removed her coat. She was wearing her scrubs. The pant legs had been frayed where she'd fallen. Rafe rolled her pants legs to look at her knees.

Though her pants were likely ruined, the skin beneath was red, but not torn.

"Why don't I ask Anand or Felicia to come talk to you?" Rafe asked. Gemma had reassured him she wasn't hurt too badly, but sometimes talking to a friend was easier than talking to a doctor, and Rafe didn't know if Gemma considered him a friend. He didn't give Gemma a chance to say no.

He found Anand working in the triage area. After he'd finished with his patient, Anand went to speak with Gemma, and Rafe took over with the patient.

They'd been lucky that a few bumps and bruises were the extent of how hurt Gemma had been. It could have been worse and Rafe refused to let it escalate. Gemma was coming to live with him or he and Danny would live with her.

Rafe had given her a pair of his scrub pants, which were too big, but after tightening the drawstring and rolling the legs, they'd worked. He'd wanted her to go to his place and even after her protests of her home being safe, Gemma didn't feel like being alone.

Since her shift had ended, she decided to help the ongoing effort to clean up the patient records area. Their front desk admin, Cathleen, had picked up most of the paperwork from the floor, but the files and folders were disorganized in stacks on her desk. She was working through filing them as her time allowed.

Gemma had only started on a few folders when she heard shouting from the doctor's office area. Worried it was another attack, she grabbed a pair of scissors from Cathleen's desk, the only weapon in sight. Dread in her stomach, Gemma ran to investigate.

Felicia was standing in the doorway to Lucas Rand's office.

"I quit! I can't do this anymore! Working all the time and being exposed to that virus. We'll all catch it and die. There's nothing anyone can do to stop it!"

Gemma couldn't hear Dr. Rand's reply.

Felicia threw up her hands. "You can't know that. No one can know that. This virus will kill everyone in this town."

"We need you, Felicia. Please don't give up," Dr. Rand said.

"I have to give up. I can't take it. I can't live like this anymore." She turned on her heels and left.

Felicia stopped as she passed Gemma. "If you're smart, you'll quit too and spend what's left of your life having a little fun."

Felicia stormed out of the clinic. Dr. Rand came out of his office. He looked exhausted and frazzled. As the director of the clinic, he'd been in charge of arranging the staff's schedules. Dr. Goodhue had had some say in it, but they were already stretched thin and if today wasn't just Felicia blowing off stress, they were in deeper trouble.

Gemma considered returning to her filing task. Since her brother and Mimi's brief affair had become public, her relationship with Dr. Rand had been awkward. Gemma had never asked him why his ex-wife's affair bothered him, and Gemma wondered if he'd been harboring unresolved feelings for Mimi. She decided she could be a friend. Dr. Rand looked like he needed one. "What was that about?" Gemma asked. It wasn't like Felicia to scream and lose it.

Dr. Rand looked at Gemma. "She was at her breaking point. Working too hard. She asked to talk with me and then she got more and more upset. I tried to calm her down, but she wanted to quit." His words were clipped.

Gemma nodded. "Maybe she needs a couple of days to cool down." Sleep and rest could help. She was needed at the clinic.

Dr. Rand shrugged. "She doesn't believe we'll find a cure. I know that we will."

Dr. Goodhue joined them in the hall, and Gemma was grateful for the lessening of awkwardness. Dr. Rand wasn't over Theo and Mimi's affair and he somehow held it against her. Dr. Goodhue appeared flustered. "I overheard part of what Felicia said. We can't think that way. We can't think a cure won't be found. But morale has taken a few hits lately and I've been thinking about our situation. It's hard on everyone. I'm going to convert our storage trailer into a doctor-and-nurse lounge. We can move the remaining supplies into the clinic. When you need a break, please go out to the lounge and take it. We can't keep working this way without everyone losing it."

It was a gesture that could help. Being in the clinic, the lab and the virus wing for so much of the week was wearing them down and exhaustion could lead to mistakes. A few minutes away—and not a few minutes standing in the Wyoming cold, outside the clinic—could help. Maybe even twenty minutes to sit and eat or to lie down and take the edge off their stress. "That's thoughtful of you, Dr. Goodhue."

"Wouldn't that space be better used for more patient rooms?" Dr. Rand asked.

Dr. Goodhue shook her head. "I don't have the

equipment or ventilation to extend the virus wing any further. I've requested more BSL-4 space and I've been told the CDC is working on it. If we don't keep our staff on board, I don't have to remind you of the consequences."

Consequences like no cure being found. Lives at stake. Families torn apart.

Molly Colton picked up an orange crayon to color the picture on the opposite side of Annabelle's coloring book from where the little girl was scribbling. Molly could see Danny through the bay window at the front of the house, dribbling a basketball in the driveway. Rafe Granger, the sexy doctor at the clinic, had asked her to keep an eye on him and since Molly was already watching Annabelle, she was double-babysitting. Gemma and Rafe'd had some trouble—even more trouble—at the clinic and it had everyone worried.

In Molly's thinking, the whole town was nothing but trouble and no one could escape it. Maybe if she saved her waitressing tips for the next gazillion years, she could take a trip far away. That is, if the quarantine was lifted before the virus killed everyone.

A man walked up the driveway and Molly rose to her feet. She didn't like strangers approaching the house or Danny. Though it didn't look like an escaped killer—*alleged escaped killer,* she sarcastically corrected—she hadn't gotten a good look at his face and too much weirdness was going on in Dead River.

"Annabelle, I'm going to check on Danny. Stay here, okay?" Molly grabbed her coat and her cell phone and dashed outside.

"Danny!" she called.

He was already at the end of the driveway talking to the stranger. Danny looked over his shoulder and the other man lifted his head.

Molly's breath caught in her throat. Not the face of a killer. He had the face of an incredibly, strikingly handsome man, strong jaw, chiseled cheekbones and a straight aquiline nose. Not that Molly would let herself be tricked again by a pretty face. This man's build and outfit spoke of hard work, whether it was the muddy jeans or the worn cowboy hat on his head. Molly walked down the driveway, her shoes feeling clunky.

"Danny, come in and have some juice." Her voice wavered with nervousness. In ten seconds, she had a crush on the mysterious stranger. But she wouldn't let that change anything. No more too-fast relationships. From here on out, she was Gram Dottie–slow, like she needed fifteen dates before a man could kiss her hand.

She was talking to Danny as if he was a five-year-old, but Gemma and Rafe had put her in charge and she wouldn't let them down.

Danny jammed his hands in his pockets and looked between the two of them. "It's okay, Molly. This is my brother, Matt."

Molly paused. Sounded innocent enough. Should she call Rafe or Gemma? She couldn't leave Annabelle alone inside, but she couldn't keep a close eye on Danny. What if Danny walked away with his brother? Though Rafe had been vague about the details, Molly knew that Danny was somehow involved in the problems at the clinic.

Making a decision, she peeked back into the house on Annabelle. Still coloring.

"Why don't you come in for a drink? Of juice. Or milk." She wanted to be clear she wasn't offering alcohol, but in the presence of the other man, she felt tongue-tied. The last man who had left her tongue-tied on first meeting was Jimmy Johnson—the cad. She had other nastier names for him, but she was trying to be more positive and put her anger with Jimmy behind her.

It wasn't easy. Misplacing her trust in a thief, con man and liar had made her look a fool in front of her family and the town and had broken her heart.

Matt touched the brim of his cowboy hat. "Much obliged."

He threw his arm around Danny and they strode onto the porch.

"I'm sorry for dropping by without calling first, but I had the afternoon off and I wanted to see my little brother." Deep voice. Too good-looking. Red danger signals flashing everywhere.

Molly straightened. "Where do you work?"

"At the animal rehab center with Cole Colton," Matt said.

Molly's anxiety lowered. "Cole is my cousin. Distant cousin." If Cole had hired Matt to work with him, Matt had to be all right. At least, not likely a criminal, unlike her ex.

"Come on in and I'll fix snacks," Molly said, hoping Dr. Granger had refreshments in his pantry.

She lucked out and found a box of cookies. She set them on the table.

Annabelle grabbed a handful and Molly laughed. "Just one, Annabelle. Your dad will be here soon to pick you up and you'll have dinner with him."

The little girl appeared sad. "I miss Mommy. When is she coming home?"

Molly's heart squeezed. "That's why we're making her these pictures. Aunt Gemma will take them to your mom and then you can talk with her on the computer."

It seemed to cheer her and Molly mouthed "the virus" over her head to Matt. Matt nodded. Almost everyone in Dead River knew someone with the virus and the prognosis wasn't good for anyone.

Matt sat across from Annabelle. "Hi, Annabelle. I'm Matt. Danny is my brother. I know it's hard when families have to be apart. My brother and I love each other, but we can't be together as much as we want to be."

Annabelle took a bite of her cookie and watched Matt. "Why?"

Danny and Matt exchanged looks. An undoubtedly complex situation. How to explain it to a five-year-old?

Molly waited, seeing a kindness and warmth in Matt's eyes. "I have to work and Danny has to go to school. One day, we'll live together again and we'll take care of each other. But you have your dad and Molly and your Aunt Gemma to take care of you. You're lucky to have so many people who love you."

Annabelle nodded. "That's what Mommy says too. When I saw Mommy on the computer she said I was brave."

"You are brave. I bet you're the bravest girl in Dead River," Danny said.

A knock at the door and then Annabelle's father came in. He looked tired. "Molly, Danny, thank you again for looking after Annabelle."

Annabelle ran to her father, throwing herself into his arms and hugging him.

Molly gathered up the pictures she and Molly had colored and handed them to Tom along with her camera's memory card. She had taken photos of Molly playing to share with Jessica. "I love spending time with her. She's fun."

After gathering Annabelle's toys and belongings, she and Tom waved goodbye. Molly stood on the porch and watched them drive away. Her chest felt tight thinking of what it had been like when she'd lost her own parents. She had been older, but it was pain no child should have to experience so young.

Molly went back inside to clean up and start dinner. Matt and Danny were talking in the kitchen. They went quiet and looked up when she entered.

"Danny, will you give me a hand with dinner? Tacos," she said.

Danny rolled his eyes. "Again?"

"Hey, it's what I know how to make." With the limited food and supplies coming into the town, it was also a dish she could gather the ingredients for because she could make do with beans or meat and whatever toppings were available.

"Matt, would you like to stay for dinner?" she asked.

Danny looked at her gratefully and Matt appeared surprised. "If I'm not intruding."

Molly shook her head. "You're not intruding. I make extra because I don't know who will be here for dinner and it's great as leftovers."

"You work for Rafe Granger?" Matt asked.

Molly shook her head. "Nah, I'm a waitress at the diner. Just pitching in to help Gemma with Annabelle. We're doing a little extra because so many people are having a hard time."

She didn't mention her own hard time, her stupidity for falling for the biggest jerk in the state and losing her money and her heart to him.

"Molly is the girl who was supposed to marry that guy from the auto shop," Danny said.

Molly cringed. She didn't know that Danny had connected her and Jimmy Johnson. Danny hadn't said anything to her. It had been in the news when Jimmy became a person of interest in the theft of her grandmother's heirloom engagement ring. People who knew her were aware she was the victim. Flint had managed to keep her name out of the news, but word spread fast in a small town.

She waited for Matt to speak disparagingly. Living in Dead River, the theft was big news for a while, at least before the virus had taken over the headlines and Hank Bittard had escaped the jail. She'd heard remarks ranging from pity for her foolishness to blaming her for being blind to implying the theft was a carefully hatched plan to defraud her extended family. Ridiculous of course. Jimmy had taken the ring and her money and run.

"That guy is a real piece of work," Matt said. "Who treats a woman that way? From what I hear, he's on the run with some killer, so I say, what a grand pair the two of them are. Maybe they'll disappear together."

"If he disappears, my grandmother won't get her ring back. He took it when he left." A major source of guilt for Molly.

"It will turn up. Maybe in a pawn shop," Matt said.

She recoiled thinking of her grandmother's engagement ring sitting in a seedy shop, waiting for someone to buy it, likely at a tenth of its value, not knowing how much it would mean to her to have it returned.

Even if the ring did turn up, her savings would be gone. She had put Jimmy's name on her bank account, thinking they would be a real family. He had taken everything. Everything. She unrolled her fists. Getting angry wouldn't help. She had been making progress in getting over what had happened and learning to accept it. It didn't seem like she had another choice.

Danny and Matt were staring at her. She felt she had to speak. "I can't believe I was duped. Jimmy seemed so honest and nice."

"Some guys have the 'honest, nice guy' routine down pat," Matt said.

"Like you?" Molly asked, feeling unreasonably hostile and defensive.

Matt and Danny laughed. "Thank you for the compliment. I don't think a woman has ever called me honest and nice. Rough around the edges and rude, sure."

Matt could use a shower and a shave, but she didn't think he looked ragged. "I don't think you're rough and rude."

"You're too much of a lady to say anything even if you did," Matt said.

A lady? That description made her feel a little better about what had happened with Jimmy. She *had* been a lady. She could have torn through town badmouthing him and raging like a lunatic, but she had kept her composure, at least in public. "Lately, I've been blunt with people," Molly said.

"Just lately?" Matt asked.

"I figure with the virus loose, I don't have time for games."

"I'm with you there," Matt said.

"I missed the warning signs with Jimmy." She took a deep breath, suddenly not feeling an enormous weight when she spoke of him. Matt was easy to talk with. Nothing in his face reeked of judgment. "It moved too fast. It was too perfect. He was too nice and accommodating. Liked the same music I did and wanted to see the same movies." He said romantic things. He had once read her poetry, which she had thought was his own work, but was stolen from a famous poet.

"Sounds like you're a nice girl who gave the wrong guy a chance," Matt said.

She liked how that sounded over the ways others had described it. "I'll be more careful next time."

"You should be careful. You're a beautiful woman and some men will want to take advantage of you. But don't be too careful. You'll end up alone, shutting everyone out."

She had felt alone for a long time. Since her parents had died, she'd had her grandmother and her cousins, but that gaping hole in her heart was painful and raw. Jimmy had filled that hole; at least it had seemed as if he had. He had given her hope that they would have a family of their own and the idea of holding a baby in her arms, maybe naming him after her father, had been salve on a deep wound. "My parents died when I was eighteen. I haven't made the best choices since then."

Matt inclined his head toward his brother. "Welcome to the club. It's a crappy club filled with lots of sad kids that miss their parents, but at least you won't be judged."

Could Molly trust Matt? Despite rumors floating

around town about Danny and trouble at the clinic, Molly liked him. She liked his older brother Matt even more.

She could always use another friend, but was she repeating the mistakes of her past and trusting the wrong man?

Gemma sat at the foot of Jessica's bed.

Jessica was sipping some freshly brewed herbal tea. She was too thin, but she swore food sounded disgusting. Not even the decadent foods of the Blue Bear Restaurant could entice her.

That was most worrisome to Gemma. Jessica had always had a healthy appetite, and she couldn't get her friend to eat anything. Not even chicken soup or fresh veggies or applesauce.

At least Gram Dottie forced herself to eat the chicken soup that the Dead River Diner had become known for. According to Nina, they were making it by the stockpot full and selling out on a regular basis.

"I heard that some men were planning to climb the Laramie Mountains to escape," Jessica said.

"Who told you that?" Gemma asked. She wasn't as looped into Dead River gossip as she once had been.

"Tom mentioned it on the phone last night. Some of the wranglers were talking about it. He also mentioned thinking it was a bad idea. If they make it, what will they do on the other side?" Jessica asked.

"Have their freedom? Not come back to Dead River?" Gemma asked.

Jessica held her tea in her lap, cradled between her hands. "Is your sexy doctor still planning to escape?"

"I know he's not planning to scale the mountains or

slip past the patrolled border, but he still can't wait to leave. He's also not *my* doctor." Although he was sexy.

Jessica smiled. "You like him."

"Of course I do." She wouldn't lie to her best friend. "Something happened though."

"Something good, or something bad?" Jessica asked.

"Not really either. Just confusing. Are you sure you want to hear this?" Gemma asked. Her relationship issues with Rafe seemed silly compared to Jessica and her family's current struggles.

"Please tell me. I want the sexy details."

"We were driving to see a patient and we got into a heated conversation. He told me he thought I was sexy and obviously you know how I feel about him. One thing led to another and..."

"You had sex?" Jessica asked.

"Sort of. I got on my knees in front of him and..."

"No!" Jessica's eyes appeared wide and bright for the first time that day. "You are so bad and I mean that in the best possible way."

"I wasn't thinking about the consequences, like how weird it could make things between us at work or how it would impact our friendship. It's been a while since I've had a good fling and once he was touching me, all I could think about was how much I wanted to."

"Good. You should take what you want if it's being offered," Jessica said.

"But that's the thing. He wanted to return the favor and I wouldn't let him."

"Because you want to call in the favor on your terms?" Jessica asked.

Her friend knew her so well. "That's part of it. As long as I don't let him touch me, then I can't fall for him. That's screwed-up logic, I know, but I loved doing it to him, and I was thinking if we kept it one-sided then we have some boundaries."

Jessica inclined her head. "Why do you need boundaries? You know he's leaving. Why not have fun with it?"

"If it was any man but Rafe, I would. But he's always been this demigod in my world and now that he's paying attention to me, it's almost like he could reciprocate my feelings." In which case, she would fall for him. She knew it.

"He must reciprocate your feelings, at least somewhat," Jessica said.

That should make her happy. But it didn't. "That scares me. I like him. More than just for sex."

"You're worried he'll stomp your heart like Jackson did?" Jessica asked.

"Yes." Had she learned enough from Jackson not to fall into the same emotional traps?

"This is different. You're older and worldlier now. Unlike Jackson the snake, Rafe isn't lying to you."

"What do you think I should do?" Gemma asked.

"I think you should enjoy yourself. Relax with the little free time you have and let your inner vixen have some fun."

"My inner vixen?" Gemma asked.

"Every woman has one. Some men can handle her. Others can't. Based on what I've seen of Dr. Rafe, he can most definitely handle her."

"Gemma, I need to speak you, please," Rafe said. His tone was sharper than he'd intended. He'd wanted to speak with her, to clear the air, to unwind the tension that had been escalating since their encounter in his car.

He couldn't get her off his mind. He needed to find out if she was thinking the same.

With a development in the lab, he'd lead with that.

They were nearing the end of their shift and Gemma appeared tired. Despite his and the rest of the staff's urging, she hadn't taken off any time in the last several days. Rafe wondered if her bruises from the attack on Main Street were bothering her.

"If this is bad news, I'm not sure I can handle it," Gemma said. Her hair was knotted in a messy ponytail and pieces had escaped and fallen down her shoulders.

He kept his hands at his sides. He wouldn't touch her until he knew how she was feeling. "Can we talk in the lounge?"

"Only if you promise you won't try to convince me to nap. Lately, everyone keeps telling me I need to take a break. I'm starting to feel like you," Gemma said and gave him a small smile.

They put on their coats and walked to the recently converted doctor-and-nurse lounge. Dr. Goodhue had done a nice job with the lounge. She'd found a few cots, a small table and a couple of chairs.

Rafe closed and locked the door behind them. He didn't want any interruptions to their conversation. If their patients needed them, his pager, which was connected to the virus wing's alert system, would go off.

When they were alone in the lounge, Rafe took her hands in his. "I think I have good news."

Gemma leaned forward. "About the cure?"

"I made progress in the lab."

Gemma's face filled with excitement. "What did Dr. Goodhue say?"

Rafe paused. "I haven't told anyone but you. We don't know who is trying to sabotage us."

"It's not Dr. Goodhue. She's built her career finding cures for illnesses. She wants a cure found," Gemma said.

Rafe didn't think it made sense for anyone to destroy their lab results or attempt to stop them from finding a cure, but just the same, someone was.

"Rafe, Dr. Goodhue might be able to help," Gemma said.

Rafe shook his head. "I'm in the early stages, but I've found a few common sequences in our samples. If I can match those to other strains of viruses, we're closer to a cure."

Gemma's face darkened. Rafe reached for her instinctively, sensing her unhappiness. "Tell me what you're thinking."

"A cure will save Gram Dottie and Jessica. But a cure also means you'll leave. I'm happy to think about life getting back to normal."

"I'm not part of your normal," Rafe said.

His relationship with Gemma was the most complex he'd had with a woman. They had a history dating back to their childhood, they had mutual professional interests and his attraction to her was off the charts. But she was also his good friends' little sister and his colleague and a nice, sweet woman. And a sexy woman. That last trait would be his undoing.

"What if I left tomorrow? What if this was over? How would you feel?" Rafe asked. He wouldn't put his lust ahead of Gemma's feelings.

Gemma shifted on her feet. "I'd miss you."

"Why?"

"Because you're a good man. You're interesting. Fun."

"Can't we stay friends?"

Gemma looked away and pulled her hands free of his. "That's a tricky proposition. Once you're in New York, you'll be busy. We'll grow apart. It's hard to make a friendship work when we'll live thousands of miles apart."

He understood and agreed with her assessment. Connecting over social media wasn't the same as sharing drinks with friends on a Friday night. In the past, when Rafe had left Dead River, he hadn't wanted to look back. He'd wanted to put as much space between him and this little town as he could. "Then tell me what you want. If you tell me, I'll give it to you."

Heat flared in her eyes. "Rafe, you'll crush me."

Rafe shook his head. He didn't know what exactly she meant by that, but he wasn't planning to hurt her. "I haven't lied to you. I haven't pretended to be anything other than me."

Gemma set her hands on his chest. "I've always tried to be a good person. I've always tried to make decisions that would ultimately lead to happiness. For me. For my brothers. For my grandmother. But I've been thinking about my life and I'm not sure if I haven't been using the idea of a good decision to give me a reason to make the safe decision."

"Taking a chance can have a huge payoff."

"Or it can be devastating."

"I won't devastate you."

"You already have," Gemma said.

Rafe startled. "I didn't mean to hurt you, and if I have, I am deeply sorry."

"I thought I wanted stability and a family and to date a nice, safe guy. But having you around makes me want to forget those things, and be a very, very bad girl."

Gemma grabbed the front of his jacket and pulled him to her. He didn't resist. Their mouths met in a hungry, wild kiss.

His male brain had trouble thinking about anything except that he was going to sleep with Gemma. She was pressing her petite frame against him and her tongue was stroking his. He couldn't slow this enough to think, let alone stop it.

The trailer had two cots set head to foot along one side of it. Gemma pulled him toward the one farthest from the door.

She surprised him by pushing him onto the cot. He sat and she climbed on top of him. Her fingers brushed at the hair at his temples.

"You are beautiful," she said.

"You stole my line," Rafe said.

Gemma kissed him, shifting closer. He took her hands from his shoulders and kissed her palms. "You smell good."

"It's hand sanitizer and soap," she said.

He laughed. "Not that. Just you. Clean and refreshing."

He ran his hand along her hair, taking the elastic holding her hair back and pulling it free. "You are so sexy when your hair is loose around your face and you smile."

She blushed. Her humility made her more stunning. Did she know how beautiful she was? "You really don't know, do you?" he asked. He shed his coat, feeling entirely too warm.

She reached for the hem of his shirt and he held it in place.

"I could look at you all night. You are beautiful."

"I want to see you naked," she said.

He released his shirt so she could pull it over his head. She looked from his face, running her fingers along his hair, then down across the day's worth of beard that had grown, down his body. She seemed captivated.

Had he ever been with a woman who had looked at him how Gemma was?

She dropped his shirt to the floor and he captured her mouth in a demanding kiss. She sank into him and he let her set the pace.

He had much to say, but he would show her instead. She reached for his pants and hooked the sides in her hands. She drew them down his legs, pulling off his shoes. They hit the floor.

She lowered her body between his legs and he stopped her, taking her hands. "No, Gemma. Let me make you feel good."

She shivered and he knew it was from passion, not cold.

He removed her clothes, piece by piece. When she wore only her bra and underwear, he enjoyed the sight of her. She wrapped her arms around her midriff and he removed her hands.

"Let me look. You are turning me on."

She glanced at his erection and her eyes got wider. He guided her to the cot and removed her panties and bra.

He brought his hand between her legs. "You are so wet."

"I want you, Rafe. I've told you that all along."

He thought he would spill on her thigh from her words. He hadn't had a woman be so honest about her attraction to him.

He slid a finger inside her. "Tight." He moved his fingers slowly, watching her face for a reaction, studying what she liked, learning from her moans and cries how fast to move and how deep to go.

Then, unexpected words from her mouth. "I need you inside me. I want to come with you deep inside me."

He fumbled for a condom, hearing the urging in her voice. Making sure she was wet enough, he entered her and she trembled in his arms, her body contracting around him. He went still, then pulled out, unsure if she was too sensitive to continue.

"More," she said. She rolled over and presented her perfectly round rear end to him.

He hadn't known many women who liked this position, but he moved behind her and pushed inside her. Slamming himself home, he sensed she liked it the harder he thrust.

The goal of having her orgasm caught in his mind and he refused to finish until she did again. He reached between her legs and stroked her until she was moving wildly beneath him. Then he lightly slapped the side of her behind and she exploded again, this time, taking him with her.

They collapsed on the cot and he shifted her, rolling to the side, keeping her tucked in front of him.

Sex had never been this soul-shaking. Hot sex with

someone he liked, someone he enjoyed talking to, was almost a novel concept. This wasn't just attraction and it wasn't just a meeting of the minds. With Gemma, it was everything in the same woman.

Chapter 6

Gemma could hear Lucas Rand swearing from behind the door to the virus wing. She hurriedly cleaned her hands and raced to the small corridor to the doctor's offices.

"Dr. Rand? What's wrong?"

Another outbreak somewhere in town? Had someone died?

"The shipment that came from the CDC was destroyed." He was pacing in his office.

Her heart sank. They had been waiting on equipment to replace the items that had been broken in the lab. "Destroyed? How?" Gemma asked.

"It was torched," Dr. Rand said.

"As in set on fire?" Gemma asked. She didn't understand what he was saying. Shipments into the town were slow due to the overhead of clearing items entering Dead River, and the need for a drop-off point and for someone to pick up the materials and deliver them.

"That's what torched means!" Dr. Rand said. His angry expression morphed to remorse. "I'm sorry, Gemma. I didn't mean to snap at you. I don't know how many more setbacks I can take."

The shipment they were waiting for had their replacement lab equipment, but also food, medicines, clothes and a hundred other items the residents of the town needed.

Anand appeared in the entryway of the office. "I heard some commotion. Tell me no one else has died."

Gemma shook her head. "No new casualties, but our supplies shipment has been destroyed."

Anand closed his eyes and took a deep breath. "Why? How?"

Dr. Rand stopped pacing. "I was waiting for Dr. Goodhue to return with the supplies. She called from the delivery point. Everything is gone. Someone sabotaged the shipment."

"Everything? Sabotaged?" Gemma asked. Was the same person targeting the clinic targeting the town's shipments?

Shelves in stores were becoming more and more bare. Medication at the pharmacy was near depleted as some residents had begun hoarding in anticipation of worsening conditions. The town had had to implement a rationing system, which had been an administrative nightmare.

"Food. Medicine. Supplies. Destroyed," Dr. Rand said.

Gemma couldn't understand who would do this. It was as if someone wanted everyone in the town to die.

Rafe appeared in the hallway, tablet in his hand, tapping at the screen. It was their first encounter since they'd slept together in the doctor-and-nurse lounge. He looked up and lowered the tablet when he saw Anand, Dr. Rand and her staring at him.

"What's happened?" he asked.

"The supplies that were sent from the CDC were

destroyed," Gemma said. She didn't have another way to break the news to him. She wished she could soften the blow. Rafe would take it hard.

He took a deep breath. "I see." He handed Gemma the tablet as he walked by. "Patient charts have been updated." He strode into his office and shut the door. It closed with a heavy thud.

Anand gestured to the door. "Talk to him. He needs a friend."

Rafe had indicated he wanted privacy, but she hated to think about him alone. She walked to the door, tapped once and entered. She shut the door behind her.

Rafe looked up from his desk. The dark circles under his eyes were more prominent. "We won't find a cure at this rate. I needed that shipment to keep working on the sequences."

Gemma leaned against the edge of his desk. "We will find a way. Everyone is working on it."

Rafe slammed his fist against the desk. "Not everyone."

That was true. Someone in Dead River didn't want a cure found.

"I convinced Dr. Goodhue to order some video surveillance equipment. Nothing fancy, but I want eyes on the lab and the clinic," Rafe said. "Those cameras were in that delivery."

Gemma rubbed her forehead. "What about setting up our own surveillance equipment using computers or video cameras? We could ask around for spare equipment."

"If we make the announcement public, it will tip off the attacker and he'd be more careful. We could ask around discreetly," Rafe said. He smiled at the idea.

"But we can't have eyes and ears everywhere in town at the same time. I wouldn't have imagined someone would sabotage the delivery."

What could she offer to help them with the cure? They'd been counting on the shipment to make additional progress.

Gemma tried to clear her mind. Every time she did, she saw Rafe pushing into her. Not an image that would help her focus on the virus.

"What's the matter?" Rafe asked, coming around the desk to stand in front of her.

In the small confines of his office, their thighs brushed and heat torpedoed through her. A stress reaction to bad news or perhaps her reaction to Rafe in general. He was too close.

"I'm upset."

"You're breathing heavier. Are you dizzy?" he asked.

Her heavier breathing wasn't about being upset. "I'm trying to think what we can do. I am sure another delivery will be arranged, but we don't know how long it will take for it to arrive. We can't sit around and twiddle our thumbs waiting." It was hard to think with him staring at her, especially staring at her with that intense look in his eyes, but she had a lot at stake. "Maybe we're thinking about this wrong. Maybe instead of analyzing the virus, we should be working to figure out where Mimi Rand became sick."

"I like that idea too. You're on fire today."

She lifted a brow. He had no idea.

"I haven't told anyone else, but I was in the lab this morning before my rounds. Some of my samples are different."

"Different like someone sabotaged them?" Gemma asked, keeping her voice low.

"Different like the virus is changing. It's morphing. I want to take another sample from our patients to confirm and get a sense how quickly it is changing."

"If it keeps changing, how will we track a cure for it?"

"I don't know," Rafe said.

The news had other disturbing implications. "How do you think the virus changing will affect our patients?"

Rafe scrubbed a hand over his face. "Could make it more lethal. Stronger. Different symptoms. It could spread in a new way. I need to know if the virus is morphing in the samples because of the medium we have it growing in or if it's also mutating live."

"We're still being cautious about exposure," Gemma said.

"We'll continue to be cautious, but I don't like the direction this is headed. I thought by now we would be closer to a cure." He looked at the wall where a calendar was posted. "Do you know Christmas is in a week?"

She didn't. Christmas had been almost off her radar. She hadn't put up a tree or strung lights or baked cookies. She didn't have the energy most days and it seemed strange to celebrate anything while the town was in dire straits. "It will be a crappy Christmas." Christmas had been a happy holiday for her growing up. She, Gram Dottie and her brothers had exchanged presents and they'd attended service at the local church together. Gemma and her grandmother often bought dresses for the occasion, always green because they thought it brought out their eyes. She wouldn't have those traditions this year.

"I shouldn't have pointed it out. It's a downer for everyone," Rafe said.

"Maybe we can have a Christmas do-over when this is resolved," Gemma said.

Rafe nodded, though a faraway look came into his eyes.

"You're thinking that the moment a cure is found, you're running for the border," Gemma said, feeling hurt even though he hadn't said the words.

"I can come back for Christmas do-over. Bring you a nice gift from Manhattan."

Gemma didn't want a gift from Manhattan. "Do I strike you as a Tiffany's girl?"

Rafe took her hands in his. "That's a complicated question. If you are asking that question because you think Tiffany's is classy and elegant, then yes, you most assuredly are. If you're asking it because you think I'd try to buy your friendship, then no, I don't think you can be bought."

"I'm holding you to a Christmas do-over. You don't have to bring a present. Just bring you."

She kissed his cheek and let her face linger close to his. When she drew away, she released his hands. "How can I help?" Gemma asked.

Rafe cleared his throat and seemed to gather himself. "Talk to your brother. Find out if he knows anything else about Mimi. He was leading the investigation into the last days before her death, trying to track the origins of the virus. Baby Amelia managed to avoid it as did Theo, but people Mimi came into contact with at the café were affected."

A more complete picture of the days and hours leading to Mimi's death could help them establish how she had contracted the virus. "If she caught the virus in another town, why haven't we heard of an outbreak outside Dead River's limits? Dr. Goodhue would be among the first to know if other towns were affected."

A dark expression crossed Rafe's face. "I'll speak to Dr. Goodhue later and make sure she isn't holding anything back from us."

"Why would she do that?" Gemma asked.

"I'm not accusing her of doing anything wrong, but if this virus is worse than we believe, the CDC may not want everyone in America to panic. One small town in Wyoming under quarantine is bad enough. Two becomes scarier. More towns being affected is worse."

A chilling sense of foreboding streamed through her. "It would be difficult to hide an entire town being sick from the media."

"I need to ask the question," Rafe said.

He circled his desk and sat heavily in his chair. He set his elbows on the desktop and put his head in his hands. "I haven't been this paranoid in my life. I'm questioning myself and my decisions and the people around me."

"Are you questioning what happened last night?" Gemma asked. She had wanted to ask him about it since she saw him. She hadn't meant to speak the words, but now that they were out, she had to deal with them.

Rafe stiffened. "Last night was great."

Did he want it to happen again? Had he been thinking about it? "But…"

"Not so much a 'but.' It's an 'and.' It was amazing

and I want to do it again. But I don't want to lose sight of our top priority. Finding a cure."

She had felt like this once before, when she had been dating the surgeon. He had been evasive, giving her reasons he couldn't commit to their relationship. She should have seen the signs before her pregnant friend was standing in front of her with the evidence.

The cure was her priority too. "Let me talk to my brother about the surveillance equipment and what he knows about Mimi," Gemma said.

"I'll walk you to your car."

"You don't need to," Gemma said, sensing strangeness between them. He was pushing her away again by reminding her they had no future.

Gemma felt the beginnings of frustrated tears forming behind her eyes. Pride held them back. She hurried to her car, Rafe following.

She unlocked her car door and before she could open it and climb in, Rafe set his hand on the door, stopping her.

"Talk to me. Don't run away when you're upset," Rafe said.

Gemma faced him and cursed the tear that escaped. In his hurry to follow her, he hadn't grabbed his jacket and was wearing only his scrubs in the Wyoming cold.

"I am not running away. You asked me to talk to my brother and I will do that."

"You're upset."

"Yes."

"Will you tell me why?"

"You don't know?" Why were the men she dated so dense? Why did they overcomplicate things?

"If I knew, I wouldn't ask. I want to know. Tell me."

"You love to give commands," she said.

"Do you want me to ask nicely?"

It wasn't how he'd asked it. It was what he'd asked. "We slept together. Now you're acting dodgy. I don't want to be involved in that again, in a relationship or even a fling with a doctor who cares more about himself than anyone else." Even in her emotional state, she knew part of her accusation was about Jackson, not Rafe. She didn't apologize though. Rafe was behaving almost as badly.

Rafe stepped back. "I care a great deal about you. About Danny. About my patients. What do you want from me?"

"If that's true, why don't you stay?" Gemma asked.

Rafe appeared bewildered. "Stay where? In Dead River? In the town I have been trying to escape from most of my life? Not a chance. I have a good job waiting for me. I can't throw that away over a few people I care about."

She wouldn't change his mind. He was making it too complicated. If he couldn't have a brief relationship with her because it was too much, what could she do? "There's nothing more I can say to you."

Gemma pushed Rafe's hand away and opened her door. He didn't stop her from leaving this time. She started her car and pulled away from the clinic. A piece of chocolate cake and some wine were waiting for her at home.

She was halfway home, before guilt got the better of her. She had asked Rafe to stay in Dead River after he had told her repeatedly of his plans to leave. Trapping him in Dead River wasn't her intent. Sleeping together had been as much her idea as his. She pulled to the side of the road and took out her phone so she could apologize and admit she had overreacted. She dialed Rafe. He didn't answer. She disconnected and then dialed him again.

He could be working in the lab for hours. At this rate, she couldn't sleep with the fight, a fight she had picked, lingering between them. She pulled a U-turn and headed back to the clinic.

Parking in the same spot she'd recently vacated, she climbed out of the car. Someone was sitting on the lot. After the recent attack, fear clutched at her. But she recognized the shoes. They looked like Rafe's. What was he doing sitting in the parking lot?

She walked close and let out a shriek. Rafe was lying faceup on the ground. Rushing to his side, she felt for a pulse. He was breathing, but he was cold. She tore off her jacket and tucked it under his head. Though it was difficult to see in the dark, she saw blood running down his temple. She had to take him inside and get more help.

Not wanting to leave him, but unable to lift him herself, she ran to the clinic's front door and called for help. "Anand! Please, someone! Help me!"

Anand and Dr. Moore raced into the parking lot. Dr. Moore fell to her knees and looked at Rafe. She shined a light in his eyes and then looked him over. "Help me carry him inside."

Together, they hoisted Rafe off the ground, Anand taking the bulk of his weight, and brought him into the clinic.

* * *

Rafe's head was throbbing when he opened his eyes. The lights from the ceiling were too bright, intensifying his headache.

"You're awake!" The squeak of chair legs against the vinyl floor and then Gemma was standing over him.

Rafe oriented himself. He was in the clinic, lying in the triage area on a cot.

"Rafe, do you remember what happened to you?" Gemma asked, looking down at him, her green eyes coming into focus, her hands moving to his pulse and then along his limbs. "Tell me if this hurts."

Too many questions. Why was she poking and prodding him? Slowly, the events of the night replayed in his mind.

Rafe had been watching Gemma drive away from the clinic, thinking about pursuing her and weighing whether it was best to give her space, when he'd heard footsteps approaching from behind him. He'd turned around, but had seen nothing. He remembered a sharp pain on the side of his head and then darkness.

"Someone hit me on the side of the head." Was that all he could remember?

"Dr. Moore put in a few stiches. The laceration was either from being struck or from when you hit the ground."

Gemma's voice choked and she brought her hands over her mouth. "When I saw you laying in the parking lot, I thought the worst had happened."

Rafe reached out to touch her arm, but she pulled away. "I was scared for you, Rafe."

He hated seeing her upset and he hated that he was frequently the man making her upset, even if he didn't always understand the reasons. "I understand. I was upset when I heard you'd been attacked."

Dr. Moore entered the room. "I thought I heard voices. How are you feeling?"

As if he'd been hit in the head. "A little like a sucker. I should have seen it coming." If he hadn't been distracted by Gemma's departure, he might have.

"Nausea? Dizziness?" Dr. Moore asked, taking his chin in her hand and looking in his eyes with her pen flashlight.

"Vision is clear. I've got a headache, but that will go away."

Dr. Moore nodded. "I'd prefer to send you to Cheyenne Memorial for a CAT scan, but that's not an option right now. I need you to be on the lookout for any symptoms and report them immediately."

He knew what to look for. "Aneurism, stroke, dying in my sleep," Rafe said.

Gemma did not appear amused by his words.

Dr. Moore shook her head. "Just take it easy, Rafe."

"I already called Flint," Gemma said. "He said he would come by tomorrow morning and get a report from you."

Home. Danny! "I should get home. Danny will be waiting for me."

"I called him too," Gemma said, touching his arm. "Molly agreed to stay with him until you were feeling better. She's crashing on your couch. I hope that's okay."

Rafe appreciated Gemma's thoughtfulness. Being a foster father under the conditions in Dead River was difficult. "Of course that's okay. Thanks, Gemma."

"I'll drive you home," Gemma said.

"You should try to keep him awake," Dr. Moore said, looking up from the tablet where she was adding information into Rafe's patient chart as she walked away.

"That will be near impossible," Rafe said. Even when he'd been a resident doctor at Johns Hopkins in Baltimore he hadn't worked this many long hours. When he went home, he was ready to crash.

"Molly is working the morning shift at the diner tomorrow. I'll send her home and stay with you and Danny," Gemma said.

Rafe wasn't sure why she was volunteering to stay with him, especially after their last conversation, but he didn't question her.

Gemma helped Rafe out of the bed. Rafe sat at the edge of the cot, allowing some dizziness to pass. "Why did you come back to the clinic?"

Gemma shifted. "I felt bad about what I said to you."

He hadn't enjoyed the conversation much either. "What in particular?"

Gemma sat next to him. He was reminded of being with her in the doctor-and-nurse lounge. Nothing would happen here, with only a curtain between them and their colleagues, but he was keyed into the idea.

"I shouldn't bring up the idea of you staying in Dead River."

When she did, he felt guiltier than he already did. "It's not an option." Rafe liked to think of himself as flexible, but remaining in Dead River wasn't negotiable.

He stood and Gemma set one hand on his lower back and one on his stomach.

"Are you okay? We'll go as slow as you need."

"Move your hand lower and we can make this go faster," he said, trying to think about sex and not the sharp pain in his head.

Gemma laughed quietly. "It's not an option." Echoing his words back to him.

He harrumphed. He put on his jacket and they walked to Gemma's car. They climbed inside and Gemma turned the key in the ignition.

Rafe didn't want Gemma to feel obligated to take care of him. He could take care of himself and Danny. "Why are you doing this? You don't owe me anything."

Gemma pressed her lips together and then glanced at him. "Danny deserves better. He deserves breakfast on the table in the morning and hugs before school. I know he's a teenager and maybe he thinks he's too old for that, but it's how I feel."

"Is that how your grandmother sent you and your brothers to school in the morning?" Rafe asked, trying to gain some insight into Gemma's thoughts.

"Most mornings. I remember a few times when my father would come around and cause a problem. Those mornings were chaotic and tense. When it was the four of us, Gram Dottie and my brothers and I had some nice family time at the breakfast table. My grandmother did her best to keep us together and strong."

"Is that why you're so angry at me? You think I'm doing to Danny what your father did to you?"

Her brows furrowed and then she sighed. "I hadn't thought about it that way. Maybe it's a bit of that, but also a little of what happened with the last doctor I dated. That relationship crashed and burned. My dad was a jerk and while my brothers are good men, they have their relationship issues too."

Rafe's headache intensified. He wasn't sure he liked being lumped into a group with her father and the doctor who'd cheated on her. He expected better of himself. She deserved better. "That's harsh, telling me I'm like a cheater and a liar."

"You're the one who told me to speak my mind," she said.

Though he didn't like what she'd said, he did prefer honest Gemma to peacemaker Gemma. "At least you're telling me how you feel."

"You haven't lied to me about your plans. What you do after a cure is found is up to you."

She said the words, but he knew she didn't feel them. She thought less of him for leaving, maybe because of Danny and maybe because of her. He didn't like being less in her eyes, but he wasn't willing to do what was necessary to change it.

Chapter 7

Gemma drove Molly home and then returned to Rafe's house. He had changed into athletic pants and a white cotton T-shirt. He looked rugged and handsome. He hadn't shaved in a while and she liked the roughened look on him.

"I woke Danny and told him I was home so he didn't worry," Rafe said.

"When I spoke to him earlier tonight, he was concerned about you."

She was concerned about him, too. A head injury was nothing to take lightly and without the proper screening equipment, they had to monitor symptoms and hope nothing serious occurred. "What can I fix you to eat?" Gemma asked.

"You'll be sorely disappointed with the ingredients I have to work with," Rafe said.

"We can make it an adventure."

"You don't have to stay awake with me. Being here for Danny is enough."

She had said her motives were to make sure Danny was okay, but she was also here for Rafe. He knew it. "If I go to sleep, you'll fall asleep."

Rafe rolled his shoulders. "You're welcome to curl up in my bed and relax. You need to sleep sometime."

His bed. With him? She read it as an invitation, but because it was Rafe, she might have been extrapolating. "Let's see about food first." Going into his bedroom would be akin to relighting the smoldering fire between them.

"I'm not hungry," he said. "But you're welcome to eat."

"Not hungry or are you nauseated?" Her worry intensified.

"Not hungry," Rafe said, reassuring her. "For someone who is mad at me, you're awfully concerned about my well-being."

Gemma stuck out her tongue. "Flint told me to take care of you."

"Then this is a favor to your brother."

Being here wasn't only because of Flint's request. She had needed to see for herself that Rafe was okay. "Perhaps."

"Then it would be wrong of me to ask you to come to my bedroom, but not to sleep. To spend time with me."

Gemma laughed softly. "Even when you've been knocked unconscious, you're still thinking about sex."

Rafe touched the side of his head. "It will make me feel better."

Gemma shook her head. "No strenuous activity."

"I can do laid-back sex," Rafe said.

"With Danny home?" Gemma asked.

"Our bedrooms are on opposite sides of the house and my doors lock," Rafe said.

"I think we know what will happen if we go to your

room alone. Are we sure it's what we want?" She had to think it through while clothes were on and they weren't horizontal.

"Of course I want you. I've always wanted you. I'll always want you. I've made that clear, haven't I?"

They were words that could melt her where she stood. Her unwillingness to say no when confronted with sex with him was telling.

He moved quickly, crossing the room and putting his arms around her waist. His arousal pressed against her belly and the reasons for not having sex became nonexistent. "We have to be quiet."

He nodded solemnly. "Of course."

She took his hand and led him upstairs. At the landing at the top of the stairs he pointed to the right. She walked to his bedroom and opened the double doors to the master suite. She inhaled when they entered the room. "I didn't think your room would look like this."

"It's a rental, remember?" he asked.

"It's like from a Victorian novel."

She closed the first door, sliding the lock up into the frame. She closed the second door and locked the knob.

She faced him and took his shirt in her hands, pulling it over his head. "I love seeing you naked."

She lowered his pants, kneeling on the floor to help him step out of them, worried he might feel off-balance from his injury. Her mouth was level with his hips, and she brushed against him as she stood.

"Are you playing nurse to me?" he asked.

"I don't have to play nurse. I am a nurse," she said.

"Why don't you ever wear a white outfit with a little cap?" he teased.

"When is the last time you saw a nurse wearing a short, white skirt?" she asked.

"Come to think of it, never in real life," he said.

She backed him to the bed, but before she could push him onto it, he took her arms and spun. "Let's play this differently. Let me play nurse to you."

It had interesting possibilities. "So you want to wear a white skirt?"

Rafe laughed. "No. I want you in bed and me waiting on you."

"You're the one with a head injury."

"Don't worry about that." He lifted her legs and set them on his mattress. His pillow and sheets smelled of him.

Rafe slipped his hand under her pants and lowered them down her legs. Then he removed her shirt. "How do you feel about being blind-folded?" he asked.

Her senses went on alert. Blind-folded? She hadn't been blind-folded in bed before. "We can try it."

He reached into his bedside table and removed a black box. A black box of exciting possibilities. He opened the lid and removed a dark purple slip of fabric. He held it up and she nodded. He slipped it around her eyes.

Completely in the dark, she felt him run his hand down her body. Without seeing him, without being able to anticipate what he was planning and doing, she found his touch made her skin tingle more. Then his lips brushed her neck and her hips lifted involuntarily from the bed.

He set his hand gently on her waist and lowered her flat onto the mattress. His mouth moved down her body, past her breasts and then lower, down her side, along her thigh and to her feet.

He kissed the arches of her feet and then moved his body between her parted thighs. She reached for him, wanting to draw him close, but he resisted, not giving her the full body contact she craved.

Rafe removed her bra and then her underwear. The scent of him washed over her and lust enveloped her.

He covered her with his body. The heat of his skin scorched her.

He reached between her legs. "I love the way you look when you're turned on."

"How do you know I'm turned on?" she asked.

He laughed as he slid two fingers easily inside her. "I don't know all there is to learn about your body, but I'm a quick study."

Drawing away again, she heard the opening of a condom and then he was nudging at the entrance to her body.

"Open your legs for me. Let me inside you."

She did as he asked.

He slid into her and went perfectly still. She pushed her hips against his, bringing him deep. Gemma accepted him as part of her. Tilting his hips, he moved slow, too slow. She felt a release building inside her but out of reach. He needed to move harder, faster.

She undulated her hips and he stilled her movements. "You will do nothing to hasten this. I want every moment to last."

She needed to see him. She removed the cloth from her eyes and as they adjusted to the light, she met his gaze. He was watching her, an expression of pleasure on his face, the beginnings of a smile and enough intensity for her to know the power wasn't lost on him.

He spun her, dangling her legs off the mattress, and he stood at the edge of the bed. Reaching between her legs, he made small circles with his thumb and then he began to move, faster and harder.

She pressed her lips together to keep from screaming. Looking to where their bodies met, she couldn't believe this was happening, that she was having sex with Rafe Granger. Again.

He slowed. "Hey, where'd you go? Look at me."

She lifted her face. "I don't know how this keeps happening."

"You are irresistible," he said. "As soon as you said you were coming home with me, I knew this would happen."

He moved faster and she tried to keep the thread of the conversation. "Sure of yourself."

"When it comes to us, to this, yes I am."

He grabbed her legs behind the knees and brought them close to her body. The tightness increased and the feeling of fullness sent her body into fulfillment.

He slid her back onto the bed and collapsed next to her.

"What about you?" she asked. Her sight was still cloudy, sparks dancing in her vision.

"What about me? Finishing? Didn't you notice?" he asked.

"No."

"Too much thrashing."

"I was not thrashing," she said.

"As the man holding you, I can assure you that you were."

"What are we going to do now?" she asked.

"Are you asking for an encore performance? Because if you give me a few minutes we can go again."

She was more thinking that they shouldn't stay in bed and risk falling asleep with his head injury. But as long as they were moving and awake, she didn't see the need to hurry out of bed. "Okay, but this time, I want the blindfold on you."

"Sure."

"What else is in your box?" she asked, glancing over at it on the nightstand.

"You'll have to stick around and find out." Then he rotated, getting on top of her. He rocked his hips, giving away he was ready again. "Look at that. Just needed to catch my breath. That's what you do to me, Gemma."

"Then lay back and let me see if I can live up to your body's expectation."

Gemma opened Rafe's refrigerator. She was wearing a pair of his flannel pants and a T-shirt. He would prefer her in less, but as she'd reminded him, Danny was asleep upstairs and if he came down for a midnight snack, he'd be traumatized at the sight. "I would have a criticism about the state of this kitchen, but I know grocery shopping is probably low on your to-do list, in addition to the stores running out of staples on a regular basis."

The last time he had been to the grocery store, the bare shelves had been a disturbing sight. "The destruction of the latest shipment won't help that," Rafe said.

"Who do you think is doing this?" Gemma asked, taking a few items out and setting them on the counter.

"A psycho," Rafe said.

Gemma gave him a look. "No, seriously. Do you think it's Hank Bittard?"

"The escaped killer? I don't see what he stands to gain by keeping us trapped in Dead River without supplies."

"What about Jimmy Johnson? Trying to create a distraction so he can breach the perimeter and escape Dead River?"

"What I know of Jimmy Johnson implies he's too stupid to mastermind this. But the town is locked down. I can't see anyone getting out without risking their life. Causing a distraction in the town won't divert the National Guard patrolling the border outside Dead River."

Watching her in the kitchen was as interesting as watching her with her patients. She was methodical and tidy.

Gemma prepared him an omelet and then made one for herself. It was tasty and he found himself eating despite not feeling hungry. His head was feeling better and his vision was clear.

When they were done eating, he had the strange realization that he had talked with Gemma for over two hours. They'd had no awkward lulls in the conversation and he was enjoying himself. His physical hunger was sated and the time he'd spent in bed with her had satisfied a deep-seated longing.

He'd connected with her. She was a friend and his lover. He couldn't point to a past relationship that had ever been both.

"Is your head throbbing? Do your stitches hurt?" Gemma asked, standing and circling around his chair to look at his head.

She must have noticed the expression on his face. "My head is fine."

"Maybe we were rough with you too soon," Gemma said. She lightly touched his hair around the injury.

Rough with him? "If anything I was rougher with you," Rafe said.

Gemma lightly squeezed the back of his neck. "I'm a big girl. I can take it."

He admired her courage. She was made of stronger stuff than he would have guessed. She took life and the inevitable problems in stride, including his.

Flint was not happy that she'd answered Rafe's door wearing a pair of Rafe's pajamas pants and his T-shirt. But her only other clothing choice was her scrubs. She hadn't planned to stay the night.

"I thought I warned you to keep your distance from him," Flint said.

"You're overreacting to nothing."

"I will arrest him. Might be illegal, but who will stop me?" Flint asked.

Gemma rolled her eyes. "Stop. You told me to take care of Rafe. After the incident in the parking lot, I stayed to make sure he didn't slip into a coma. Besides, I wanted to help Danny get ready for school."

Flint didn't look like he believed her, but he wasn't planning to press his sister for details about her personal life. Her brothers saw her as pure and virginal and she was content to let them think whatever they wanted as long as they didn't interfere.

"What did you make for breakfast? Pancakes and sausage?" Flint asked.

"Pancakes and turkey bacon. No sausage in the house," Gemma said.

Flint waited a beat. "Do you have leftovers? I had breakfast with Nina, but you flip a mean pancake."

Gemma waved him in. "There's more." She always cooked extra, a habit of growing up with brothers.

Flint sat at the table and Rafe joined them a few minutes later, his hair wet from the shower. He smelled good, like spices and oranges.

Gemma rushed to check his stitches, but Rafe waved her off. "It's okay. They're in place."

She checked that the wound was sealed and then sat. Fussing over him was unnecessary. He was a doctor. He knew his physical limits, even if he chose to test them.

Rafe poured himself a cup of coffee. "Every time I see you, Flint, it's bad news."

Flint drizzled syrup over his pancakes. "Sorry to say I have more to share about last night. You weren't the only one at the clinic to have trouble. I received a call this morning from a patrol car. Colleen Goodhue was in a car accident. Her car went off the road and into a ditch."

Gemma felt sick. "Is she okay?"

"Banged up pretty bad," Flint said.

It was too strange to be a coincidence. Everyone at the clinic knew what was happening and was being careful. How was this assailant continually getting to everyone?

"Is she awake? Have you spoken to her?" Rafe asked.

"She is awake. She said her brakes weren't working. I had the car towed to the auto body shop. They confirmed her car had no brake fluid."

"Poor maintenance or do you suspect someone?" Rafe asked.

"Based on what's been going on around here, I assumed the latter and it looks like I was right. The car had a puncture in the brake line."

Rafe shook his head. "Who wants us to fail this badly?"

He nodded his thanks when Gemma set some pancakes on his plate. He didn't delve into them.

"What makes you think the attack on Dr. Goodhue is about the virus?" Flint asked, taking another forkful of pancake.

Rafe lifted his brows. "You don't?"

"Oh, I do. I think it's about the virus that's terrorizing everyone. But I want to know why you think so. You work at the clinic. Have you seen something? Heard something?"

Gemma liked that quality about her brother. He listened well and he talked to the people closest to the problem. It was how he closed so many cases successfully and found so many criminals.

"If I had, you would be my first call," Rafe said.

"Maybe someone wants one of the victims to die who hasn't," Gemma said.

Rafe and Flint turned to her, matching startled expressions on their faces.

Gemma shrugged. "What?"

"That's pretty dark coming from you," Flint said.

Her family still saw her as an innocent. Though she wasn't quick to talk about the disappointments and hurts in her life, she'd had enough of them that she no longer wore rose-colored glasses. She was a nurse in the only clinic in Dead River. She met and talked to people in many walks of life. Some of them were cruel, awful people. Her innocence card had been trampled and torn long ago.

"If someone doesn't want a cure found, they probably aren't a victim themselves of the virus. Which means they need some reason why they care about a cure being found. Which means they have a vested interest in at least one of the patients." Gemma didn't like to think about someone actively targeting her patients, but if they wanted to keep their patients safe and find a cure, she had to be realistic and protective.

"Could be," Rafe said.

Flint took a sip of his orange juice. "I'll look into the victims starting with the first ones and see if any of them believe someone is gunning for them."

"Maybe Mimi wasn't patient zero. She could have been the first to die from the virus, but she could have contracted it from someone else," Rafe said.

"Or from something. I read a study that Dr. Goodhue provided about a case of Ebola that was transmitted from bats to a human," Gemma said. "Could Mimi have been in the mountains hiking somewhere and come into contact with the virus?"

"From what Dr. Rand and Theo described, Mimi isn't the type to go hiking, especially since she recently had a baby," Flint said. "But I'll talk to Dr. Rand and Theo again. We've been filling in the blanks on where we believe each patient contracted the virus and then warning the people who were with them at that time. Maybe we're missing an obvious connection," Flint said.

Flint then turned the discussion to Rafe's attack. Rafe provided what information he could, which was next to nothing.

Flint finished his pancakes and Gemma walked him to the door.

"Be careful with him," Flint said quietly, slipping his cowboy hat back on. "He's not sticking around for long. This little picture of domestic bliss you're painting will suck you in and you'll be hurt."

Except she knew where she and Rafe stood. She knew what was at stake. "I know what I'm doing."

"You know Rafe is my friend. But he came back to Dead River for a short time. He's leaving the first chance he gets."

"Thanks for the reminder," Gemma said.

"Just take care of yourself," Flint said. "With Gram Dottie sick..." He swallowed, unable to continue.

She hugged her brother. "I will be careful. I'm sad about Gram Dottie too." She visited with their grandmother far more than her brothers were able to, and each visit, she saw changes in her grandmother. Though her emotional strength was ironclad, her physical health was failing.

"I don't like the idea of you working at the clinic. If I could, I would drive you to and from work every day," Flint said.

Gemma laughed. "Like when I had that job working at the Dead River library when we were young? You acted like every ride was a huge inconvenience."

"It was! I was a teenager with a car. A crappy car, but a car. I wanted to use it to cruise around with girls, not with my sister."

Gemma kissed her brother's cheek. "I will be fine.

The staff at the clinic is looking out for each other. Rafe is closer to finding a cure every day."

Surprise registered on Flint's face. "Is he? He hasn't said anything."

"He's keeping it quiet. He doesn't want anyone to know. Just in case the person committing these crimes amps up their efforts in stopping him."

Though Gemma couldn't imagine anyone she worked with intentionally hurting someone, paranoia might keep her safe.

"Dr. Rand said he was happy to take the first part of your shift and Dr. Moore is taking the second half," Gemma said.

Rafe groaned. "Don't treat me like a patient on bed rest. I am fine. I can work."

"You've suffered a head injury. Take a break."

"What am I supposed to do? Sit around the house and watch television?" Rafe said.

Gemma shook her head and handed him some paperwork. She knew better than to think Rafe would sit around and stare at a screen all day. "I have some light reading for you."

Rafe took the folder and opened it. "What is this?"

"Copies of the relevant information about our inpatients related to the virus. I've input the data into your computer so you can graph it and analyze it in different ways. Also, I have the profiles from the CDC of the ten most similar viruses and papers published about them."

Rafe seemed to cheer up at that. "Will you check our samples in the lab and take the recordings? Check the temperatures and the humidity levels?"

"Of course. Immediately after my rounds with the patients," Gemma said.

"You're a life saver," Rafe said.

"That's what I was trained to be," she said.

Before she left for the clinic, she kissed his cheek and waved. The moment could have been awkward. How did lovers part ways? But too much analysis would land them in trouble. With her brother's warning in her head, Gemma promised herself she would keep it light and carefree. She wouldn't fall for Rafe Granger anywhere except bed.

Gemma hated wearing the protective gear while in the virus wing. It was uncomfortable. It was loud. She wanted to hug her grandmother and her best friend without what felt like a spacesuit between them.

Gemma was tempted to tear off the protective gear and throw her arms around her friend. Only knowing that she would be forced into a quarantine area for monitoring and that she had work to do stopped her. If she did catch the virus from the virus wing, the clinic would have one less person to help in the lab.

Gemma stopped in each patient's room, taking the patient's vitals and recording them in the computer. The results were uploaded at the end of the week to the CDC.

Gemma stayed with each patient for a few minutes, taking some notes on their requests and finding out what was new in their lives. Monitoring their emotional health was as important as their physical health. Being separated from their families and friends was hard and the strain was showing in some of the patients.

Though most of the patients spent their days watching television, sleeping or reading, a patient requested paper and paints. Gemma couldn't see why she couldn't have them, but requests had to be approved by Dr. Goodhue. The staff was limiting factors that agitated or spread the illness and the more items brought into the virus wing, the more variables at play.

Gemma sat next to Jessica, who was sleeping. She laid her hand on her friend's and said a quiet prayer, asking for the strength and knowledge she needed to heal her.

Jessica opened her eyes and smiled. "I love when you're on shift. You stick around and keep me company."

"I love that I can visit you," Gemma said.

"How's Annabelle? How's Tom?"

Gemma had good news to share on that front. "Tom took her to sit on Santa's lap at the hardware store and he snapped a few pictures. I uploaded a bunch of new ones for you." Trying to keep Jessica looped into what her daughter was doing was critical to keeping her friend's spirits high.

"I can't wait to see them," she said. She looked away and then she broke down into tears. "I can't believe this is happening. I'm going to miss Christmas with my family. My daughter is going to decorate our tree without me."

Gemma didn't tell Jessica that most traditions were on hold. Residents of the town couldn't get specialized food for holiday treats and baked goods. No one felt like hanging wreaths on the street lamps. Few people had decorated their homes.

Gemma hugged her friend. "We'll get you out of here."

"I've been here forever. I'm missing my little girl. I miss my husband. I miss my bed. I miss sex!"

"It will be okay. Everyone in town is banding together. Molly has no problem pitching in to babysit Annabelle until Tom can pick her up after work. The other day, Danny was even playing dolls and ponies with Annabelle. He'll deny it if you ask him, but I saw it with my own two eyes."

Jessica laughed and wiped at her cheeks. "You must think I'm deranged. I feel like my emotions are being jerked around everywhere." She looked at her hands folded in her lap. "Can I ask you a question and get a straight answer? I need to know that you'll tell me the truth."

"That's a loaded request," Gemma said. She didn't like lying to anyone, but Rafe wanted to keep their progress with the cure under wraps. If Jessica asked about that, could she tell her? "What are you worried about?" A careful way of answering the question.

"Am I going to die?" Jessica asked.

The adamant no had to be stamped on her face. "You are not going to die. I will not let that happen."

"Will you find a cure?"

"We are trying." How much could she say? She wanted to put her friend's mind as ease. But they didn't have a cure yet. They had been working on it. Setbacks and sabotage were slowing them down.

"Is it realistic? I've been sitting here and thinking about Annabelle and Tom. What will they do without me?" Jessica's tears started over again. Gemma felt her own eyes well with tears and she couldn't hide them or wipe at them from inside her suit.

"They won't have to answer that question. They

won't have to live without you. We have the CDC expert and the doctors and nurses are working on a cure," Gemma said.

Jessica shook her head. "I've been trapped in this trailer for too long. I want to walk around outside. I picture just opening the door and leaving. I want to see my husband and daughter. Other people are sick in town. Why aren't they in isolation? Why am I forced to stay here?"

Gemma could hear the hysteria in her friend's voice. "We don't have enough room at the clinic to keep everyone in isolation. Those who are ill are staying in their homes and trying not to spread the virus. The entire town is under quarantine. If you leave here, you won't be able to stay away from Annabelle and Tom and they could get sick too."

Jessica lay back against her pillows. "Tell me some good news. All I can think about is missing Christmas with Annabelle. I already missed Halloween and Thanksgiving with her."

"Tom and I already talked about that. When you're cured, we're having a holiday do-over."

"What's a do-over?" Jessica asked.

"We'll put Annabelle in her princess costume and make a turkey dinner and Santa will have to visit again," Gemma said.

Jessica coughed, which turned into a fit of coughs. Her eyes watered. Gemma waited until it passed and then handed Jessica a cup of water.

"Please drink if you can," Gemma said.

Though she hadn't weighed Jessica, her friend looked more gaunt. It was difficult to tell if the dark shadows under her eyes were malnourishment or exhaustion.

"What can I bring you for dinner? Tonight, the diner is bringing the meals and I have an in with the owner." The diner's owner, Nina, was her brother's girlfriend.

"Nina and Flint are still doing well?" Jessica asked, sounding tired.

"They are. I've never seen my brother so happy."

"What about you? Are you happy?"

"I worry about you and Gram Dottie and my patients. I know it's hard on you to be here," Gemma said.

"What about Dr. Granger? What's new with him?"

A lot was new with Rafe. New levels of sexual experiences and uncharted territory, at least for her. "We had a few moments of passion."

"Define moments of passion and do not leave off the details."

"We slept together," Gemma said. Multiple times, in the doctor-and-nurse lounge and then all night long at Rafe's house.

Jessica's eyes widened. "Finally. How was it?"

"Great, except after the first time, I got clingy and told him to stay in Dead River, which is absolutely the last thing he wants to hear."

"After the first time? You had sex with him more than one time?" Jessica asked.

"Yes. Several times," Gemma said. She wanted to tell her friend about the black box in his bedside table, but wasn't sure if that was crossing the line between gossiping with a friend and divulging intimate secrets about her lover.

"Are you falling for him?" Jessica asked.

No. Never. She knew that would lead to her heart

being broken. "We're not in love. We're two colleagues who have been spending an inordinate amount of time together and there's always been a connection between us," Gemma said.

"How did you leave it with him?"

They hadn't defined their relationship. Why did it matter how they thought of it? The only word she needed to describe it and keep it clear in her mind was fleeting. "We've formed a quasi-friendship," Gemma said.

"Next time Dr. Granger comes in here, I will ask him about it," Jessica said.

"You cannot! This is not high school. And we were planning to keep it a secret. You can't mention anything to him," Gemma said.

Jessica frowned. "Too bad. I think I could make him squirm and I could use the entertainment."

"I don't want him to squirm. I want him to admit that Dead River isn't so bad. With a virus and murderer loose it's not on anyone's top ten travel destinations, but it's a great place to live."

"The smallness isn't for everyone," Jessica said.

"What some may see as small, I see as close-knit," Gemma said.

Jessica closed her eyes and Gemma knew she was drained.

"Let me finish up in here and then you need to sleep." She grabbed the trash from the can, placed in a new bag and tidied up. By the time she was finished, Jessica was asleep.

Gemma visited her grandmother last. Before stepping into her room, Gemma looked through the window. The lights were dimmed and her grandmother was sleeping. She looked frail and pale beneath the white linens on her bed. Under other circumstances, Gemma would not be providing direct care to the people she loved since it was hard to be objective in those cases, but the clinic didn't have anyone else. No one had heard from Felicia, which left only Gemma and Anand.

Gemma entered her grandmother's room quietly, not wanting to wake her.

She stood at the foot of the bed. Her eyes darted to the cross that Gemma had brought from her grandmother's home. It had belonged to Gram Dottie's husband and Gemma hoped it brought her comfort.

She recorded the results of her examination in the computer, concerned about the spike in her grandmother's temperature. One hundred and two point seven wasn't alarm worthy, but she'd ask Dr. Rand about it.

She didn't note any other changes in her health. "We'll find a cure, Gram. I promise." Then she slipped out of the room.

After completing the procedures to safely exit the virus wing, she went straight to Dr. Rand's office, thinking of her grandmother's high temperature. He was working at his computer.

"I finished my rounds," Gemma said. "I put a couple of notations on the patients who had marked changes. My grandmother's temperature was high and I'm concerned about that."

Dr. Rand nodded sympathetically. "I'll check on her. I know you've been worried about her."

Dr. Rand was behaving warmer toward her than he had since learning his ex-wife had slept with Theo. Had Dr. Rand finally come to terms with what had happened with Mimi, both the end of their marriage and her death? "Thank you, Dr. Rand. And thank you for picking up the extra shift for Rafe."

"It's frightening what's been happening around here. We're trying to bring this to a speedy conclusion and put it behind us," Dr. Rand said.

Gemma held onto the idea of the quarantine being lifted and normalcy returning to the town. "I'm going to take care of a few patient requests."

Dr. Rand nodded. "I'll review your notes and then I'll suit up and follow up on these cases."

He returned to his computer and Gemma hurried to call Nina at the diner.

Fifteen minutes later, Gemma was chatting with Nina, who promised to bring over the specially prepared dishes for the patients as soon as they were ready. The line to the phone in the virus wing lit up. It was their policy to answer immediately. "Nina, I've got to go. Talk soon." She pressed the button to connect to the line in the virus wing.

"Dr. Rand? Everything okay?" Gemma could hear machines beeping uncharacteristically loudly.

"Not okay. Get in here. Your friend Jessica is in distress."

Chapter 8

Gemma dropped the phone and raced to the virus wing. With quaking fingers she dressed in her protective suit, hating she was losing precious seconds. Her patients had been stable when she checked them a few minutes ago. Had she been distracted and missed a critical symptom? Too tired to be sharp? She had spoken with Jessica and hadn't noticed anything.

She had promised Jessica she would be okay and Gemma could not break a promise to a friend.

Finally in her gear, she entered the virus wing through the double door enclosure. Dr. Rand was in Jessica's room.

"Patient has low oxygen levels. Her lips were blue when I came in," Dr. Rand said.

"Did the oxygen sensor alarm?" Gemma asked, wondering how long Jessica had been lacking oxygen.

"Her pulse ox wasn't on her toe. It was on the floor," Dr. Rand said. "It's lucky I was here. I decided to look in on every patient, otherwise…"

He didn't need to finish his statement.

He was holding an oxygen mask over Jessica's face and Gemma took it from him. Had she knocked her friend's sensor off her foot? That wasn't like her. Had she made a mistake that would cost her friend her life?

* * *

Gemma was raw and shaken when she exited the virus wing. Dr. Rand had stabilized Jessica and Jessica had woken for a time. Her vitals were stable and she didn't appear to have suffered any severe neurological impacts from her oxygen deprivation, but time would tell.

They would keep Jessica under close watch for the next forty-eight hours. Gemma had to call Tom and let him know what had happened, but she needed someone to talk to first. She had gone over and over the time she had spent with her friend and she remembered checking the monitors. Had she bumped one on her way out? Pulled a cord free? Missed an alarm? Had the ventilation system misfired?

Rafe's office door was unlocked and his office was vacant. She sat at his desk and lifted the phone receiver. She could call her brothers. She could call Anand. But she wanted to talk to Rafe. He answered his cell on the first ring.

"Strange receiving a call from my office," Rafe said.

At the sound of his voice, she felt tears spill down her cheeks. "Everyone is okay now, but something bad happened to Jessica."

"Tell me," Rafe said.

She explained about her rounds and what Dr. Rand had found when he'd gone in for his follow-ups. "Thankfully, Dr. Rand was there. What if I had reported no issues? Would Jessica have suffocated in her room?"

"You are a good nurse. I am glad Dr. Rand was there too, but this is not your fault. Jessica could have kicked the sensor off. She could have had a seizure and the sensor disengaged."

"That doesn't make me feel better," Gemma said. Could the Dead River virus have caused the oxygen deprivation? They hadn't seen the symptom in any of their other patients yet.

"It's hard caring for friends and family. It's impossible to be detached. But I can say with confidence that you did not do anything to cause your friend harm. We are dealing with a dangerous, unknown virus. Some of the symptoms are manageable, others are terrifying. We've been lucky to keep as many people alive as we have."

A depressing thought. "Again, not making me feel better."

"I'm sorry. I don't think lying to you will make this easier," Rafe said.

She didn't want lies, but she wanted to know that they would find a cure. "Can you tell me more about the sequences?"

Though he wouldn't have been conducting experiments at home, Gemma wanted to think about anything except her friend's near death. "The initial sequences I found haven't matched to every sample." As Rafe reviewed what they knew about the virus, Gemma focused on his words.

"I still have hours left on my shift, but I feel sick," Gemma said. She didn't know how to get through them.

"Take a break. Walk away for a few minutes. Go to the lounge and lie down."

At the mention of the lounge, the steamy memory of being there with Rafe sprang to mind and heat flamed up Gemma's neck. "Maybe that's wise." She wished

Rafe was with her. She wouldn't ask him to come to the clinic when he needed rest, but being near him had a relaxing effect on her. She wished he was in the lounge and she could lie next to him.

"Don't let it shake you. We need you, Gemma. You're smart and good at what you do. You've got to hang in even though I know this is hard."

Gemma thought of Felicia Martin, the nurse who had quit. To Gemma's surprise, the woman hadn't returned to ask for her job. Gemma had been sure her quitting was a stress reaction. But it looked like they'd be down one nurse for the duration.

She said good-bye to Rafe and hung up the phone.

Gemma wouldn't leave the main clinic in case she was needed, but she would take a break and clean up the patient files that were still out of order behind the reception area. As hard as Cathleen was working to sort them, they had a decade of lab notes, doctors' notes and test results to file with the proper patients.

The phone rang at the reception desk and Gemma answered.

"Hey Gemma, it's Levi Colton. Katie and I have been following the problems in Dead River on the news, but I wanted to call and find out how you were doing. We've been worried."

Her cousin Levi was a doctor and he and his wife, Katie, had moved from Dead River six months ago to a town in dire need of a doctor.

"We're doing everything we can. I wish you were here. We could use an extra set of capable medical hands."

"I wish I could help. I've been told no one in and no one out."

"That's been hard," Gemma admitted. She gave him an update on the virus and their research. Unfortunately, he didn't have much that could help them.

"If there's anything I can do, please don't hesitate to call," Levi said.

"Thanks for calling. If I think of anything, I'll be in touch." She wrote Levi and Katie's home number on a slip of paper. A phone consult with another doctor might come in handy down the road.

After she hung up with her cousin, she returned to her filing. Gemma sat on the floor and started with the top piece of paper. Lab results with the patient name across the top. It was easy to file. Same with the next dozen sheets of paper. The next sheet was notes from a case several years ago where the patient had died. She thought of Jessica and how close she had come to death. Gemma shuddered.

The patient's name wasn't typed across the top of the sheet. Gemma flipped the page over. Dr. Rand had been the physician of record and Gemma remembered the case. The clinic had their share of deaths and the staff took each one hard.

Finding the patient's name, Gemma filed the paper and returned to the stack. Though she shouldn't read a patient's file without a legitimate medical reason, some pages weren't labeled as well as others and she had to scan for a patient name. An hour later, Gemma had worked through a number of papers and felt more depressed than before she had begun.

In the hectic day-to-day life in the clinic, she felt they helped most of their patients. Looking at the results on file, it seemed like they had too many to help and in some cases, the patients were worse upon receiving treatment than before entering the clinic.

The practice of medicine wasn't an exact science. Patients didn't all react to the same medications in the same way. Some patients lied about their symptoms or if and how they'd taken their medications, which could prove a nasty surprise to the clinician. But Gemma was seeing cases that had turned on a dime.

A patient had entered the clinic needing a tetanus shot because he'd been cut by a rusty nail while installing a roof. He had developed hand tremors and sweating, which had led to Dr. Rand administering antibiotics and a sedative. The patient had gone into respiratory arrest and had died. Though Gemma hadn't known the man, she was bewildered by someone dying of tetanus. She remembered hearing about the case. Dr. Rand had been inconsolable after it had happened.

In another case, a patient with type 2 diabetes had come into the clinic with hypoglycemia. She had been in the area shopping and had felt shaky, sweaty and nauseated. Concerned, her friend had brought her to clinic to be examined. Soda, a glucose tablet or a handful of raisins and then monitoring her sugar levels should have helped. It hadn't. The woman had suffered a seizure, slipped into unconsciousness and died. Gemma had been working that day, although she'd been assisting Dr. Moore with another patient at the time of death. Dr. Rand had been distraught. He'd followed procedures and something had gone wrong.

Gemma set aside the papers. The clinic couldn't help everyone, but some of the more straightforward cases should have been resolved with the proper treatment. It boggled Gemma's mind that it hadn't worked out that way.

Before Rafe had arrived, Dr. Rand had been the star of the clinic, performing life-saving procedures. A perceived mistake or an unintentional oversight were hazards of the job. In some cases, a doctor had to choose treatment from a variety of acceptable options and they sometimes chose wrong.

A dark thought crossed her mind. What if Dr. Rand had done wrong and then had tried to cover it up? He couldn't prove he had provided treatment or that he'd provided the right treatment. Gemma returned to the patient records and looked at the list of signatures on the pages. For legal reasons, in situations that resulted in a patient death, the clinic kept detailed notes on which staff members had treated the patient.

In both cases, the nurse of record was Felicia Martin.

An even darker thought crossed Gemma's mind. Had Felicia known about a mistake that Dr. Rand had made and had covered it up? Had that played a part in her stress and reasons for quitting her job?

Gemma couldn't imagine a doctor intentionally harming a patient, but she knew gray areas in patient care existed. A doctor who'd been up all night on call, a doctor who had worked thirty hours straight without sleep or a doctor who had misunderstood a patient's symptoms could result in tragedy.

Doctors couldn't be held to an impossible standard, but they could be held liable for recurring mistakes or gross negligence.

Gemma was running on fumes after the incident with Jessica. Was she looking for problems and someone to blame or was Dr. Rand not the superstar doctor everyone believed him to be?

Rafe felt strange having a day with nothing to do. Since arriving in Dead River, he'd been working too much at the clinic and tying up loose ends with his parents' estate. With Danny at school, Rafe figured it was a good time to clean the house. He and Danny had an agreed-on chores schedule, which they somewhat stuck to, but the house was messy. Rafe liked to give Danny his privacy and space in his bedroom, but laundry was everywhere: on Danny's bed, on the floor, on his desk chair. Rafe grabbed an empty clothes basket and began tossing in dirty items. When he'd picked up the laundry, he started a load in the washing machine. Good thing he had a big washer. With football practice, Danny had enough muddy, sweaty gym clothes to fill the load. Rafe added extra detergent.

Rafe also picked up in Danny's bathroom, pleasantly surprised it was reasonably clean. He'd thought he would have needed to drag in the garden hose and coat the room in bleach before squirting it down.

Danny was a good kid. Not a huge bombshell based on who had raised him, but Rafe had expected some acting out. Grief was a complex emotion and adolescents often had difficulties dealing with it. For that matter, so did most adults.

When he'd tidied up, he decided to spend time in his office. A friend from New York had emailed him some journal papers discussing cutting-edge virology and epidemiology breakthroughs and he had the files that Gemma had given him to read.

Though he found the articles interesting, especially

in light of his progress in the lab, Rafe's thoughts returned to Gemma again and again. She'd been in his life for so long, from the time they were children onward, but some of his strongest memories of her were from high school.

Back then, she'd been innocent and sweet, a quality missing from most of the women Rafe had known. He was interested in her, but she was off-limits. She was Theo and Flint's sister, she was younger and he didn't want to be involved with a woman who came with complications. Even when he was a hormonally-charged teenager, he'd recognized she wasn't a woman whom he could take out for the night and be hot and heavy with and then forget about.

Same applied now, which made it more bewildering that he was sleeping with her. He knew better. He knew he was leaving. He didn't want any more ties to this place.

It was a point of contention between him and Gemma, even if she acted as if she was fine with it. They'd addressed it poorly, so they would either ignore it for the rest of his time in Dead River or eventually discuss it calmly and reasonably.

The hard part was that he wanted to do it again. He wanted Gemma in his bed, preferably for the duration. He felt like a jerk asking her to carry on with him when he knew no future could come of it.

But all the rationalizations in the world didn't make the desire go away.

Gemma was overreacting. No chance an employee of the clinic would intentionally harm patients. Why would Dr. Rand? If he had made a mistake, she understood. Everyone did and despite some patients' expectations, doctors were human. It was a huge leap to move from a mistake to intentionally harming someone.

They had taken the Hippocratic oath, swearing to practice medicine honestly and help those they could. None of them were working at the clinic for the money. Big-dollar salaries weren't available in Dead River.

Gemma decided to put her mind at ease. She would check their computer records. It was faster than looking through the paper records, and unlike paper records that could be altered or destroyed, their computer records were backed up and any changes recorded. She'd need to be careful though. Every record accessed was tracked for patient privacy purposes.

Though she knew it was wrong to review Dr. Rand's cases without a medical reason, she felt it was a matter of life and death. If Dr. Rand was hurting patients, either through negligence or overt actions, she had a moral obligation to stop him.

Gemma opened the medical records application on the computer in the reception area. She started her search, selecting the patients who had been more critical and whose cases had been noteworthy enough to stand out in her memory.

Case after case of Dr. Rand coming to the rescue. But she couldn't find the same types of incidents for Dr. Moore and Rafe. They'd also had their share of tough cases and judgment calls that could have gone either way, but none where heroic measures taken to save a patient resulted in the patient dying.

Rafe had only worked at the clinic for a short time. He didn't have nearly the number of cases that Dr. Rand had. Before they had hired Rafe, they'd had an open position on the staff and with it going unfilled for so long, Dr. Rand and Dr. Moore had worked longer hours. Occasionally, they'd hire a temporary doctor to fill in over vacations and holidays, but otherwise, Dr. Rand and Dr. Moore had been a capable, committed doctor team. Dr. Rand had more experience as a doctor. Perhaps Dr. Moore more often referred difficult cases to Dr. Rand, forcing him to make the hard treatment decisions for patients at the clinic.

Had Dr. Rand been attempting to play hero with Jessica because they were otherwise powerless to stop the virus? Finding a cure wasn't going well. Dr. Rand hadn't spoken of it to her, but he had worked diligently in the lab without results.

Gemma felt disloyal for questioning him.

Mentally arguing it didn't lead her to any conclusions. Her gut told her something wasn't right. Maybe she could take a look at Dr. Rand's job history and call someone he previously worked with to find out if any strange incidents had occurred. She'd have to be careful. She didn't want to smear Dr. Rand's reputation if she was wrong.

Normally, Gemma chose the safe, stable option. Sleeping with Rafe had been a lust-based decision. Was pursuing this also emotion-based? It had been her best friend who'd been the patient who had almost died. Gemma had no objectivity about the matter.

Gemma called Rafe. He sounded distracted when he answered the phone.

"Rafe, I have a string of suspicious cases," Gemma said.

"Is this Chief Colton or Gemma? Since when does a nurse work suspicious cases?" Rafe asked.

Gemma was standing outside the clinic with her cell phone so that Dr. Rand couldn't overhear her. She would have laughed, but she was too worried and too cold.

"I didn't review every case Dr. Rand has handled, but I found a few where the results don't add up. Wrong diagnoses or incomplete treatment or bizarre turns of events leading to someone being hurt or killed."

"Gemma, we're tired and overworked. I don't think it's fair to look at another clinician's records and scrutinize them. We've all had those tough cases, when we gave it everything we had and it wasn't enough."

He was understandably defensive. In a litigious world, doctors had to protect themselves and stand up for each other. They weren't miracle workers. They were people with education and experiences that should allow them to make the right calls.

But Gemma didn't think this was a case of wrong decision-making. "I'm not accusing a good doctor of practicing bad medicine. I'm saying there's a pattern of behavior that needs another look."

"I'm not the person to talk to about this. After what Dr. Rand accused Danny of, I don't like Dr. Rand as a person, but I can't find fault with him as a doctor. His methods are good. His patients like him. Maybe you should bring it up with Dr. Moore. She's worked with him longer."

Gemma couldn't believe what she was hearing. He was blowing her off. "You're my friend, Rafe. I'm bringing this to your attention because I trust you. If you don't want to be involved, I understand, but you can at least be my sounding board."

"I can listen, but I can't be objective."

"I understand." Gemma told Rafe what she had discovered in the various cases.

"It does sound strange," he said, conceding the point. "I'll be aware and maybe I'll talk to Dr. Rand about some of his cases," Rafe said. "Especially what happened with Jessica. If respiratory distress is a new symptom of the virus, we need to be prepared to address it with our other patients."

She liked the sound of Rafe asking some questions. Dr. Rand didn't like her after the incident with Theo and Gemma guessed that Dr. Rand would point the finger at her or Jessica as being at fault. If Rafe pressed Dr. Rand about the incident, maybe he'd learn something important.

"Gemma, still there?" Rafe asked.

"I'm here," she said.

"You want to come by after your shift?" he asked.

She did. Having dinner with Rafe, maybe watching a movie with him and Danny would be a great end to the day. A sleepover with Rafe was better. She stopped herself before the thought ran away with her. After the day she'd had, she was better off going home, eating dinner alone and going to bed early. "Maybe another time. I have to go. I've been outside long enough, and Dr. Rand will be looking for me."

She and Rafe said goodbye and Gemma returned to the clinic.

Though she dreaded talking to him, she needed to check in with Dr. Rand to find out what he needed her to do.

"Gemma, are you okay?" he asked, meeting her in the hall outside the virus wing.

"I'm shaken and worried," she said. It wasn't the reaction she had expected from him. She had expected him to be accusatory and his dislike for her to be more plain. He seemed sympathetic.

"I know Jessica is your friend. I may have reacted harshly to you in her room, but I was worried about her. Now that she's stable, I think she'll be fine."

He was being nice. Gemma had been involved in every-moment-counted medical issues where she had been rude or sharp and it wasn't a personal attack. Dr. Rand almost seemed apologetic, though he hadn't said the words. Was she wrong about him?

Gemma stripped off her scrubs and took a hot shower. She should have taken Rafe up on his offer to visit after work. She didn't feel like being alone. Too much work and no play left her a lonely woman.

It was part of the reason she had reached out to the wrong people in nursing school and why she hadn't seen Jackson's betrayal coming. When she'd left Dead River, it was the first time she had been away from home for any lengthy period of time. Away from her grandmother and brothers, she had felt a freedom she hadn't before. No expectations and no judgments from others. What she hadn't expected was how behind she was in school. Her small high school hadn't been state of the art in science or math and her education was lacking. She'd scrambled to keep up with her peers.

Gemma climbed out of the shower, dried off and changed into warm pajamas. A quick dinner in front of the television, a little reading and then she'd sleep.

An hour later, Gemma returned to her bathroom to brush her teeth before bed.

She froze in the doorway to the bathroom.

In pink lipstick, her pink lipstick, words were written on the mirror. "Shut up or die."

Gemma ran from the room. She had been home all night. The message hadn't been on the mirror before dinner. Someone had been inside her home.

Rafe waited with Gemma on her neighbor's porch while Flint and his deputies looked around her home and took pictures of the scene.

"I'm so sorry this happened, Gemma," Rafe said. She'd been upset earlier in the night about Jessica and the possibility that a mistake had been made. Now, someone had come into her home and left a warning.

"Do you believe me now?" Gemma asked.

"About Dr. Rand? You think he did this?" Rafe asked.

"He knows I was looking at his patient files."

Rafe didn't think she could automatically assume the threat had been left by Dr. Rand. She had brought her concerns to Rafe earlier that day. When would Dr. Rand have had time to plan this? "He has no reason to do this to you."

"Unless he thinks I suspect him," Gemma said.

Rafe didn't know what to believe. Who wanted Gemma to shut up and about what? "Flint will speak to everyone at the clinic, at least to warn them." Again. "If Dr. Rand did this, he won't have an alibi."

"You don't believe me," Gemma said.

He didn't want to upset her further by casting doubts on her suspicions. "I believe everything you've told me. What I don't believe is that Dr. Rand is the person behind the attacks against the clinic and the town."

"We should start keeping a running list of the suspects," Gemma said. "We have Hank Bittard, the murderer, Jimmy Johnson, the thief, Dr. Rand, questionable medicine, and the person who attacked me, you and Dr. Goodhue."

The number of problems in the town was stacking up. Rafe blamed the quarantine. It was making people crazy to be trapped in Dead River, and they were acting out.

"There's enough going on that you should stay with me. You've been attacked twice and tonight is another warning."

"Whoever came into my home could have attacked me. They didn't. Maybe you're right and we're dealing with multiple criminals."

"That doesn't do anything to convince me that you're safer alone. Someone managed to break into your home without you hearing them. It could have been worse than make-up on a mirror." Whoever had left the message could have killed her. Rafe couldn't stand the idea of Gemma alone in her house.

"Okay," Gemma said.

That easy? "You'll stay with me?" Rafe asked.

"I could stay at Gram Dottie's, but it's too far from the clinic. We can look out for each other and I can make breakfast for Danny."

"I make him breakfast," Rafe said.

Gemma lifted a brow. "Cereal isn't making him breakfast."

She was right, but Rafe didn't want her to think he was a negligent foster parent. "You can make him breakfast if that's what he wants."

"He's a teenaged boy. Of course he wants food," Gemma said.

Flint crossed the yards between them, a serious expression on his face.

"Find anything?" Gemma asked.

"We're analyzing the scene," Flint said.

"In the meantime, I'm planning to stay with Rafe. I don't feel safe here."

Flint looked as if he might throttle Rafe. "You should stay with Nina and me."

"I'd feel weird, like I'm in your way. Rafe has offered to let me stay with him. We have similar shifts, sometimes the same shift, at the clinic, so it's more convenient."

"I don't know, Gemma. Rafe was attacked the other night too," Flint said.

"I could be attacked anywhere. It's safer to be together. I'll be fine with Rafe and Danny."

At the mention of Danny, Flint seemed to relax. Probably because Flint figured the teenager would be a good barrier between them.

Gemma faced her brother. "Can I grab a few essentials?"

Flint nodded. "Sure."

Gemma smiled at Rafe. "Give me five minutes and then I'll meet you at your place."

Rafe nodded and waved once. Flint turned to him and Rafe waited for Flint to lash at him. When he spoke, Flint was surprisingly calm. "What are you doing with Gemma?"

Rafe knew Flint wasn't asking about tonight. He was asking what they were doing together, for a definition of their relationship. "We work together. We're friends." Friends who were sleeping together.

"Rafe, this isn't high school. Gemma's not a notch on your bedpost."

Flint was protective of his sister, but his assessment of Rafe's intentions was unfair. "I'm not interested in Gemma for sport."

Flint tilted his hat back on his head. "Gemma's been hurt before. I don't want her hurt again."

"What makes you think I would hurt Gemma? I care about her."

"If you care about her, then maybe you'll keep your distance. If she falls for you and you leave, then it's the rest of us who have to pick up the pieces," Flint said.

Gemma knew that Rafe wasn't sticking around. She also knew not to fall for him. "Gemma and I are adults. We have it under control."

Except as he walked away from Flint, he knew when it came to Gemma, he didn't have control.

Annabelle was sitting quietly in the corner of Rafe's living room, playing with two dolls she had brought from home.

"How was school today?" Molly asked Annabelle.

The little girl had been uncharacteristically quiet since Molly had picked her up from school. Danny was upstairs doing his homework.

"Fine." She didn't look up from her dolls.

"Do you want a snack? I think Dr. Rafe has some oranges," Molly said, knowing it was one of Annabelle's favorite foods.

"No."

Molly crossed the room and sat on the floor in front of Annabelle. "Do you not like playing here? Because we can go play at your house if you want." Gemma's was off-limits after the break-in, but a quick call to Tom and they could relocate. Danny could either come with them or be alone for a few hours.

"No."

"You don't want to go home?" Molly asked.

Annabelle broke down into tears. "I don't want you. I want my mommy."

Molly's heart tripped. The depth and strength of the little girl's hurt was palpable. Molly would do anything to make it stop. "Let's call your mom, okay? Dr. Rafe has a computer we can use to video-chat with her."

Annabelle whimpered her agreement, but at least she'd stopped sobbing.

"I know it's not the same as being with your mom. I'll call Dr. Rafe to ask for the password for the computer." Molly tried to inject some warmth into her voice, but she felt defeated. It was getting harder and harder for people in the town to cope with the virus and the effects it was having on families.

Molly had been at the grocery store earlier and it had scared her to see how bare the shelves were. What if Dead River ran out of food? It was too cold to start a garden and she wasn't sure if she had enough talent to grow enough food for herself much less for Rafe and Gemma and Danny and Annabelle...

Molly collected herself. Any sign of additional stress and Annabelle would know something was wrong. She called Rafe at the clinic and he gave her the password so Annabelle could video-chat with her mom.

When Molly returned to the family room, she stopped in the hallway, hearing Danny talking to Annabelle.

"I don't think my mom will come home," Annabelle said.

"No way. She'll be home soon. Dr. Rafe is the best doctor and Aunt Gemma is a great nurse. They're taking good care of your mom," Danny said.

"What about your mom? Does she live at the clinic too?"

Molly's breath caught. How would Danny answer? Should she step in?

"No, she doesn't. That's why I live with Dr. Rafe," Danny said.

Molly thanked Danny for not mentioning that his parents and grandparents were dead. That concept would be frightening for Molly.

"My daddy is sad," Annabelle said.

"He misses your mom, just like you do," Danny said.

"He cried," Annabelle said, sounding solemn.

"Everyone cries sometimes. That's okay."

"Big boys don't cry," Annabelle said.

"Sure we do. All the time. I don't tell people that, but sometimes, before I figure out what to do, I cry."

"When I cry, my daddy hugs me," Annabelle said.

"Hugs are good for helping crying and for making us feel better," Danny said. "But I like fist bumps."

"What's that?" Annabelle said.

"I can show you, but it's a super cool big kid thing."

"Show me! I want to do it!" Annabelle sounded thrilled.

"Are you sure you can handle it?" he asked.

"Yes! Yes! Yes!"

Molly smiled at Annabelle's excitement.

Danny rolled his hand into a fist and tapped it

against Annabelle's tiny one. "That's a fist bump. You can do that with your mom over the computer."

Molly entered the room, carrying the laptop, feeling choked up about what she had overheard. Danny was a nice kid. He'd reached out when Annabelle had needed someone to be a friend.

"Thanks, Danny. We're going to call Annabelle's mom," Molly said.

"Sounds good. Did my brother call you?"

Molly's heart rate escalated. She hadn't heard from Matt since the first time they'd met. "He doesn't have my number."

"Sure he does. I gave it to him."

Disappointment speared through her. She thought they'd had a connection, but she could have been wrong. Her judgment with men was way, way off. He had her number and did not call. That made the picture clear enough. "I haven't heard from him."

"He knows you're too good for him."

"What? That's not true," Molly said. She was talking to a teenager and she didn't want him in the middle of anything, but could he talk to Matt on her behalf? Would Danny repeat to Matt anything she said? "I had a good time talking to Matt. I would like to see him again. Maybe for coffee. He could come by the diner sometime."

The diner was a friendly place. Maybe meeting again on neutral ground would give Matt the courage to ask her out. Although she should still be licking her wounds from what had happened with Jimmy, she got excited whenever she thought about Matt. Maybe they had a connection or maybe like everything else in her life, she had been completely wrong about him.

Chapter 9

"Flint, what are you doing here? Checking up on me?" Gemma asked, opening Rafe's front door to her brother.

Flint removed his hat. "Sadly, no. Can I come in?"

Fear overtook her. "Is it Gram Dottie? Jessica?"

Flint shook his head. "You'd know more about the virus wing patients than I would."

Rafe joined her at the door. "What brings you by, Flint?"

Flint took a deep breath and let it out. "I got an anonymous tip that Danny confessed to someone that he was responsible for the break-in at the clinic," Flint said. He sounded tired and weary.

"Why would he say that? Why would he do that? You said his teachers vouched for him, that he was in class during the break-in," Rafe said.

"They did. But now there is some question and I am following up on every lead. I need to talk to him."

Rafe appeared unsure if he would allow it, but then he turned away from the door. "Danny, can you come here for a second?"

Danny clambered down the stairs and came to the front door. "Chief Colton. Hi."

"I'd like permission to search your room," Flint said.

Rafe stepped between Danny and Flint. "I cleaned his room yesterday. I didn't see any notes or lab equipment."

"I didn't take anything from the clinic!" Danny said. "Why doesn't anyone believe me?"

"I believe you," Rafe and Gemma said at the same time.

The accusation was ridiculous. "Did you trace the call from the anonymous tip?" Gemma asked. Maybe the real thief was working to pin the robbery on someone else and had found out that Danny was named as a suspect in the attack on Dr. Rand.

"The call came from a burner phone," Flint said.

"You don't find that suspicious?" Rafe asked, crossing his arms over his chest.

"I do. Of course I do. But I'm working this case as hard as I can," Flint said. "I have a warrant, but I'd prefer if you'd allow me to search the room."

"Go ahead," Rafe said, setting his hands on Danny's shoulders. "Check his room. We have nothing to hide."

Gemma felt sick. How could someone point the police at a child?

Flint wiped his feet on the welcome mat. "Thanks, Rafe. You could have been unpleasant about this. I feel unpleasant even coming here tonight."

Two deputies followed Flint upstairs.

Gemma waited, giving her brother space to do whatever he needed to do. "Who is doing this? How could someone accuse Danny of robbing the clinic?" She wrapped her arms around him and hugged him.

"You know we believe you, right?" Gemma asked

him. Danny had to be terrified. He had gone quiet, but Gemma read fear in his expression.

Rafe remained stone-faced and silent. Flint came down the stairs, holding a notebook and some empty test tubes. "Can you explain these?" He directed his question at Danny.

Danny's mouth dropped open. "Those aren't mine."

"You're right. They aren't yours. They're notes from the lab that belong to the doctors at the clinic."

Danny appeared bewildered. Unless he was a sociopathic liar, he was as confused as she was.

"First of all, if those are the notebooks and supplies taken from the lab, they'd be contaminated and Danny would be sick," Rafe said. He almost sounded panicked. Rafe, panicked? It was unsettling. His medical training had taught him to stay put together and calm in emergencies. Danny being accused and Flint finding evidence to support the claim had shaken him.

"Can the virus be transferred by paper?" Flint asked, looking at the notebook and test tubes warily.

"The virus only lives a couple of hours without a host. But the live virus was taken," Rafe said. "Those tubes are empty."

"Do I need to quarantine your home? Are we in danger being here?" Flint asked.

Rafe narrowed his eyes. "No." The word was glacial. "If we had been exposed, we would have presented symptoms in six to twelve hours. As you can see, we are fine. The clinic was robbed over a week ago."

Flint slipped the test tubes into a plastic bag marked with the word evidence. "I hate to do this, but I need to arrest Danny."

"No!" Danny yelled, moving behind Rafe.

Rafe wrapped his arm around Danny protectively. The image almost tore Gemma's heart out. Flint couldn't separate them. She had known for a long time that Danny needed Rafe, but now she saw how much Rafe needed Danny.

Gemma stepped in, her heart in her throat. She had a lifetime of experience with her brother in talking to him and trying to reason with him. "Flint, please don't take Danny away. Danny didn't do this. Don't split up their family."

Flint cringed at the word family. "I'm sorry, Gemma. I really am."

"You can't put a boy in jail!" She worked to stay calm, but she was almost shaking with anger at the injustice of the situation. Rafe looked ready to kill someone to protect Danny and Danny appeared terrified.

"I am not putting him in jail. I'm taking him to stay at the youth center."

"He is better off here. I will take responsibility for anything Danny does because I know Danny didn't do this," Rafe said. Gemma had expected anger. She heard only heartbreaking sadness.

"You're not here around the clock. You're needed at the clinic," Flint said.

Rafe swore. "If I quit my job at the clinic to stay here with Danny, then can he stay?"

Flint shook his head. "I have to follow the law."

"This town is backward. This entire place is screwed up. Is it any wonder I can't wait to leave? Maybe I'll take Danny with me. He deserves better than this place."

Danny brightened at the prospect.

"Let me pack his bag," Rafe said.

He and Danny went upstairs. One of Flint's officers moved to follow them and Gemma stepped between him and the stairs. "Give them a few minutes to talk. They aren't going anywhere."

When Danny and Rafe returned to the front door, they hugged. "I will find who is doing this. I know it isn't you, buddy," Rafe said to him.

As Flint led Danny outside, Gemma hugged Rafe wishing she could have changed Flint's mind. "We'll prove he didn't do this."

Rafe's expression darkened and rage traversed his face. "Dr. Rand called in the tip. He's trying to frame Danny."

It was her turn to defend Dr. Rand. "Come on, Rafe. Why would he do that?"

"Because he's a weasel who likes to get what he wants. He runs the clinic like it's his little fiefdom. He couldn't stand me from day one because I don't care what he says or does. I do things my way. He's convinced Danny attacked him and he wants to see Danny locked away."

"The youth center is not a bad place for him to stay," Gemma said.

"He deserves a home," Rafe said.

Her words echoed back to her. She agreed, but she didn't press the point.

Her cell phone rang, and Gemma hurried to answer it. Maybe it was Flint calling to say he'd changed his mind.

It was Tom. "Gemma, you need to come now. Bring Dr. Granger. I think Annabelle is sick."

Gemma looked like she was about to come out of her skin. Annabelle had contracted the virus. She had been taken to the virus wing for isolation and her father was remaining at home after promising to stay away from everyone until he had been medically cleared.

Tom hadn't wanted to leave Annabelle, but Gemma had convinced him that she and Jessica would make sure Annabelle was cared for. In the virus wing, she would receive around-the-clock care.

Gemma paced in Rafe's living room. "How was Annabelle exposed, but the rest of us are fine?" Since they had been exposed to Annabelle, they were staying at Rafe's house in case symptoms appeared.

Rafe didn't have answers for how Annabelle had fallen sick. He'd been thinking about the possibilities. Molly had collected Annabelle from school and they had picked up Danny. It had been too cold to walk.

Someone could have sneezed on Annabelle. She could have touched infected materials. The staff didn't have a clear answer on how the virus was transmitted.

Everyone who may have had contact with Annabelle had been notified, including the youth center and Danny. Danny was asymptomatic, but Rafe would go by later to examine him to be sure.

Dr. Goodhue tested the vials that Flint had found in Danny's bedroom. If they had contained the virus, they were now clean. Annabelle hadn't been exposed through the stolen materials.

"I don't have answers. Gemma, this is a terrible situation. People who you love and care about are in danger. But you have to be their rock," Rafe said.

Gemma blew out her breath. She looked defeated. "I don't know if I have it in me to be this strong."

She underestimated herself because others did. "You do. I've seen it. You're strong for Jessica's husband and

Annabelle and your brothers and your grandmother. You are the picture of grace under pressure. You have a core of iron."

Gemma blinked at him. "You are the only person who has ever called me strong."

"Then either everyone else is blind or I'm the only person who's ever voiced it."

Gemma hugged him and slipped her arms around his neck. He felt the wetness of her tears at his neck. "Everyone I love most in the world is in this town and the virus is infecting everyone. We're lucky no one else has died. We're lucky that everyone isn't sick by now. How much longer can this go on? How much longer can we live this way?"

Rafe held her, not knowing the right words to say, but wishing he could do something. His efforts at finding a cure hadn't been enough. He hadn't been enough. "I know you feel powerless. It's okay to be scared. Fear isn't a weakness. Quitting is. We're going to stay together on this and we'll find a cure."

Gemma leaned away to look at his face. "Where do you get your confidence? When you say it, I almost believe it."

"I want you to believe it because it's the truth." Just as he believed Danny was innocent. As he believed that the person who was sabotaging their efforts would be caught. As he believed that he could make things right in Dead River and still live the life he'd dreamt of in New York.

"I am not happy that Annabelle is sick, but the silver lining is that Jessica and Annabelle seemed happy to be together," Gemma said, wiping at her cheeks.

Rafe smiled at the memory of when Jessica had first

laid eyes on Annabelle. Her expression had flashed with joy before turning to terror, but she was a good mom and knew how to feign calm in front of her daughter.

"Thank you for putting both beds in that room," Gemma said.

"It made sense for them to be together."

He had violated Dr. Goodhue's rules by rooming patients together. Each was supposed to be housed in separated containment rooms, but in this instance, following the rules wasn't as important as making his patients happy.

"Their vitals were stable and they were sleeping when I left," Gemma said. "Jessica had her hand over Annabelle's."

Rafe nodded. "There is no one better to look after her than her mother and you."

Gemma straightened and Rafe saw a change in her. No evidence of the breakdown remained. "Are you ready for bed?"

Rafe nodded. He took her hand and led her up the stairs. They were beyond exhausted and heartbroken and worried. They fell into bed and Rafe slipped his arms around Gemma and held her.

It was the first time he had slept in the same bed with a woman whom he hadn't had sex with first. It was a strange intimacy and he enjoyed it. The alternative, being alone in a house far too big for one man, was depressing.

With Gemma in his life, he didn't feel so lonely.

When Gemma arrived at the clinic, Flint was installing cameras in the lobby. He had a box of what looked like webcams. She noticed one over the entryway as well.

"Ramping up security?" she asked.

"You put the idea in my head and Rafe suggested webcams. I finally put my hands on this equipment. It networks together and will stream to a computer I'll set up in the reception area and at the station."

"Nice work."

"Does that mean you're less mad at me for what happened with Danny?" Flint asked.

Her brother preferred to put problems out in the open, rather than let anger fester between them.

Gemma knew he was doing his job, but she wasn't happy about Danny being taken from Rafe's home. "I know you're doing your best. Do you want help?"

"I could use a hand. This isn't my area of expertise. Mounting them is the easy part. Getting them to work is another story."

"How did you get this system?" Gemma asked.

"I've been making some discreet inquiries. Betsy Morris helped me figure out how to set this up," Flint said. "She has a son who's a technology whiz and he had some old webcams."

"Maybe this will help us catch the criminal in action," Gemma said.

"Or at least discourage him. I don't have a way to hide these well."

"Maybe putting them out in the open will discourage someone from causing any more problems."

"Gemma, could I talk to you for a minute?" Gemma's heart thumped at the sound of Rafe's voice. She turned to see him in the doorway of his office.

He was wearing a pair of green scrubs and a white

long sleeved T-shirt underneath. Despite her aversion to doctors, seeing him dressed that way, looking every bit the confident, good-looking doctor, had her heart racing.

"Hey Flint, what are you working on?" Rafe asked.

After Flint told him, Rafe nodded his approval. The two men didn't talk about Danny. No good could come from addressing the heated topic.

Gemma followed Rafe to his office. "The other day, you called me about some suspicious medical cases related to Dr. Rand. I looked at some of the cases you mentioned and I have to agree with you."

Gemma wasn't happy to learn that she might be right about Dr. Rand not being the magnificent doctor he claimed to be, but she was relieved that someone had taken her concerns seriously. Most especially that the someone was Rafe.

Rafe pointed to the computer on his desk. "I have more questions about these cases. But my biggest question is why he would hurt his patients. He's a good doctor. I've seen him in action."

"Maybe it wasn't his intent. Maybe he makes mistakes and then tries to cover them up."

Gemma circled around to look at what Rafe had open on his computer. "Thank you for doing this, Rafe."

"For doing what?" he asked.

"For believing me. For taking this seriously. We could be wrong about him. I don't know how often a patient dies in a clinic and if those numbers are higher for Dr. Rand, but it warrants another look."

"If we open an investigation, every clinician who works here will be put under a microscope," Rafe said.

She didn't relish the idea of being questioned by lawyers and the inevitable lawsuit that would result, but she couldn't allow anyone to harm the patients at the clinic. "Even if we report him to the medical board, they can't examine his cases now. An investigator can't do anything until the quarantine is lifted."

"That means we need to watch our patients and be sure that Dr. Rand doesn't have a chance to be careless with anyone else."

The house was too quiet when they arrived home. Rafe had left on the front porch and living room lights, but without Danny, the house felt empty. Danny wasn't always home when Rafe was, but signs of him usually were. Rafe missed him.

He wouldn't have expected that. Their arrangement was temporary and Rafe had tried to keep it that way in his mind. But he'd gotten accustomed to having Danny around.

Gemma entered behind him. "You doing okay?" she asked.

She could pick up on his moods as no one else could. It was the peacemaker in her. She was adept at reading people and interpreting situations. It was a good skill to have as a nurse, and as his friend. "I miss Danny."

Why lie about it? She likely had already known.

"I'm sorry, Rafe."

"Let's go to bed. We have a million things to do tomorrow and I can't think if I'm tired." He sounded cranky and he knew it.

"How about a back rub? You seem tense."

Rafe trod carefully. A back rub sounded great. But from a woman he had slept with, it could turn heated and as good as Gemma was at reading people, he was equally dense at misinterpreting them. "Only if I can return the favor. You've had a hard time, too. Let me grab a shower and I'll meet you in my bedroom."

He shaved and showered and when he got out of the bathroom with a towel around his waist, Gemma was seated on the brown leather wing chair next to his bed, where he occasionally read or worked before going to sleep.

"You take a long shower for a man," Gemma said. She had changed into his T-shirt, her legs bare. It would be cold in the room except she had turned on the electric fireplace across from his bed.

This had the makings of a promising situation. He shifted, hiding his body's reaction. "Let me grab some pants."

"You don't need them," she said.

Every nerve in his body anticipated sex and lust consumed him.

She beckoned to him and he knelt at her feet. She kissed his forehead. "Why don't you lie down on the bed and I'll take care of you?"

He couldn't have denied her if he'd wanted to. He was so keyed into her and what she was doing, he was ready and wanting. He flopped stomach down on the bed and waited.

Gemma hung his towel in the bathroom and returned.

"Why don't you take off that shirt?" he asked.

"Not yet," she said. "I want to talk first."

He groaned. "Was this a trick?"

She playfully dug her nails into his back. "Not a trick. I need to make sure you're doing okay."

"I would be doing better if you were naked."

Gemma laughed. "If I were naked, then you'd forget about talking. How are you feeling?"

Rafe wasn't feeling any better than the night before. "I think Flint made the wrong call in taking Danny. Why does it matter if Danny stays here or at the youth center?"

"Flint is doing his job. Dr. Rand had been complaining about the lack of progress in the investigation into who attacked him."

Bitterness and anger streamed through Rafe. "He imagined the whole thing. Maybe he fell on the ice and dreamed up a scenario to explain his klutziness."

Gemma's hands were working the tension out of his shoulders, but the more they spoke of Dr. Rand, the more amped up Rafe felt.

"The video cameras will help. Whoever is trying to spoil our progress will try again, and when they do, we'll have them on video," Gemma said.

Rafe turned to his side, pulling Gemma in front of him. "Now, tell me how you're feeling." She had been through a lot in the last twenty-four hours as well.

"I'm scared. Worried. But mostly scared."

Rafe wrapped his arms around her, pulling her down next to him on the bed. "You don't believe I'll find a cure." It felt like a failure to let her down.

Gemma's green eyes grew wide. "I believe you will. But what will happen if you're too late? This virus is harder on the elderly and children. Now Annabelle is sick."

"I will do everything I can to keep her well until we have a cure."

Gemma kissed him and tickled her fingers down his arm. "We should try yoga to manage our stress."

"I liked to run." If he wasn't working so much and if the sidewalks weren't in a constant state of half-ice slicked, he would make it a higher priority.

"Yoga is good for relaxation," Gemma said.

"This is good for relaxation."

"I won't be in New York to do this," Gemma said.

"In New York, I can hire someone to do this anytime I want."

Gemma inhaled sharply and removed her hands from him.

"What did I say? Why are you mad?" The mention of New York upset her.

She folded her arms over her chest. "You don't want to see anything good about Dead River. Can't you find anything you like about this town without comparing it to the high and mighty New York? We don't have round-the-clock masseurs and big hospitals with prestigious jobs, but we have heart. We care about each other."

She was taking his leaving as if it was personal. "I like things about this town. I like Danny. I like my patients at the clinic."

Gemma looked away from him and stared at the fireplace.

"And you. I like you." *Like* might not have been the best word. *Love* was too strong, and saying "I dig you" sounded juvenile. He'd have to show her how he felt about her. He pulled her on top of him and kissed her.

When Gemma was in his arms, he couldn't think logically and rationalize why what they were doing should or shouldn't happen. He wanted this and he wanted it now.

He lifted his hips, wishing she was already naked. He'd show her another side of him, the caring, soft side. He wasn't a rebel in high school with something to prove. He was a grown man making love to a woman he cared about.

That meant more than the act.

When had he started caring about that?

He lifted the hem of her shirt and tossed it away. She was wearing nothing except a pair of pink thong underwear.

"You shouldn't be allowed to dress like that under your scrubs," he said.

"I don't. I changed," she said.

Then she was thinking about sex with him. That was good because he couldn't have derailed his brain's process to save his life.

"I'm still mad at you," she said. But the look on her face told him he could convince her otherwise.

"I know. I think you'll be mad at me and New York for a while," he said. "Let me see if I can make you a little less mad." He removed her panties and brought his mouth between her legs.

In moments, he had her gripping the sheets and screaming his name.

Gemma pushed her coffee cup back and forth between her hands. The Dead River Café was slow, no doubt because the police had traced Mimi Rand, the first known victim of the virus, to the café and suspected she had infected others at this location.

Colleen Goodhue had instructed the Dead River

Café on how to sanitize any remaining virus and the café had passed the CDC testing for sanitation. They also now knew the virus couldn't remain alive without a host for longer than several hours, but the stigma about the place remained. Rumors suggested the café could have been where Mimi became infected, as opposed to where she had spread the virus.

Gemma didn't know what to believe, but as a nurse, she thought patronizing the café would give the residents some confidence. After all, she was working with the virus. She was in the know more than most about how it worked and how it spread. If she found the café safe, hopefully so would others.

Flint was four minutes late for their meeting. When he arrived, he sat across from her and picked up the coffee she had ordered for him.

"One packet of sugar, just the way you like it," she said. Both a peace offering and a bribe so that he would hear her out. Her brothers had always listened to her, but they sometimes dismissed her ideas as harebrained. If she pitched her concerns about Dr. Rand, she wanted Flint to keep an open mind.

"Tell me you have good news about the virus. And thank you for this," he said lifting the cup. He didn't need to mention that his days were long. Everyone in town was having longer, harder days.

Gemma leaned forward. They were the only two people in the café, except for the sole employee who was sitting behind the counter on a stool reading on her tablet. "It's not bad news. It's about what I found while I was working."

Flint rubbed his face. "A cure?"

Gemma rolled her eyes. "I'd be shouting that from

the rooftops if we had a cure. We're working on it," she added. Always working on it and trying to keep the faith that they would find it.

"I think Dr. Rand is involved with the strange incidents that have been going on around the clinic," she said.

"Dr. Rand? The doctor who was attacked? Whose office was trashed?" Flint asked.

Her brother would want facts and evidence and she didn't have them. She had intuition and a lead, maybe the only one Flint had in finding the saboteur. She didn't know what he and the other police officers had found at the crime scenes. Flint wouldn't share details of an open investigation with her. "The other night, a patient went into distress minutes after I had checked on her. Dr. Rand was in the virus wing doing his follow-ups at the time."

By the look on his face, her brother had doubts, but he was hearing her out.

"I don't see how a patient could be stable and then in utter distress," Gemma said. She'd seen it happen in her career, but not with this virus, not in fifteen minutes.

"Is this patient someone you've grown attached to?"

Jessica was her best friend, yes. She still had to honor patient confidentiality and telling Flint that Jessica had been the patient would undermine the information she had about Dr. Rand. "It is someone I like. What does that have to do with anything?" She felt her defensiveness rising. Her brothers sometimes still treated her like a little girl who needed to be told what to do.

"I want to know if you're seeing the situation clearly. Do you have any proof?" Flint asked.

"He went into her room. She went into distress. It's in her case notes. That's my proof."

"I can't investigate every medically unstable patient who has a rough day," Flint said.

Gemma curbed her temper. "I have some additional medical cases that are suspicious." Cases that required more review and more questions asked.

"Dr. Rand has worked at the clinic for a long time. He's a good man. A tad arrogant maybe, but I expect that from people who are good at their jobs. Why would he harm a patient? He has his reputation and insurance rates to worry about."

Flint was making good points, but Gemma knew Dr. Rand was up to no good. "Every doctor and nurse with any experience has had their share of difficult cases that have gone wrong through no fault of their own. But I think Dr. Rand likes the more challenging cases because when he rides to the rescue, he's the hero."

"Doctors are heroes, even without difficult cases."

Gemma gripped her coffee cup and then released it. Her brother was frustrating her. Would he talk to someone else like this? Or was his refusal to believe what she said because she was his sister? "He has helped many patients. But I think he's not as grand as he pretends to be."

"If you have evidence, I can work with that," Flint said. "Anecdotal evidence won't hold up in court or grant me a search warrant." Flint took a sip of his coffee. "I will look into it."

Gemma's irritation tweaked at her nerves. "Is that a blowoff?"

"It's not. It's a promise to my sister that I will do what I can, but I can't make any guarantees. I am forehead-deep in problems in this town and I don't have the resources to investigate a suspicion without proof."

The proof was somewhere, in medical notes, in an autopsy or speaking to patients who had been treated by Dr. Rand. But tracking them down would take time. "Then I'll look into it myself and call you when I have more substantial evidence."

His hand reached across the table and covered hers. "Gemma, promise me you will not. Do not go snooping around playing amateur investigator into a dangerous situation. You've been attacked twice and I don't like you working at the clinic with a deadly virus, much less telling me your intention to poke a bear."

At least he seemed to think she had some validity to her concerns, if not completely believing her accusation. "I will be careful. I need to go. I promised Rafe I'd helped him in the lab tonight." Rafe had spent the day with Danny at the youth center and planned to meet her at work afterward.

"Stay safe, Gemma," Flint said and hugged his sister. He walked her to her car and then followed her in his police cruiser to the clinic. He didn't leave until she was inside.

Gemma pulled on her protective wear and entered the lab through the double door enclosure. Inside the lab, Dr. Goodhue was working on the computer modeling system and had her microphone off.

Gemma took a seat next to Rafe. "How's it going?"

Rafe was testing swabs from locations where Annabelle visited in the last forty-eight hours, looking for the presence of the virus. They also needed to test new blood samples that Anand had collected from patients who were sick at home. "Tedious. The results are negative for existence of the virus, which I usually prefer, but this time, it's frustrating."

If they didn't know how Annabelle had gotten sick, they didn't know who else could have been exposed. They were most worried that the virus could have originated from someone in Annabelle's school, putting children in danger.

"In good news, I have samples from at least two patients who have quarantined themselves in their homes because they suspected they had the Dead River virus, but my tests show one has strep throat and the other has a nasty infection, likely sinus-related. I've called them and asked them to come to the fire station on Saturday during drop-in hours for a proper diagnosis. If they can't make it, I'll make two house calls."

Fire Chief Stan Burrell, paramedic Kit Wheeler, EMT Josh Hadaway and holistic healer Betsy Morris were helping at the fire station running a small clinic for less serious cases. Another retired doctor who lived in Dead River was also lending a hand. The clinic's three doctors were donating their limited free time to assist during scheduled times to oversee patients.

Though he was focusing on the positive, Gemma heard the defeat in his voice. "We will find the antidote." She told herself that a hundred times a day and she would tell Rafe and the staff the same until it was true.

Rafe wrote another note on his notepad. "That's the only end game that doesn't result in every person in this town falling ill."

And dying, Gemma added to herself.

Gemma looked over at the files they'd created on each patient. Some files were marked expired. Their families were grieving. Some who had died also had friends and family who were sick. The number of folders grew each day. Tracking the patients infected with the Dead River virus was becoming a full-time job.

"It's a lot of people," Rafe said, looking at the stack and then catching her eye.

More were being added every day. "When I studied viruses in school, cases of Ebola and Lassa fever happened in faraway places. I never imagined we'd have a dangerous virus in Dead River."

"We need one patient to recover. Just one. Then we can use that person's antibodies to create a cure and distribute it."

He sounded shredded. Gemma touched his gloved hand with hers. "Someone will get better or we'll figure this out. I have faith in you. I'll be here and we'll do this together. We won't give up until we get it right."

Rafe needed to find one common sequence from his samples, one pattern to use to identify the virus. He and Dr. Goodhue believed they were close and neither was giving up. Gemma had stayed with them, acting as a lab assistant. She was unfailing in her devotion.

They were using a DNA sequencer, which worked well in theory. But they continued to encounter problems. The computers were searching the CDC database for gene commonalities, but little was coming back as similar. They repeated the process many times, each time resulting in different readings and unclear results.

After six hours without a break, Rafe needed to walk away from the lab. He needed to think. He couldn't do that in the confines of the lab with his failures staring him in the face.

He exited the lab, stood in the chemical shower and then removed his suit, hanging it to dry. Then he sat in his office. It was quiet this time of day.

He heard movement in Dr. Rand's office, likely the man arriving for his shift. Could Dr. Rand be involved in something untoward at the clinic? Rafe had known doctors with a hero complex or in more extreme cases, a god complex, and some who were narcissistic sociopaths. Being good at a job didn't mean personality flaws weren't numerous. Half the time, Rafe thought he fell into one of those categories: hero complex, god complex or narcissist. He could be single-minded about his work, obsessive about helping his patients and could argue fiercely when he believed he was right about a treatment plan. He didn't like anyone questioning his medical expertise.

From the first time he had met Dr. Rand, they'd had a cool relationship. In fact, Dr. Rand seemed to have a tepid relationship with everyone at the clinic. It could be his personality to keep coworkers at arm's length. It could be that he was good at his work, but lacked social skills. Dr. Rand wouldn't be the first doctor to have that problem.

Rafe found himself knocking on Dr. Rand's office door, still not sure what he would say to the man. A quick conversation and he could get it off his mind.

"Dr. Rand, can you spare a minute?" Rafe asked.

Dr. Rand looked up from his computer. "Need a consult?"

Rafe didn't need a second opinion. He needed to know if there was any truth to Gemma's suspicions about Rand. It was no secret that Rafe disliked Dr. Rand after the incident with Danny, but Gemma's intuition was good. She read people and situations. It came with the territory of being the person who kept social order in a household of an aging caregiver, two wild brothers and an alcoholic half-estranged father. "Not a consult. I was wondering if you could tell me more about what happened with Jessica in the virus wing. I'm concerned oxygen deprivation will be the next symptom we face and I want to be in front of it." Was it a good enough lie to get Rand talking? Would Rand see through it?

If it had been a medical incident, Rafe guessed congestion or fluid in her lungs. He had seen no evidence of fluid in her lungs when he'd examined her and Dr. Rand hadn't noted it in her chart.

Dr. Rand leaned back in his chair and folded his hands across his stomach. "I was lucky to be there when I was. She was struggling to take in enough air."

"What do you think caused it?" Dr. Rafe asked.

Dr. Rand shrugged. "I checked the oxygen level in the room and the ventilation system. Both appeared to be working properly. The air recycler is at full capacity and showing no signs of slowing down." He tossed around a few ideas, but Rafe didn't like what he was saying. Dr. Rand returned the conversation to his importance in the situation and how he had taken life-saving measures. It was almost as if Jessica wasn't as important as Dr. Rand's intervention.

Gemma's suspicions might be dead on.

"When tough cases come into the clinic, you take on a lot of them," Rafe said, pushing a little harder for answers without making an accusation point-blank.

"I do. I don't fear difficult medical problems. I've handled everyone's medical issues and I've seen it all.

The people in this town use the clinic as a catchall for every medical problem possible."

Rafe was tempted to ask him about cases where a patient had died, but he decided to back off. Dr. Rand was acting strange. Perhaps exhaustion or general frustration was affecting him, which was upsetting Rafe's mood as well. He would keep an eye on the doctor. Anything suspicious, and he would be all over Dr. Rand.

Chapter 10

For every piece of paper she filed, Gemma felt as if two more appeared. Maybe one day the clinic would be completely paperless, but until then, she had to organize these documents. After completing her patient rounds, this time shadowing Dr. Rand, she used sorting patient files as an excuse to prevent herself from having a conversation with Dr. Rand. Gemma was concerned she would slip about her suspicions or unload her anger on him. Though she wasn't someone who ran off at the mouth often, when it came to her friends and family, she was fiercely protective.

The front door to the clinic opened, the bell over the door chiming. Rafe was scheduled to start his shift shortly. Maybe it was him. Gemma stood and came face-to-face with a sick man.

Her training had taught her to identify a patient in desperate need of care and this man fit the bill. He was pale, his eyes were watering, he was sweating profusely and he looked exhausted and worn. His dirty gray puffer jacket hung on him as if he had lost a lot of weight. He had the symptoms of the Dead River virus. How long had he had it? Who had been taking care of him?

She circled the desk to assist him. He looked like he might pass out. "Sir? Can I help you? Are you all right?"

The man lifted his shaking hand and held a gun at her head. "Get me the doctor." His voice was hoarse and he smelled of damp earth and garbage.

Which doctor? Who was this man? Then Gemma remembered the sketch that Flint had posted at the clinic a while back. This man, though thinner and wearier, was Hank Bittard, accused murderer and prison escapee. He was armed and volatile and dangerous. Why hadn't she been more careful? Why hadn't she locked the clinic door after the last meal delivery?

Terror shook her. Hank wouldn't hesitate to harm her. "We can help you. You don't need to point a gun at anyone."

Hank blinked at her. "Get me the doctor now."

Before Gemma could make her next move, Dr. Rand appeared. "Gemma, do you have…"

He was holding a patient file in his hand and his voice trailed away as his eyes fell on Hank Bittard and the gun.

"You the doctor?" Hank asked.

"I am," Dr. Rand said, lowering the file folder and meeting Hank's gaze.

"Get me some antidote," Hank said. "I'll never escape this place. I need you to fix me."

Dr. Rand gestured toward their examination area. "Let's go to the triage area and I'll examine you to see what you need to feel better."

"I don't need to be examined! I know what's wrong with me! I have the virus!" Hank shouted. He was shaking and Gemma feared the gun in his hand would go off.

"We are treating patients with the virus. We can help you," Gemma said, trying to calm him. He was growing more agitated. What did he expect them to do? If he had been following the news, he had to know they didn't have a cure. What was he anticipating would happen?

"Give me the cure! I don't need your help. I need the cure. Now. I need it now," Hank said and looked over his shoulder at the door.

"Please, come with me and we'll give you the right dosage of the cure," Dr. Rand said.

Gemma was already wondering if they had an injectable sedative to calm Hank Bittard. She could dose him and then call the police. Thanks to Flint's video monitoring, they'd have the incident recorded.

Hank wiped sweat from his forehead. "Why is it so hot in here?"

He started to remove his jacket and grew impatient when it caught on the gun.

"If you'll come with me, I'll take care of everything. We'll have you feeling better in no time," Dr. Rand said.

"You're lying. I can see it," Hank said. Spit flew from his mouth and Gemma flinched. She'd been directly exposed to the virus. Though living through this ordeal was priority number one, avoiding infection was the second.

"We want to help you," Gemma said.

Hank backed away toward the door. "You and her want to hurt me. You want to trap me and do experiments on me. That's what this is about, isn't it? This is a secret facility where you test sicknesses on people and you didn't mean for your virus to escape. Well, it has! Now everyone will die! I shouldn't have come here. You'll use me as a lab rat!"

What was he talking about? He had the irrational mutterings and hallucinations of someone on the edge. Someone who was about to lose it and who had a weapon and may not care who he hurt.

Dr. Rand came forward and stood next to Gemma. "We will not hurt you. Please do not hurt Nurse Gemma. I am a doctor and I will help you."

Gemma was surprised by Dr. Rand's words. He hadn't run. He had put himself closer to Hank and he was trying to help her.

Hank Bittard brought his free hand to his head and stumbled to the left, the gun still aimed in their direction. "My head. It will not stop pounding. I can't see anything. I can't think when my head hurts like this."

Could Gemma tackle him? She was small, but he was off-kilter.

From the triage area, Rafe appeared. In a split second, he assessed the situation and rushed Hank, grabbing him around the waist and throwing him to the floor. The gun clattered to the ground and Gemma hurried to grab it. Once it was in her hands, she pointed it at Hank Bittard. She had no intention of using it, but she had to make him believe she would. She didn't want him to hurt anyone else.

Hank was screaming, accusing them of using him for testing.

Dr. Rand pulled out what Gemma recognized as a sedative and raced to help Rafe. He injected Hank and the man's mutterings stopped in seconds. Hank went limp on the floor.

Relief tore through Gemma. She had almost died tonight. She had been exposed to the Dead River virus. She sat on the floor, gun in her hand.

Rafe knelt next to her, taking the gun from her shaking hand. "Are you hurt?"

Gemma pushed him away. "He has the Dead River virus. He spit on me. Don't touch me. You'll be infected, too."

Rafe didn't move. "If we've been exposed, we've been exposed."

He sounded calm. How was he this calm under the circumstances?

Dr. Rand looked at his hands. "It was a matter of time before we contracted it."

Not an uplifting thought, but he was right. Working with patients and the virus every day would lead to an incident. It just had.

"Dr. Rand, Rafe, thank you for what you did," Gemma said. They had been brave and loyal.

"I didn't do anything," Dr. Rand said.

"You could have run," Gemma said.

Dr. Rand blushed. "Leaving you to face him alone? Never."

Gemma had second thoughts about her accusations and suspicions against Dr. Rand. He had acted nobly. Could Flint have been right? Was Gemma's affection for Jessica skewing her take on events?

Gemma called her brother and the three of them locked themselves in isolation. Dr. Rand chose his office and Gemma and Rafe secured themselves in the lab.

* * *

Hank was cuffed and locked in a room in the virus wing. They had moved two other patients together to make room for him. The door locked from the inside and outside, so he was reasonably secure.

Rafe and Gemma were confined to the lab for twelve hours, the period of isolation the CDC required before they would be permitted to return to work. If they showed no symptoms of the virus, they could resume normal activities.

Dr. Goodhue was following CDC procedures to sterilize the waiting area and anywhere that Hank could have infected.

Flint also had the idea to install webcams in Hank's room to monitor him. Though the picture was grainy, they could ensure that Hank Bittard didn't escape again.

"This is just what we need. Another risk factor to our patients," Rafe said.

"Hank Bittard is in no condition to attack anyone," Gemma said.

"He's pretty sick, but if he flies into another rage, he could hurt someone," Rafe said. "Those walls are not intended to withstand beatings."

"We'll have to keep him sedated."

"I don't want you going into his room alone, ever, Gemma. I'll tell everyone on staff to be careful around Hank Bittard. Not just because of the virus, but because who knows what he has planned. He escaped jail. It can't be hard to escape the virus wing."

Flint would be monitoring him, but Hank had proven to be wily.

"I don't think I've seen any patient in as bad condition because of the virus," Gemma said, thinking of how out of control Hank had been.

"He must not have been receiving the proper rest or care. Most of our other patients are lucid and stable."

"He was on the run. I can only imagine where he was living and how he was finding food," Gemma said. "How likely is it that we caught the virus?" It was anyone's guess, but asking the question made her feel better.

Rafe shrugged inside his suit. "I'm not convinced it's airborne. Every case we've studied and every interview we've conducted with our patients seems to point to this spreading through contact. It's also not contagious enough that everyone who comes into contact with it becomes infected."

"Which I'm glad for. Theo and Amelia would be goners if everyone caught it," Gemma said.

"That's an interesting thought." Rafe appeared to be considering it. "Is it possible that Theo or Amelia have a natural immunity to the virus?"

"Could be. Can we test them to find out?" she asked.

"I'll send an email to Dr. Goodhue about it. While we're in here, I won't waste time. I've work to do, and I haven't given up on investigating the common sequences in the samples," Rafe said.

Gemma's hands were still shaking. "I need a few minutes, and then I'll help you."

"Take your time. Rest. You've been through too much."

Gemma watched Rafe work, the intensity on his face sometimes startling. "I'm starting to think I was wrong about Dr. Rand." She didn't mean to interrupt his thought process, but she had to let Rafe know what was on her mind.

"I was starting to think you were right in suspecting him. Why have you changed your mind?"

His actions when Hank Bittard had been in the clinic. "He seemed to genuinely care about me. When Hank was waving his gun at me, Dr. Rand tried to step in and help me."

"Because if he had defused the issue, he would have been deemed a hero."

Could someone be that focused on maintaining their hero complex that they would put themselves at risk? "That's a negative way to look at it," Gemma said.

"Not being negative. Just pointing out that your original theory holds water."

Rafe returned to his work. He devoted himself with the same resolute focus that he devoted to her in bed. Bed with Rafe. They were trapped alone in the lab and trapped in their suits.

"I wish we didn't have to wear these suits," Gemma said.

Rafe gave her a long look that spoke loudly of where his mind had gone—the same place as hers. "If we don't have the virus, working in the lab without them would ensure we caught it."

Maybe they should have quarantined themselves in Rafe's office as Dr. Rand had, in his own office.

"What are your plans for when we're cleared?" Gemma asked. She would think positive about the possibility they did not have the virus. She would think about having dinner with Rafe and maybe turning on the fireplace in his bedroom and celebrating that they were healthy and safe.

Rafe grinned. "I'm thinking about you and me in bed without these suits. Without clothes at all. But we've got another ten hours and thirteen minutes to go and your brother has cameras in here."

Excitement washed over her. Only Rafe could take her mind off a deadly virus and instead direct her toward the idea of another romp in Rafe's bed. "When the suits are off…"

"I'll race you to bed."

Rafe had been recording his lab results, tossing his samples when a hypothesis didn't work out, and starting over, trying a variation in temperature, humidity or density of cellulose. With the range of results from the samples and without consistency, he wasn't gaining any ground.

He and Gemma had two more hours in the lab. As yet, they'd presented no symptoms.

Looking at the results of the last iteration, Rafe did a double take. He'd hit a pattern across several samples. He slowed his breathing. He needed to check the samples again and then run several more to validate his results.

"Gemma," he said.

She was sitting at the lab station behind him, but their microphones were on. "Are you okay?"

"I think I found a lead."

Gemma moved to stand at his side and watch him.

He worked quickly and methodically, mentally checking every step twice. No mistakes and no false hope.

Three hours later, they had a pattern that existed between the samples. A common strain. Still unsure who he could trust, he uploaded the file to the CDC database for cross comparison. He snapped pictures of the samples and of what he was seeing under the microscope.

"We have to call Dr. Goodhue. First, I want out of here. Second, she needs to know."

Gemma nodded enthusiastically. They called Dr. Goodhue who was at the Round-Up motel.

She answered on the first ring, sounding groggy. "Everyone okay?"

"Gemma and I have been working in the lab and we discovered something."

"Tell me." She sounded wide awake now.

"A common sequence in the strains." One that he could define and map.

"Across multiple samples?" she asked, sounding even more excited.

"Yes." He could speak the words with confidence. He and Gemma had checked and rechecked their process. They could replicate the lab results. They were finally on the right track, no fumbling, bumbling, stumbling with a theory or a hope.

"I'll be right in," Dr. Goodhue said. "What about you and Gemma? Are you feeling okay?"

"We're fine. Great actually."

Rafe hadn't felt this good in months.

As excited as Gemma, Dr. Goodhue and Rafe were about their progress, they agreed to keep their breakthrough amongst themselves.

If and when the CDC found a virus with similar patterns or could make a recommendation to counter the Dead River virus, they would inform the staff they were changing directions from identifying the virus to manufacturing a cure.

It had been a quiet few days as Rafe and Gemma waited for the CDC to respond with more data. No one else knew about the sequence they had found and it was hard not to share the good news. Gemma only hoped that the CDC would respond with helpful information.

In the meantime, they had plenty to keep them busy. After visiting Danny early that morning, Gemma and Rafe were working at the Dead River fire station for the Saturday clinic. The line of patients wrapped around the building. Anand and Cathleen were already working triage, separating the cases and assigning priority. Gemma knew they were also confirming no one waiting for care had the symptoms of the Dead River virus. Those cases needed to remain quarantined and would be referred to the clinic immediately. Dr. Moore and Dr. Goodhue were working at the clinic today to help with any referred cases and to watch over the patients in the virus wing.

Stan Burrell and his firefighters had organized a section of the firehouse to act as a clinic. He, Kit, Josh and Betsy had hung sheets to provide privacy between cots. They had gathered medical supplies and had stocked them on rolling carts.

They had a table and chairs set up and Nina was providing coffee, hot tea, hot chocolate and snacks.

The firefighters had brought in a few evergreens and had decorated them with ornaments, tinsel and gold garlands. They had hung Christmas decorations and lights. In the back parking lot, they had gathered greenery and were planning to hang it throughout the town. Although helping the residents of Dead River with their medical issues was their first priority, Stan and his firefighters had created a pleasant and warm atmosphere. It was good for the morale of the town.

"This is really special," Gemma said to Stan.

"There's not much to celebrate in Dead River. We thought if we could do nice things for the town it would help matters, get people's minds off the virus."

The gesture was unexpected and, added to her knowledge about the progress with the virus, it had Gemma floating on air. She looked across the room to where Rafe was simultaneously washing his hands and talking with a patient.

A surge of warmth rose in her chest and she was taken aback by the sensation. Normally, when she looked at Rafe, she felt lust. She wanted him alone and flat on his back. She wanted to explore his little black box and some of their fantasies together.

But this was an entirely different emotion. More terrifying than the intensity of her lust. This was love.

Gemma knew she had fallen for Rafe. A huge mistake, of course, since falling in love with him meant it would end with her heart being broken. While that was how her relationship with Jackson had ended and she had survived it, she had promised herself the next time she fell in love, it would be for keeps. She'd fall for someone safe and simple when it was easy and complication-free.

Rafe was the opposite of those things. He was a bit dangerous, definitely complicated and their relationship was futureless. Not what she had been looking for, but she hadn't been looking for a long-term relationship at all. She had known when Rafe came back to Dead River that she wanted him. Hadn't she always? But she had thought she could keep their emotions locked into lust and desire. This soul-shaking, heart-all-in was unexpected.

"What's going on with you guys?" Anand asked, coming to stand next to her.

"What do you mean?" Gemma asked, pasting on a smile. She had plenty of reasons to smile. She would think of those and not of Rafe leaving.

"Come on, Gemma. We've been friends a long time. I know you and Dr. Granger have something between you two."

She had thought they'd been careful to hide their relationship. "Is it that obvious?"

"To me," Anand said.

If Anand knew, she could count on him not to spread it around town. "That's because you're a sweetheart."

Anand pressed a finger over his lips. "Shhh, don't tell anyone."

It was the town's worst kept secret that despite his formidable size suggesting otherwise, Anand was an incredibly warm and gentle person. "It doesn't matter what I feel for him. He's leaving."

"Eventually," Anand said.

"The moment he can," Gemma said.

"You're a good reason to stay," Anand said.

Rafe wouldn't give up his job in New York for her. He'd be trading in a dream position for long hours and low pay at the clinic. "He doesn't see it that way."

"It's one-sided?" Anand asked. "I could be wrong, but I've seen some looks coming your way from him and it didn't seem one-sided."

Those looks had everything to do with desire. Rafe wasn't in love with her.

"We've been spending time together. We've known from the beginning what we have. But it's gotten mixed up."

"Because you love him," Anand said.

"Yes."

"I'm there," Anand said.

Gemma whirled to look at him. "You? In love? With who?"

Anand gestured in Cathleen's direction. Gemma's mouth fell open. She had seen them talking and laughing, but Anand was friendly with everyone. "Since when?"

"Since forever."

"Does she know?"

He shook his head. "We've had dinner a few times. I don't think she had any idea they were dates." He sounded sad.

"Are you going to tell her?" Gemma asked.

"Are you going to tell him?" Anand asked.

She wouldn't. She remembered how angry Rafe had gotten when she'd told him he should stay in Dead River. How would he react if she told him she was in love with him? She didn't think the conversation would end well. It would push him away or force him to close the door on their fleeting relationship.

Thinking of losing Rafe to New York hurt. Thinking of being in the same town, working in the same clinic and being unable to connect with him hurt worse.

"I can't. It's complicated," Gemma said.

Anand smiled. "Exactly."

"So, we're two suckers in love?" Gemma asked.

"Looks like it," Anand said.

"What do we do in the meantime?" Gemma asked.

"What we've been doing. Work."

At some point in the long line of patients, Rafe realized that even those patients who recognized him from his childhood or adolescence had said nothing about the trailer park where he'd grown up. No one mentioned his less-than-spotless reputation. They had conveyed sympathy for his parents' passing. A few people mentioned they missed seeing his mother at the liquor store where she'd been a clerk and that they missed his father's sense of humor. He might not have been able to keep a steady job, but the odd jobs he worked meant he'd met a lot people. One of Danny's teachers thanked him for taking Danny in and remarked how well Danny was doing in her class.

His patients listened to his advice with due respect. For the first time in his life, even though he thought of himself as an outsider, he was treated like one of the town.

Was this why his father had wanted him to return to Dead River? To see the small town differently through the eyes of someone who belonged, not someone who felt judged and excluded? He had avoided visiting Dead River, using the excuse of his work and his studies. He'd paid for his parents' plane tickets to come see him and they'd spent Thanksgivings in restaurants in New York because Rafe didn't want to spend any time in the small trailer they'd called home.

Guilt slithered over him and he felt like a snake. Why had he turned away so fully from the town where

he'd grown up? He'd had his share of bad times and in-
stances he wished he could forget, but didn't everyone?
As a teenager, he'd been so consumed with his own
issues and problems he hadn't taken the time to see
himself through the eyes of others. He'd been moody,
quiet and he'd had a bad attitude.

After Rafe finished with his patient, he removed
his gloves, cleaned his hands and walked to Nina's refreshment area.

"What can I get you, Doctor?" Nina asked. She was
wearing a festive red shirt and an apron with a red-
nosed reindeer stamped on the front.

"Some water would be great," Rafe said.

"Coming right up," Nina said. She returned with a
cup of water.

"You're thinning the line," Nina said, gesturing to
the patient-waiting area. "When I saw the crowd this
morning, I thought you'd never get to everyone."

"This is long overdue. People are afraid to come to
the clinic for help and they don't have anywhere else
to go."

He was facing another long night. He'd had to be
creative with many of his patients. The Dead River
pharmacy wasn't fully stocked. He couldn't send patients for testing at the nearest hospital or diagnostic
center. He had to rely on his instincts, the patients'
descriptions of their ailment and even a few holistic
remedies.

He wrote notes in his patients' files with recom-
mendations for more thorough follow-ups when the
quarantine was lifted.

When the quarantine was lifted, not *if* it would be
lifted. Knowing it would happen was a secret that was

keeping him going. As the thought crossed his mind, he saw Dr. Rand enter the fire station.

"Thanks for the drink," he said to Nina.

"Sure thing!" she said and returned to fixing refreshments for others.

Dr. Rand strode directly to Rafe. Though he wasn't scheduled to work at the clinic today and he hadn't mentioned his specific plans to come to the fire station, it was good of him to help. It would cut Rafe's patient load in half. Could Rafe trust him or was Dr. Rand at the clinic to drum up some hero worship?

He and Dr. Rand had been circling each other carefully since the incident with Danny. Rafe nodded once at Dr. Rand, acknowledging him. It was the most the other man would get from him. Despite his actions with Hank Bittard and not having hard evidence to prove he was either negligent or intentionally harming patients, Rafe didn't trust Dr. Rand.

"How can I help?" Dr. Rand asked, looking at the crowd.

"Cathleen is buzzing around. She has the priority list. Please jump in with whatever cases you feel like handling." When he said it, he was relieved to know that none of their cases were too serious, or he would have seen to them earlier in the day. He would alert Gemma to stay close to Dr. Rand if she could.

"I'll start right away," Dr. Rand said and walked in Cathleen's direction.

Gabriella and Trevor Garth entered the fire station. Trevor looked around and lifted a hand in greeting to Rafe. Gemma hurried over to speak with her cousin.

Rafe watched Gemma's face shift from happy to concerned. Rafe joined the threesome. Foursome, he amended thinking of Gabriella's baby. When he had visited her at her husband's ranch, she had seemed in good health. Her blood pressure had been elevated, but she hadn't been leaking protein into her urine.

"Hey, Gabriella, Trevor. Everything okay?" Rafe asked.

Gabriella laughed nervously. "I am sure it is. But I've been having some abdominal pain and I wanted to be sure nothing had changed since I saw you last."

Stress could cause Braxton-Hicks contractions. They wouldn't necessarily lead to labor, but Rafe would take a look. "We'll see what's going on."

As they walked to an open exam room, Rafe could almost hear Trevor worrying. "We have to get out of this town, Doc. If Gabriella and the baby had a problem, I don't know what I'll do."

"We'll do everything we can for your family," Rafe said.

"You should have called me if you were concerned," Gemma said to her cousin.

"I didn't want to bother you. I had some early contractions with Avery that went away on their own. I was hoping these would too," Gabriella said.

Rafe gave Gemma and Gabriella some privacy to help Gabriella into an exam gown. Rafe retrieved the ultrasound equipment and the heart rate monitor. He was glad he'd brought it with them today. It had seen a lot of use.

"Avery is with her Uncle Cole and Aunt Amy," Trevor said. "She wanted to come with us, but I have a bad feeling about this."

He was concerned about his wife and their baby.

Rafe understood. "It was a good idea to bring her in if you were worried. That's why we're here."

Gemma poked her head out from between the privacy curtain and she motioned it was okay for them to come in.

Rafe didn't want to alarm Gabriella, but he was concerned to see her blood pressure still high. "How long have you been having cramps?"

Gabriella glanced at Trevor, concerned about worrying her husband. "A while."

Rafe needed to speak with Gabriella alone so he could get the information he needed without her censoring herself to keep her protective husband from becoming upset. "Trevor, Gabriella needs some water. Hydration could be a factor here. Nina in the refreshment area can help you."

Trevor slipped out of the room, eager to help.

"How long have you had the contractions, Gabriella?" Rafe asked again.

"Two days."

Rafe didn't like the sound of that. She could be in pre-term labor. "Have you noticed any fluid leaking? Either clear fluid or blood?"

She shook her head. "No, no fluid."

Rafe checked the baby's heartbeat, happy to hear it strong and solid. He had done a rotation in obstetrics, but he was not an expert. He'd need to be overcautious. "This might be hard for you to hear, and I don't want to alarm you, but I'm going to recommend bed rest."

Gabriella sat up. "With a toddler at home?"

Trevor entered the patient room. "What about Avery? What's wrong?"

"I want Gabriella on complete bed rest. I want her to

lie on her left side as much as possible, stay hydrated, drink at least a glass of water or juice every hour while you're awake and sleep as much as you can."

"What about Avery? She needs me," Gabriella said.

Trevor put his arm around his wife. "That's why I'm here. I'll make sure Avery has everything she needs."

Gabriella leaned into her husband. "I know you will. But I'm scared."

"What does this mean, Dr. Granger? Tell me what you're thinking," Trevor said.

He was thinking he wasn't an OB-GYN. He didn't have access to an operating room. He couldn't perform a cesarean section in a case of extreme distress for the baby or Gabriella. They didn't have a NICU to keep a pre-term baby healthy. Throwing out that list of terrifying possibilities would only upset the Garths further. "I am thinking we will minimize our risk factors. I'd like for you to stay here and rest for a couple of hours. We'll keep stopping in and checking on how you're feeling. Trevor, I want you to write down every time she has a contraction."

Rafe gave a few more instructions and then he and Gemma stepped away from the Garths.

"You think she'll go into labor too soon," Gemma said.

"That's my concern," Rafe said. "We don't have the facilities to deal with a baby who is only thirty-four weeks and a mom who might lose a lot of blood."

Gemma nodded, her brows furrowed with worry. "Can we do anything to prepare?"

"I'll talk to Dr. Goodhue about what we can do if Gabriella needs to be evacuated. Perhaps Cheyenne

Memorial could make arrangements for her to be dealt with in isolation. I will make some calls."

It was another of the thousands of reasons Rafe needed a cure for the virus. The longer they were trapped inside Dead River, the more victims the virus would take, directly and indirectly.

Chapter 11

Flint and his officers had created a large map of Dead River and had it hanging in the police station. They had posted colored push pins in various locations to indicate an outbreak, a death from the virus, an illness and possible places of exposure to the virus.

The number of pins on the map was disturbing. Gemma stared at it before turning away. They were close to a cure. She would focus on that.

Flint had asked her to come to the police station.

"Gemma, thanks for coming." He hugged her and she read his need for comfort in the hug. Principal Lewis had passed away that morning. The doctors had not performed an autopsy, but Gemma knew the much-loved principal had a history of heart problems and hadn't given up smoking even though he had promised he would after his second heart attack. The Dead River virus may have overwhelmed his immune system.

"We think we traced Annabelle's exposure to the school. We've had seven reports of students contracting the virus. I received a report this morning from Dr. Goodhue that the CDC would like for us to close the school for the time being," Flint said.

"Close the school?" Gemma asked. The students

would be on winter break in a few days, but the finality of Flint's words resonated through her. If they started shutting down the school and businesses, conditions would worsen in Dead River. Boredom and worry would escalate and trouble would follow.

"We're asking people to report any and all illnesses and symptoms in their children, but that's creating a mass panic. Every kid who sneezes is being reported as a possible victim. If parents can't send their children to school, they won't have anyone to watch them during the day." As her brother's dire predictions grew more severe, Gemma felt a sharp headache spear into her.

They needed a plan and they needed a cure.

"Let's call Cole and Amy. They've run summer programs at the rehab center before and we think animals are safe from the virus. After twenty-four hours, we can screen the kids and send some of them during the day to the rehab center."

"That would be a great idea, except I heard from Eric over at the gas station and they're almost out of fuel. The tanks are low. I can imagine the panic when I announce that gas will be rationed. We won't have fuel to bus anyone to Cole and Amy's rehab center."

She put her arm over her brother's shoulders. Like Rafe, he took on problems as if he was ultimately responsible. "We'll be okay."

"If people start to riot, I can't control them," Flint said.

"No one will riot," Gemma said. "At the clinic and at the fire station, everyone worked hard to keep spirits up. Did you notice the wreaths on the street lights? Stan organized his firefighters to do that. They carried their fire ladders up and down Main Street. The virus has been unrelenting, but it's brought out a good side in people."

Flint gave her a half smile. "You're always trying to fix things. To fix people. Speaking of that, and bearing in mind that I am your brother and need no explicit details, how are things with Rafe?"

"Things are great with Rafe." She wouldn't give her brother another reason to worry and she wasn't exactly lying. The best part of their relationship, the time they spent in the bedroom, was going well. Perfect. Mind-blowing. The rest of their relationship was chugging along, likely fueled by that bedroom attraction.

"You can't fix a man like Rafe," Flint said.

"Who says he needs fixing?" Gemma said.

"He's pretty angry at this town."

"I wasn't planning to change that," Gemma said. Or was she? She liked living in Dead River, but when she was around Rafe, she did make it a point to be more rah-rah about the good things and downplay the bad ones.

"I don't want to see you hurt," Flint said.

"You don't have to worry about me. I have everything under control."

"Famous last words," Flint said. "I thought working in a small town would be easy. I thought I'd spend my days with a coffee cup in one hand and a donut in the other."

"How's that working out?"

Flint sighed. "Haven't sat to have coffee and quiet in months."

Gemma wanted to tell her brother they were close to a cure. She had promised Rafe and Dr. Goodhue she would keep the secret. "Trust me when I tell you this won't be forever."

Flint lifted a brow. "Is that your way of telling me the clinic may have good news soon?"

"It's my way of telling you to have faith in your sister."

"I've always had that. What I don't have is a cure."

"Please calm down!" Betsy was shouting over the wave of people clamoring to climb into the delivery rig. Betsy had driven it from the drop-off point into town. Word had spread about the supplies and people had rushed to Main Street. The last, destroyed delivery had left people that much shorter on basic necessities and desperation was growing.

No one was listening to Betsy. Rafe and Gemma were waiting to be sure their lab equipment was removed safely off the truck. They had their eyes open for Dr. Rand or anyone looking like they intended to start a problem. That was the entire crowd.

Shoving, pushing and shouting surrounded Gemma. She was jostled forward in the crowd and barely kept her footing. Telling her brother the virus had brought out the best in people hadn't taken into consideration that it was hard to be civil when shortages were high.

The back of the rig slammed to a close behind Betsy and then Rafe stepped to her side. He said nothing but everyone went quiet and looked at him.

"Are you ready to listen?" Rafe asked.

He could command a crowd as quickly as he could her and his patients. Gemma watched, half-riveted, half-afraid for him that he'd be trampled.

Murmurs of anger rose.

Rafe spoke over them. "This truck contains supplies destined for the clinic, the pharmacy, the police department and the fire station, facilities that every member of this town needs and uses. We'll keep those services up and running by ensuring they receive their deliveries undisturbed. Then we will deliver the remaining items, including the groceries, and every person in this town will have enough to eat. No hoarding. No stealing."

"Who are you to decide that?" A shout from the crowd.

"I am the person who will need to treat people if this gets violent. I'm the person who will have to handle finding a cure for the virus and stitching people up at the same time. Gemma Colton is always telling me how wonderful this town is. She's always telling me that the goodness in this town is in the hearts of the people who live here. If you care about your neighbors, your friends and your families, then you will take nothing more than what you need. You will not turn into savages. This will be orderly and no one will be hurt. When we're done, Gemma and I can transport our medical equipment and return to the lab so we can work on a cure for the Dead River virus."

Murmurs of approval rolled through the crowd.

Gemma was transfixed.

Rafe waited until the crowd was silent. Then he opened the back of the truck. "First box is marked for the pharmacy. Is Gloria here?"

The crowd parted to allow Gloria Hitch, the pharmacist, through. "I brought a hand truck, but those boxes are larger than I thought."

"Ma'am, we'll help." Two men who looked like father and son stepped forward to assist Gloria with the boxes.

As Rafe distributed the boxes, groups worked together to take the crates to the proper locations.

When they found the boxes for the clinic, Gemma hurried forward. Some of the equipment was delicate and they needed it now more than ever. Broken syringes, scratched lenses or unsterilized bandages would set them back.

They placed their boxes to the side of the truck and when the rig was emptied, she and Rafe hefted the boxes onto hand trucks to transport them to the clinic.

"You were exactly what this town needed today," she said.

"I can't take credit. It was all you. You're the one who told me the people of this town were good. I would have let it erupt into chaos, thinking no other outcome was possible. But I had your voice in my head."

"It could have been almost as bad as the last shipment that was sabotaged," Gemma said.

"That crowd wouldn't let the supplies be destroyed this time," Rafe said.

"No, but I think they would have raided the rig and taken anything they could."

At the clinic, they inventoried their supplies, restocked the closets and set up the new equipment in the lab. When they were finished, they retreated to his office.

Rafe closed the door and she reached up, taking his tie in her hands and pulling him to her for a long, slow kiss. She let her tongue tangle with his. She knew a kiss like this one had the potential to turn incendiary and she was okay with that possibility. So much affection for Rafe swelled up in her.

"I've wanted to do that since I saw you directing the crowd at the rig," Gemma said.

"All this for organizing a little supplies distribution?" Rafe asked.

For that, for helping at the fire station and because she'd realized she was in love with him. That realization had been freeing and terrifying. "You believe in Dead River."

Rafe turned his head quickly and darkness came into his eyes. "Don't do that, Gemma."

"Do what?" she asked, releasing his tie.

"I know what you're thinking and where this conversation will lead and I already told you I was leaving Dead River. I agree that the people of this town acted civilly, even honorably, today, but that doesn't mean I've fallen in love with this place or that I want to stay. I do not want to fight about it again."

Why was he quick to draw a line in the sand? He wasn't in love with Dead River, but what about her? Did she mean anything to him? "Is this about being worried about my feelings or being worried about your own?"

He narrowed his gaze on her. "What do you mean by that?"

She went for broke. She needed to know if any of her affections were returned. "Are you worried that you have feelings for me?"

It was a hot button question to ask. Their affair hadn't been about emotions and she had escalated it to that point.

Rafe said nothing.

"Are you worried that if you stick around you'll fall in love with me? This town? Maybe even see yourself as Danny's father?"

Rafe went still. "Why are you always pushing?"

"Why are you always pushing me away?" Gemma asked.

"I am not pushing anyone away. We had sex this morning," Rafe said.

Sex. He brought the conversation and their relationship back to that. She had believed she could handle sleeping with Rafe, without her emotions getting in the way. Lust had ruled her thinking. Now she had no idea how to respond. She had told Rafe she could sleep with him and be okay with it. The way she was feeling now was decidedly not okay. "I wasn't talking about sex." That wasn't the closeness she was referring to.

Rafe's expression softened. She knew he didn't want to hurt her, but he wasn't willing to sacrifice anything for her. "Gemma, from the beginning you knew where I stood. That hasn't changed. If you thought I would change my mind and stay, I'm sorry. If you've changed your mind or I've said something that led you to believe I could be a man who would love you, then I'm sorry."

The words cut like a dagger. She didn't need his love, but knowing she wouldn't have it made the room feel like it was missing oxygen. On the heels of her hurt was anger. How could he be so cavalier about her feelings? How could he be sure he couldn't love her? Was she that unlovable? "I thought I could do this." Maybe if he had been any other man she could. But not Rafe, not the man who was standing in front of her, the man of her fantasies. "I realize now that I can't." Or maybe she just didn't want to anymore, knowing her love was unreciprocated.

She turned to leave and Rafe caught her arm. "Wait."

He looked torn between wanting to kiss her and being unsure what to say. "It always seemed to make things better when I held you. Let me hold you."

Gemma pulled free of him. "I think we've crossed a line and now we can't go back." She loved him and he wouldn't return her feelings. How could she continue this affair knowing it?

"You've always been too good for me, Gemma. I knew I would hurt you. I knew this would end badly."

Gemma wiped at a tear that had escaped. "Maybe that's been the problem. You know how good you are in medicine. You know how good you are in bed. But you don't grasp how good you are as a partner."

She slipped from the room and closed the door behind her. It snicked shut with a finality that shook her.

It took Rafe a solid hour to put his head on straight. He'd replayed the conversation with Gemma again and again looking for where he'd gone wrong.

She had implied his feelings about Dead River had changed and those words had made him feel utterly defensive. He didn't want to admit that his years of feeling slighted and hating this town had been misguided, that perhaps he'd projected his bad attitude on Dead River.

Gemma wanted him to stay. They had a good thing going. It was nice to sleep beside someone and wake up with her curled close. He liked making love with her before drifting off to sleep.

Their relationship was intense. Was it more than sex and friendship?

A tap on his door. Relief rushed through him. He and Gemma could talk this over.

He opened the door. Not Gemma. It was Dr. Goodhue.

"Am I interrupting?" she asked.

Rafe shook his head. "I was wrapping up. What can I do for you?"

"Can we speak in private?" she asked.

His office was small, but he gestured to the chair where his patients sat during a consult. "Please have a seat."

Dr. Goodhue looked at her notes several times before she spoke. "I heard from my contacts at the CDC. The sequences you submitted were flagged by the federal government."

"In what way?" Rafe asked. He assumed someone at the federal level was aware of the situation in Dead River and was hoping it didn't escalate into a statewide or nation-wide problem.

"From the military. The virus has some similarities to classified government research."

Classified government research? "The government already knows what it is? They've been working on it?" Classified or not, if the government had a cure, they had to share it, didn't they?

"They know what it is because they manufactured it," Dr. Goodhue said.

"A man-made virus?" Rafe asked. He'd heard that the United States government experimented with strains of viruses in their top secret labs.

"I don't know what to think. I don't see how a virus

that's classified and contained in isolation in a government lab would spread to Dead River."

The government could have a lab nearby. Mimi Rand could have known someone who worked in a top secret lab and some of the virus escaped on that person. While most labs were fastidious with their safety precautions and contaminations were rare, they did happen. "Did your contact speculate on that?"

She shook her head. "They've escalated the matter up the chain of command and we should be receiving more information soon."

The government could make cutting through red tape to find answers a time-consuming process. "Soon? Are your contacts aware we'll have ten more deaths this week if we don't find a cure?"

She nodded, looking perplexed. "I don't understand it either. We've stumbled onto a lead and it seems like everyone is worried about passing the blame rather than getting a cure into our hands."

"How the Dead River virus spread is not as important as finding a cure. Let me know when you're sent that information."

Dr. Goodhue sat for another few minutes. "I can't put my head around it. But you'll be my first call when I receive more information."

Molly was in a terrible mood. She'd heard from a friend that Jimmy Johnson had been spotted near the fire station. Then she'd heard he was seen in a crowd gathered outside the delivery truck waiting for supplies.

It had crossed her mind that unless he had some outdoor survival skills, he was either hiding with a friend or squatting in a vacant house. How else would he survive the brutal Wyoming winter?

Every time Molly thought of Jimmy, she felt stupid and used. She had fallen for him, despite the obvious warning signs. How could he use her that way?

She needed to work out her anger before her shift at the diner. Putting on a happy face for her customers was part of the job. When she thought of Jimmy, it was hard to feel good about anything.

Her car had a quarter tank of gas, just enough to drive out to Cole's ranch and back. She wanted to see Matt even if it would mean expending the rest of her gas and being forced to brave the weather to get to work by foot.

Deep in a funk, she decided it was worth it to see Matt. When she arrived at Cole's ranch, she found him working with a horse. She watched him before he turned and caught sight of her.

She lifted her hand in greeting and then strolled toward the fence near where Matt was working.

"Molly, what are you doing here?" Matt asked.

"You don't sound happy to see me," she said. A more effusive welcome or an outright joyous response to her visit would have felt nice. Molly knew she was doing it again. She was forcing giant romantic notions onto a man who wasn't interested in her. Not really interested, anyway.

"I am happy to see you. I don't want to get in trouble with Cole. He gave me this job and I want to stay on his good side."

"I can talk to Cole. He's family."

Matt's brows furrowed. "I wouldn't put you in the middle. Is everything okay? Is Danny doing okay?"

Molly smiled. "Gemma said she and Rafe saw Danny this morning and he was fine."

Sadness crossed Matt's face. "I've been worried about him."

"All of us are," Molly said.

Suddenly, she felt silly for getting worked up about Jimmy Johnson sightings and rumors. Why did it matter if he was lurking around town? He'd be caught or he'd flee town and she wouldn't see him again. Either way, he wouldn't be in her life and she had to move on. This town had other, more immediate problems and she had one big personal problem: knowing what she would do next with her life. She didn't want to work at the diner forever, but she had no cash for college and she was starting over.

"What brings you out here?" Matt asked.

She didn't want to tell him. He was watching her, his expression calm. The horse nudged his shoulder and he patted her nose gently. "Just a minute, Star Fire."

She couldn't tell him that she had needed to see him. "It's silly."

"Not to you if you drove out here. I heard there's a gas shortage."

Molly sighed. "Someone told me they saw my ex in town. It upset me."

"I'd be upset too. The guy's a tool."

Molly leaned on the fence to be closer to Matt. "It burns me that he used me and stole from me."

"If I ever see him, I'd knock some sense into him. The way he treated you was terrible."

His words were salve on her hurt. "Do you want to take a walk?" Molly asked.

Matt looked at his watch. "I can take my break a little early. Let me walk Star Fire to the barn."

Once Matt had Star Fire in her stall, he let his boss know he was taking a break for a few minutes.

They walked across the property and Matt took her gloved hand. She pulled her hand away, removed the glove and then slipped her hand into his. "I like this better."

The skin of his hands was calloused, the hands of a working man. She liked it and she liked being with him. It hadn't been this easy with Jimmy. With Jimmy, it had been exciting and fast and hurried. "Thanks for being a friend when I really need one," Molly said.

"A woman like you must have friends," Matt said.

"A few." Theo's fiancée, Ellie, and Gemma, to name two. But they were busy and being with Matt was different.

"You know I wouldn't hurt you," Matt said.

"I know. I wouldn't hurt you either," Molly said.

"I want to save enough money so that Danny can come live with me. I want us to be a family again," Matt said.

"I know," Molly said. He had talked about renting a place for him and Danny to live and then applying for custody of Danny.

"How do you feel about that?" Matt asked.

"I think you're an honorable man and Danny is lucky to have you. I'm pulling for you both," Molly said.

He stopped and put his arms around her waist. "You see me in a light that no one else ever has."

"Am I wrong to believe that you're a good person?"

Molly asked, hating the doubt that crept in and knowing it had everything to do with Jimmy's betrayal.

"I hope not. I like to think I'm a good person." Their eyes met and Molly felt the air around them heat up. He glanced at her lips and her eyes grew wide in anticipation.

Matt seemed unsure.

She gave him the green light. "It's okay if you want to kiss me."

Matt smiled. "Thank God, because I don't think I could wait much longer."

He slanted his mouth over hers and delivered a sweet, soft kiss. It was like a hundred fireworks ignited. Molly tilted her head and the kiss deepened.

When they broke apart, they were panting.

"Can I take you to dinner tonight? Tomorrow? Anytime?" he asked.

Molly grinned. "Do you have enough gas to get into town? Because I'm almost out."

"I'll walk if I have to."

"It's forty miles in the freezing cold!"

"That's nothing if I know you're waiting on the other end of my trip."

Without enough evidence to hold him, Danny had been allowed to come home. Even though Rafe was happy about that, he was brooding about Gemma. He had no outlet for his frustration over Gemma and no one to talk to. He couldn't call Theo or Flint. Not only would a call this late wake Theo's baby, Amelia, or scare them, they would kill Rafe for sleeping with their little sister, ruining the relationship and then moping about it.

He wanted to talk to Gemma and tell her what he was feeling. On the heels of their conversation earlier, she was off limits. Knowing he couldn't have her, he wanted her even more.

Danny knocked on his bedroom door and Rafe set down the book he'd been reading, or rather staring at, by the fire. Rafe was glad to have Danny home. Flint had decided it was better for Danny to stay with Rafe. Rafe had agreed to take responsibility for Danny.

"May I come in?" Danny asked.

"Of course, please. What's on your mind?"

Danny leaned against the wall. "What happened with Dr. Rand…"

Not a complete thought, but Rafe knew where he was going. "He won't bother you. He can complain all he wants about you coming home, but it wasn't his decision."

Danny shook his head, his too-long hair falling over his eyes. Rafe noted he needed to take him for a haircut soon. "Not that. I'm not worried about Rand running his mouth. I was thinking that you believed me. You know I didn't do anything to Rand."

"Of course I believe you," Rafe said.

Danny looked up at Rafe and his eyes shone with admiration. "Most people don't. I mean, Grandpa did. Matt does. But everyone else thinks I'm a screw up."

Rafe heard raw, unguarded pain in the teenager's voice. He wanted to save him from some of the hurt that he'd harbored growing up in Dead River.

"That isn't true. I saw some of your teachers around town and they complimented me on you. I don't deserve the compliment, you're your own man, but I was proud. You should know that you're a good person and people see the greatness in you."

Danny appeared surprised. "They said good things about me? Even after what happened with Dr. Rand?"

"I think especially then. I'm not sure anyone believes that you attacked him or robbed the clinic."

Danny stood straighter. "I hated living at the center."

Emotion swelled in Rafe's chest. He'd hated being separated from Danny too. "I'm glad you're home."

"Thanks, Dr. Rafe."

"You know that I want you to be happy and I want to do the right thing by you," Rafe said. It wasn't clear what the right thing was. Adopt him and take him to New York, but away from his brother? Visit Danny in Dead River?

Danny nodded.

"No matter what happens, I'll make sure you're okay," Rafe said. "You can always tell me if you run into a problem." When he left for New York, he would make sure Danny knew that still applied and he was only a phone call away.

Danny nodded again.

"Now get some sleep. We have a big day tomorrow," Rafe said, feeling himself getting choked up.

"No school," Danny said, sounding happy.

With the outbreak at the school, classes had been canceled for the duration. "I thought I would take you with me to the clinic. You can help us with a few projects."

"You'd trust me to do that?" Danny said.

"Of course," Rafe said. His other motive was to keep Danny close and therefore give him an alibi if Dr. Rand accused Danny of anything else.

Danny grinned. "Night, Dr. Rafe. See you tomorrow."

Rafe listened to the boy pad down the hallway and close his bedroom door.

Gemma was downstairs sleeping in his office. He'd heard her come inside and he'd hoped she would come upstairs to see him. He hadn't been that lucky.

He set down his book. He couldn't focus. He went to the bathroom to get ready for bed. Gemma's makeup bag was sitting on his counter. He picked up a bottle of her perfume and smelled it. Knowing it was an excuse, he carried the satin bag downstairs. He knocked on the office door.

Gemma opened it wearing a pair of light green fleece pajamas. Warm and cozy, they looked inviting. She revealed next to nothing in those pajamas, but he felt hot for her.

He held up the bag. "You left this in my bathroom. I didn't know if you needed it."

Gemma took the bag from his outstretched hand. "Thank you."

"Do you want to come upstairs?"

She shook her head. "Not tonight. Goodnight, Rafe." She closed the door.

The dark throb of need pulsed inside him. He returned upstairs to shower. A cold shower wouldn't help, but he touched himself thinking of her, wishing she were with him. If he could take the edge off, he could sleep.

Then the bathroom door opened and Gemma stepped inside. He watched her remove her pajamas and then she slipped into the stall with him.

"I changed my mind," she said.

He didn't need an invitation. He took her in his arms.

His body was primed. Gemma reached between his legs. "What were you doing in here?" A mischievous glint in her eyes told him she knew exactly what he'd been doing.

"Thinking of you."

"Right answer."

"Just the truth," Rafe said.

"I was thinking you could show me what else is in your black box," Gemma said.

"Danny's home."

"I checked on him. He's asleep in his bedroom and I locked your bedroom door."

Beyond that, he was worried about her feelings. She had said she couldn't do this with him and not be hurt. "It's not a good idea."

She laid a finger over his mouth. "I want to keep this what it should have been from the start. Just sex."

Just sex. Before returning to Dead River, those words had been the key to unlocking his libido. Now, they felt hollow. Gemma brought her mouth to his neck and sucked lightly.

Returning her mouth to him, she flicked her tongue along his chest and then down his abdominals. When she reached his navel, she moved lower and then stopped.

She would kill him with anticipation. She stood. "The black box."

Rafe turned off the water and handed her a towel. They dried quickly and climbed into bed.

He removed the box from his bedside table and flipped open the lid. Gemma took out a few condoms and dropped them onto the mattress. "We'll need these." She lifted out a bottle of personal lubricant.

"Maybe this." She dropped massage oils onto the bed and laid down, pulling him with her.

Wiggling beneath him, she hummed with anticipation. Rafe wouldn't disappoint. He picked up one of the bottles of oil. "Do you prefer lilac or cherry blossom?"

"Lilac. Please."

He massaged her body, concentrating on the tense muscles of her lower back.

When her body was relaxed, he kissed her, starting at her neck and moving along her spine. She let out a sigh of contentment.

Rolling to her back, she reached for the bottle of oil. With her hands slick, she ran them down his chest to his erection. She closed her hand over him and he inhaled slowly, trying to keep control.

He wanted her to enjoy this night and he wanted to give her more than a massage. Removing her hand, he donned a condom. Standing at the edge of the mattress and opening her thighs, he rested her ankles on his shoulders. She was hot and wet and it was easy for him to slip inside her.

He felt the power of the first full thrust and her body clamping hard around him.

"You feel great," he said.

"Careful how fast you move. You're big."

His male ego enjoyed the compliment and he felt his body growing harder.

Moving slowly at first, he increased his pace. She was moaning and chanting his name. Her feet fell to his sides, giving him complete control over the pace they moved.

He leaned forward and kissed her. She made a sound and her arms came around him. The close contact and her breasts brushing his chest amplified the sensations of moving inside her.

Rafe was close and didn't know how long he would last. Short, fast jerks and Gemma came hard. Sex with Gemma was familiar and exciting, a combination he hadn't found with any one woman.

She flipped him onto his back and impaled herself on him. Just being inside her, he wanted to come, but he grappled for control. He was close, so close.

"That was wonderful," she said. She moved up and down slowly, bringing him away from the brink of completion.

"Now, let me make you feel good." She swiveled her hips and he grasped them, wanting to draw out the pleasure longer. He felt his body tightening as she brought him close to finishing.

Her lips parted and she took his hands, placing them on her breasts. She lifted her hair and rocked her body back and forth. The steadily increasing pleasure between his hips sent a shudder over him before a powerful orgasm rocketed through him.

Gemma made a sound of contentment and lay on his chest, her wet blond hair tickling his shoulder.

"Tell me why you came in here," Rafe said. He was still hard inside her and his timing was wrong. But he needed to understand how she was feeling. It hadn't mattered much before if a woman wanted sex from him after they'd had a fight. But with Gemma, it felt like a lingering problem that had to be addressed.

"I wanted to have sex," she said.

"Is that all?" he asked, inhaling the scent of her hair. The smell would be in his sheets tomorrow and he liked that.

She sighed. "You know that I'm yours, don't you, Rafe?" She looked into his eyes and the open honesty in them shook him more than the mind-blowing sex they'd just shared.

"I don't deserve you," he said.

"Whether that's true or not, I am yours. I've wanted to be yours since I had my first crush on you in high school."

He was trying to follow her. "This afternoon you said that you couldn't be with me."

"I can't which is why this is sad for me. For us. I'm yours, but you won't be able to tell me the same and mean it."

She extracted herself from him, gathered up her clothes and pulled them on. She started for the door.

"Gemma, wait. Stay the night."

She appeared uncertain.

"If only for morning sex." He hated saying the words because they meant he was pretending right along with her that all they had was sex.

She came back to the bed, but it was an empty victory.

Rafe read the report the CDC had acquired from the United States government detailing their experiences with the virus he had been calling the Dead River virus. Pages of laboratory notes, observations, seventy-five percent of it redacted by large black boxes made it hard to read and understand.

The report had barely enough information to add anything to what he knew of the virus. To his disappointment, the report stated the virus had no known cure and cell samples inevitably died of either the virus or complications from the virus.

No known cure. Inevitable death.

It didn't bode well for Dead River.

At the end of the report, the researchers and their biographies were listed. Some names and qualifications were removed, but he noted a researcher had completed his undergraduate work in chemistry at the University of Wyoming. Could it be someone local? In a government lab, security would be tight, but could a researcher have gone off the grid or conducted research in their home? Could Mimi have come into contact with the virus that way?

The spread of the Dead River virus could have been an unintentional sequence of events.

Rafe couldn't put his finger on why that information stood out more than the graphs, charts and information about the virus.

The door to his office flew open and Anand stuck his head inside. "I've got a code blue on Hank Bittard."

Cardiac arrest. Rafe rose to his feet and hurried with Anand to the virus wing. One major downside to the safety procedures was that precious moments were lost getting into their biohazard suits to enter the virus wing.

But Rafe wasn't taking chances, not with the words "no known cure" ringing in his thoughts. He and Anand hurried to Hank Bittard's room, unlocking the door and entering. Bittard was flatlining. Rafe ran for their emergency cart.

Anand had grabbed the defibrillation paddles to try to jump his heart. They used the paddles three times and tried every medicine they had at their disposal.

After forty minutes of trying to revive him, Rafe set out his hand to stop Anand from trying the paddles again.

"Time of death: 10:41 p.m." Though Rafe knew Hank Bittard had been a murderer who had almost infected him, Gemma and Dr. Rand, he was sad to lose a patient. It wasn't easy no matter the circumstances.

He and Anand didn't need to speak. It was not the first patient either of them had lost.

They left the room, locking the door to prevent anyone from going inside, and took time to visit with their other patients to reassure them about what had happened.

Jessica was awake when Rafe entered her room. Annabelle was curled in her mother's bed. It was often how they slept, their beds pushed together with the side rails down to make a large bed for them to be together.

The whirl of the ventilation required he speak loudly, but he didn't want to wake Annabelle.

"What happened?" Jessica asked.

"One of our patients passed away," Rafe said.

"Hank Bittard?" Jessica asked.

Most of the patients had likely seen Rafe and Anand enter Bittard's room. "Yes."

Jessica blew out her breath. "I'm glad. Since he was brought here, I've been terrified I'd wake up with him waving a knife in my face."

"He was locked in his room," Rafe said, though he understood her concern.

"With my baby in here, I'm feeling a little more mama-bear fierce."

"How are you both doing?" Rafe asked.

"Annabelle sleeps most of the time. I've been encouraging her to drink a lot of liquids. Gemma brought some flavored sugar to mix with Annabelle's drinks to make it more enticing. That helped some."

"I'm glad." Rafe began checking their vitals.

"Where's Gemma tonight?" Jessica asked.

"Home."

"At her house?"

"No, at mine," Rafe said.

Jessica smiled. "How's it going with you two?"

Gemma had likely spoken to her best friend. What could Rafe say? They were having hot sex, but that was the most he would allow. He wouldn't speak that way to another person, especially not in front of a sleeping child.

"We're staying friends," Rafe said.

Jessica looked at him through curious eyes. "What does that mean?"

He felt like a jerk when he explained his job in New York. "I'm planning to leave Dead River. Gemma knows that."

Jessica frowned. "She told you about Jackson, right? That loser surgeon who broke her heart."

Gemma had mentioned him. "I know a little about it."

"He messed her up. She's been skittish for years about men. You're the first man with whom she's shown signs of getting over him. Don't hurt her and undo that."

If he could protect Gemma's feelings and pursue his dreams, nothing would stop him. But it wasn't a choice. She was clear she couldn't keep boundaries in her heart and he had a job waiting for him. "What would you suggest?"

"Let her love you."

Rafe started at the simplicity of the answer. "Won't that hurt her more in the end?"

Jessica shrugged. "Maybe. But I have the feeling that constantly reminding her that you're leaving hurts more because you're using it as an excuse to keep your distance."

Her reasoning struck him hard. He had risked nothing with Gemma because he had known the relationship would end. Keeping Gemma inside a box—his lover in Dead River and nothing more—meant he could leave her here when he left. He didn't have to think about how he would feel about a future with her because there wasn't one.

Somehow, though he hadn't intended for it to happen, he felt more for her than that.

Chapter 12

Gram Dottie had lost too much weight. Gemma didn't want to think about putting a feeding tube in her grandmother. Painful for the patient and fraught with additional medical complications, Gemma tried to entice her grandmother with Nina's chicken soup.

"Nina cooked this special for you," Gemma said.

Her grandmother watched her with tired eyes. She had swallowed a few spoonfuls, but she was looking at the bowl disdainfully. "I'll eat some in a little while. Tell me how you are doing."

Gemma set down the bowl. "I'm doing okay. I'm worried about you and Jessica and Annabelle and all my patients."

"The last time I saw your grandfather, I told him I couldn't wait to see him again," Gram Dottie said.

Gemma did not like where this conversation was leading. "Now is not that time."

"Gemma, you have to fight for what you want, but there are times when what we need and what we want aren't the same. I am tired. I've been fighting this illness. I can't fight forever."

Gemma felt tears in her eyes. She wasn't giving her grandmother the option of saying goodbye. Death wasn't a choice. "Rafe has made progress in finding a cure. We learned some information recently that might help us."

Gram Dottie smiled. "I'm old. I've lived my life. If you have a cure, it should go to the young people. The people who need it most so they can have as happy a life as I've had."

Gemma wasn't ready to let go of her grandmother. "Once we have a cure, we can replicate it."

"I don't have time, Gemma, and I won't take someone else's chance. I've been given so many happy years."

Gemma wanted to tear off her HAZMAT suit. Maybe prove to her grandmother that she had confidence in Rafe finding a cure. Her grandmother just had to fight a little longer. "Please, Gram, don't give up. Not yet."

Gram Dottie closed her eyes. "Let's talk on the computer tomorrow with your brothers and their families. I want to hear Theo, Ellie, Amelia, Flint and Nina's voices. I want to hear about you and this handsome doctor who makes your smile brighter than it's been in years."

Rafe? She hadn't told her grandmother anything was going on with him. Then again, her grandmother had always been perceptive. "I'll call the boys and we'll set it up."

As Gemma left her grandmother to rest, she hoped she could have another day with her. Lately, Gemma felt she had been hoping and pining for a little more, a little longer. Time was working against her patients and against her.

Gemma exited the virus wing and removed her

HAZMAT suit. She needed to update her patients' records in the computer with her observations and notes. For some reason, the system wasn't working in the virus wing. Every time she tried to open the medical records application, it crashed.

She rebooted the computer in the reception area and strode toward the doctors' offices. She'd update Dr. Rand on her patients verbally, and she wanted him to take a close look at her grandmother.

Dr. Rand wasn't in his office. Was he resting in the doctor-and-nurse lounge? Gemma heard a crash from the laboratory and ran to investigate.

Dr. Rand was inside the lab and not in his hazmat suit. He was throwing papers into a large metal trashcan. He was smashing their virus samples. What was he doing? What had happened?

Banging on the door's window to get his attention, he turned to face her. He had a wild look in his eyes that scared her. She stepped back from the door.

She'd call Flint. He had the video surveillance. He could see what had happened.

She ran to the reception area to the phone. Lifting the handle, she started to dial.

Dr. Rand slammed into her, knocking the phone from her hand. She hit the wall hard.

"What are you doing?" Dr. Rand screamed. He was shaking and his eyes were bloodshot, his forehead sweaty. Was he sick with the virus?

"What's the matter? What happened in the lab?" Gemma asked.

"Contaminated! Everything! The virus is loose. I can't control it. I can't contain it."

Was he having a total break with reality? A stress

reaction? "Dr. Rand, please calm down. Tell me what happened."

Dr. Rand pulled at his hair and looked around. "Mimi got sick and died. Her baby survived. How? How is Theo alive? Countless others are dead."

Gemma was cornered in the reception area. She needed to circle around Dr. Rand and flee. This might be some grief reaction to his ex-wife's death or a panicked reaction to an accidental exposure to the Dead River virus. "I know you cared about Mimi and this is hard for all of us."

"I hated her! All she cared about was your brother! She wanted some happily-ever-after with him. I told her she was a fool. Why would she think a one-night stand meant anything? She wasn't sure at first if the baby was Theo's or some other guy's."

Theo had said that his one night with Mimi was something neither of them pursued further. Perhaps having a baby had changed Mimi's mind? "I know you tried to save her."

"I didn't try to save her. Now, it's too late. The virus wasn't supposed to spread. How is it spreading? It shouldn't have gone this far. It's getting stronger. It's mutating."

He was speaking as if he had spread the virus. Old suspicions crept into her thoughts. "We're working on a cure."

Dr. Rand looked around. "There is no cure. You know there isn't. You and Rafe have been doing your secret research. You've figured it out, haven't you? Nothing will fix this. Nothing."

She and Rafe had been careful about who they'd shared their results with, but they'd been conducting their work in the lab. "We've gotten a sequence." Why was Dr. Rand certain they wouldn't find a cure? What did he know that she didn't?

"You know it will lead to Dugway and then to me. You know I injected Mimi."

Dugway? What was he talking about? He was taking responsibility for the Dead River virus and for killing Mimi. Panic rose in her throat. Dr. Rand had lost it.

"It shouldn't have gone this far," Dr. Rand said.

Then Dr. Rand lifted his hand from his doctor's coat. He had a syringe in it. "Come here, Gemma. You're too nosy. You ask too many questions. I need to start cleaning up this mess. Starting with you."

Gemma tried to run, but Dr. Rand grabbed her arm and threw her to the floor. He climbed on top of her, pinning her with his body. She felt the injection into her shoulder and cried out. Hot fluid pushed into her. Was he killing her, forcing her to overdose?

"Don't worry. If you and Mimi respond the same, you'll be dead in hours. I'll stay right here with you until that happens. I can try to save you, but we know I can't."

Gemma tried to stay focused, but her eyes began to water and her stomach roiled. He had injected her with the Dead River virus.

Then she heard Rafe's voice. Was Rafe here or was she hallucinating?

The undergraduate degree hanging in Dr. Lucas Rand's office was from the University of Wyoming, same as the government researcher who'd been listed in the bios of the document he'd been provided. Rafe didn't know how or why yet, but Dr. Rand was involved with the Dead River virus.

The moment he made the connection, Rafe remembered that Dr. Rand and Gemma were working tonight. He arrived at the clinic to find Dr. Rand on top of limp Gemma.

Rafe would kill him. What had he done to her? Rafe grabbed Dr. Rand and hurled him off Gemma. Dr. Rand swung a syringe at him. What was in the syringe?

"You picked the wrong time to check on your girlfriend," Dr. Rand said. He was sweating and his face was red.

"What did you do to her?" Rafe asked.

Gemma was motionless on the floor.

Dr. Rand smiled evilly. "Gemma got sick. I tried to help her."

He hadn't tried to help her. He had tried to kill her.

Dr. Rand seemed on the edge. Rafe was careful not to push him further. "I've already called Flint. Put the syringe down and we'll talk about this."

Dr. Rand shook his head. "The chief of police won't believe me. He didn't believe me when I told him about Danny attacking me."

"Because it didn't happen," Rafe said, realizing how sick Dr. Rand was. Gemma had been right, and it was even worse than she had suspected.

Dr. Rand lunged at Rafe again. Rafe grabbed his arm, twisting it behind his back. Dr. Rand let out a howl and dropped the syringe.

"Are you insane?" Rafe asked. "You've been behind everything, haven't you?"

"Have I thwarted your plans to have a perfect life in Dead River? The long-lost doctor returns to be hero of the clinic, winning the girl and fostering his own little family. Please, how long can you keep up that charade? I've saved you from a life of boredom."

Dr. Rand threw himself toward the syringe. Rafe scrambled for control of it. Dr. Rand let out a howl of pain as the end of the needle punctured his palm.

Dr. Rand held his hand. "I've gotten it."

"What was in the syringe, Rand?" Rafe asked.

"Dead River virus," Rand said, horror written on his face.

The man appeared surprised that he'd injected himself and Rafe took advantage. He landed a punch across Dr. Rand's face. Dr. Rand dropped to the ground, motionless.

Rafe kicked the syringe out of reach.

Gemma moaned and Rafe turned his attention to her.

He looked her over for some signs of what had happened. Had Dr. Rand injected her with the Dead River virus?

Dr. Rand rose to his feet and raced out of the room. Rafe considered chasing him, but Gemma needed medical attention.

Looking her over, he found a red spot on her arm. Dr. Rand had infected her.

"Gemma? Gemma, can you hear me?"

"Rafe? The virus. Isolation." She was mumbling, but he could make out the words and the message was clear.

Flint burst into the clinic and Rafe called out to him for help.

"Dr. Rand injected Gemma with the Dead River virus. He fled on foot."

Flint would handle Dr. Rand. Rafe had one priority: to take care of Gemma and keep her alive until he could find a cure.

The FBI had arrested Travis Kayhill, former lead scientist of the Classified Virus Center at Dugway Proving Ground in Utah. The site of the army's test facility for chemical, biological, radiological, nuclear and explosives was the source of the virus.

The FBI had Kayhill in an interview room and they were allowing Rafe to question him over a video call.

"We haven't been able to convince him to reveal how he smuggled the virus out of the lab," the FBI agent said.

Rafe didn't care about the how and the why of what Kayhill had done. He needed Kayhill to help him with the cure.

"Tell me how to cure the people who have been infected," Rafe said.

Kayhill lifted his cuffed hands and scratched his head. "There isn't a cure. The virus is resistant to antivirals."

The scientist didn't seem interested in helping. It didn't bode well for them. "How do we stop the spread?" Rafe asked.

"It's not airborne. At least, it wasn't four months ago."

"What would have changed?" Rafe asked.

Kayhill glanced at his lawyer. They had struck a deal to lighten Kayhill's sentence for his cooperation in helping Rafe and divulging what he knew about the virus. "What made it of interest to the United States—"

"The United States is not claiming any responsibility for this virus. This is a rogue scientist." The representative from the military was in the room to ensure no secrets were leaked and likely to keep the government's distance from the Dead River virus outbreak.

Rafe didn't care about where responsibility lay. He needed answers.

Kayhill cleared his throat. "What made this of particular interest in general," he glanced at the uniformed military man, "is that the virus mutates quickly and stays alive for a long period on a host, draining them slowly enough to infect many others. Except when administered in high doses. High doses are lethal within hours, maybe days, depending on an individual's immune system response."

Rafe thought of Gemma laying in a coma in the virus wing. Her vitals were stable, but Rafe knew the virus was multiplying inside her, taking over her body. If he didn't find a cure, she would die.

"Tell me how to cure it," Rafe said again. "I have hundreds of people sick. I need to help them."

Kayhill sighed. "It's not simple to explain how to find a cure. The research was started, but we weren't able to develop a cure, which made it unusable as a weapon. Until the government, I mean, until I found a cure, I didn't want to release it into the world. It could create a worldwide epidemic."

"Why would you give it to Lucas Rand?" Rafe asked. The question wasn't relevant to what Rafe needed, but he couldn't understand this man's motivations.

"He was enthusiastic about my research. He paid well. I didn't think a cure was necessary in capable hands," Kayhill said.

"Did you know that Rand planned to use it to kill his wife?" the FBI agent asked.

After conferring with his lawyer, Kayhill responded. "No."

"Tell me everything you know about the cure. I need your research leading up to it. We don't have time to cover ground you've already explored," Rafe said.

"I don't have the research. You'll need to speak to the United States government about that."

The military man looked like his head was going to blow off. "We have researchers who are looking for antidotes to the illnesses that threaten the American people. We will check our databases and be in touch with any relevant information."

Rafe couldn't hide his frustration. Dr. Goodhue seemed perplexed. They would have to cut through red tape to make this work, but could they cut through it fast enough to save Gemma?

Flint stayed close to Nina as they combed the woods for Lucas Rand. Flint had organized search parties of volunteers with an officer in each party. From what Rafe had described, Rand was not armed with a gun, but he was unhinged and he could have acquired one.

Dead River was surrounded by woods and caves nestled against the Laramie Mountains. It meant many places to hide. In the dead of winter, it was also a barren, unforgiving place to try to survive.

Unless Dr. Rand had contingency plans and had supplies out here, he couldn't last long.

"If we spot him, I need you to stay back," Flint said to Nina.

Nina had experience with search and rescue, but

looking for Dr. Rand was dangerous. He had attacked Gemma, he had attacked Rafe and he would be desperate to escape. A life in prison would be terrifying for the doctor. Flint wouldn't let Lucas Rand hurt Nina.

Flint recalled Gemma's warning about Dr. Rand from earlier in the month in the café. She believed he had harmed patients. Knowing what he did about the last several months, he could picture Dr. Rand as the culprit for the events at the clinic: the alleged break-in of his office, the trashing of Rafe's office and the lab, the "attack" on himself, the assaults on Gemma, the stolen items in Danny's bedroom and the problems the clinic had experienced.

Had Dr. Rand done this because he had wanted to kill his wife? Cover-ups could be complicated and unexpected situations were what caused a criminal to go from free to locked away.

Flint hadn't been sure what to make of Amelia's mother, the woman Theo'd had a one-night stand with over a year ago, but Flint knew she'd deserved better than to die of a terrible virus at the hands of her deranged ex-husband.

Their flashlights did a poor job of cutting through the dark. The ground was heavy with snow. Nina was calling on her tracking abilities and every eye and ear was open looking for clues. Signs of human presence, like a dropped food wrapper, broken branches or footsteps in the snow could lead to a capture.

Dr. Rand running amok in the town with nothing to lose created a desperate situation. Would he return to the clinic to kill Gemma? Flint had left two officers at the clinic and had released a warning to the media about Dr. Rand, but was it enough?

They walked deeper in the wood. Nina hurried ahead and Flint tamped down the urge to reach for her hand and keep her close. She was working, and she was good at this. He balanced the pride he felt with the worry of her being injured.

"I think I have a trail," Nina said, stopping and shining her flashlight around in the dark, keeping it pointed on the ground.

Flint saw the depressed snow, indicating someone had hiked in this area. It could have been a resident on a walk, but this deep in the woods, Flint suspected it was Dr. Rand. Fresh snow had since fallen, making the track less visible. A less talented searcher may not have seen it. But Nina was good. Nina knew what she was doing.

The searchers stayed behind Nina and she led the way. She turned and motioned ahead of her, pressing a finger to her mouth for silence.

About thirty yards away was a small cave with a light shining from inside it. A lair like this would provide shelter from the wind and snow, and while it would be bitter cold, a fire would take the edge off the freezing conditions, maybe even bringing the temperature in the cave to a bearable level.

It was a smart place to stay, but not an especially good place to hide.

Flint turned off his flashlight and circled around, staying out of view of the mouth of the shelter.

He withdrew his gun. "This is the police. Come out with your hands on your head."

No response. Silence except for the snow falling and the fire crackling. "I am armed. If you do not come out now, I will shoot." He wouldn't venture into a cave until he knew who was inside, but it was a good threat and Flint was cold, tired and angry. He didn't have time for games.

"Wait! I'm not armed." A voice from inside. It didn't sound like Rand, but Flint couldn't be sure.

"Hands on your head and come out slowly," Flint shouted.

A man emerged from the cave and Flint surged forward immediately, taking his hands and securing them behind his back. When he turned the man to face the fire, he jolted at the sight of Jimmy Johnson.

"Jimmy," Flint said. His cousin Molly's former fiancé who had stolen their grandmother's ring and Molly's savings.

"Please don't kill me," Jimmy said. He was scared. Maybe it was the cold, but Jimmy was shaking too.

Nina came forward. "Jimmy Johnson, the entire town has been looking for you."

He lowered his head. "I tried to escape."

"With Molly's ring and her money?" Flint asked. He had a job to do as the police chief and he couldn't punch Jimmy, but he wanted to. The man had hurt Molly deeply and was in need of a thumping.

"I want to talk to her. It's been a misunderstanding," Jimmy said.

Flint shook his head. No misunderstanding. If Jimmy thought he could charm Molly into not pressing charges, he had a surprise coming. His cousin was stronger than Jimmy gave her credit for.

"You're lucky that I'm the man who found you," Flint said. "There have been some dangerous, desperate people trapped in Dead River."

Flint alerted the other search parties they'd found

Jimmy. They started walking back to their car, Jimmy in handcuffs.

"I heard that Hank Bittard was out here," Jimmy said.

"Hank is dead. But another killer went missing tonight."

When they arrived at his police car, Flint patted Jimmy down and emptied his pockets. Inside he found Gram Dottie's wedding ring and wads of cash, likely belonging to Molly.

"Not a smart place to hide this," Flint said.

"I had to take it. Molly will understand," Jimmy said.

"What will she understand?" Flint asked, feeling his irritation tick higher.

"I was in trouble. I had debts that had to be paid. I took this to protect her. I didn't want anyone coming after her."

Nina sighed and touched his shoulder, a reminder to Flint to keep his temper. "Once a liar, always a liar."

"I do have debts. I have to pay them," Jimmy said.

"I don't doubt that you have debts. But I don't think you did any of this to help Molly. Do you know how much you hurt her? Do you realize what problems you've caused our family?" Flint asked.

He shoved the younger man into the back of the squad car. He'd call Molly and let her know her items had been found. He slammed closed the door, locking Jimmy inside.

Nina slipped her arms around Flint's waist. "Are we going back out tonight to look for Rand?"

Flint shook his head. "I haven't heard from the other

parties that they had any leads. It's cold and dark. We'll start again in the morning."

"Sounds good to me. I want you home and in bed," Nina said. "You've been working too hard."

Bed with Nina sounded great to him.

Molly's phone rang in the middle of the night. Gemma. Her Gram. Flint and Nina. Theo and Ellie. Ever since her parents had died, phone calls were subject to question if they would bring good or bad news.

"Hello? What's wrong?" Molly asked.

"I have good news." Flint's voice.

"Good news? What time is it?"

"Three a.m. I wanted to be the one to tell you first. We found Jimmy Johnson."

Molly's heart caught in her throat. "Thank God." Aside from meeting Matt, it was the highlight of the month.

"He had Gram Dottie's ring and your money on him."

That news was even better. Guilt over having lost the ring disappeared. "How? I mean, how did you find him?"

"We were searching for someone and Nina tracked him. According to Jimmy, he's been living in the woods, stealing food from people, sleeping in sheds and unlocked cars for months."

"Wow." She couldn't muster much sympathy for him. After what he had done, it seemed like a fitting punishment. "Who were you looking for in the woods?" Molly asked.

"We've had another incident at the clinic. Gemma was hurt and Dr. Rand is responsible."

"Dr. Rand?" The doctor at the clinic? Mimi's ex-husband?

"From what we can piece together about the events over the last several months, Dr. Rand is a dangerous and desperate man. Watch out for him, Molly."

"Thanks for calling, Flint. I will be careful."

But to be sure, before she went back to sleep, she checked that her doors and windows were locked.

Rounds in the virus wing were utterly depressing. Gemma was still in a coma and Rafe was having trouble thinking objectively about Gemma's care. He wanted to bring her home to his place and then stay and watch over her until a cure was found. The only good news was that the virus wasn't progressing as fast as they believed Mimi's had.

Dr. Goodhue was working with the trickle of information she was receiving from the government.

The vitals on every patient in the virus wing were worse by the day, a steady downward trend. More residents would die. It seemed inevitable.

Gram Dottie was writing in a notebook when Rafe entered her room. She was aware that Gemma was sick and she had taken the news hard.

"I've been praying for my granddaughter. If a life must be taken, it should be mine, not hers."

"I would like if no lives were lost," Rafe said.

Gram Dottie smiled. "I've been praying that you'll find a cure. I'm not getting better. I know I need to make my peace with my time on earth."

Rafe couldn't stand to hear Gram Dottie speaking this way. He'd been trained to do everything he could to help his patients. Knowing he couldn't heal them was hard to accept and knowing that Gemma was counting on him was driving him insane.

"I should have told Gemma how I felt about her when I had the chance," Rafe said, realizing that it was love he felt for Gemma. When he stopped thinking of her like a holdover on his way to New York, he saw her for who she was: the woman he'd fallen in love with.

"You should tell her now," Gram Dottie said.

"She can't hear me."

"Do you know that for sure?" Gram Dottie asked.

As a scientist, he didn't know what he believed. Could he communicate with Gemma on some level? Could she hear him while she was in a coma? "It's worth a try. It can't hurt."

He finished with Gram Dottie and moved to Gemma's room.

She looked small and fragile beneath the blankets. He checked her vitals and then made sure she was comfortable. He sat on the edge of her bed and took her hands in his.

"Gemma, if you can hear me, I want you to wake up. I have so many things I want to say to you. So many times during our relationship that I could have told you how I felt, but I was too afraid of what it would mean for my career.

"I will find a cure. I will find a way for you to get better. I will save your grandmother and Jessica and Annabelle and every person in this town."

Rafe hated to make promises to her that he couldn't keep, but her life hinged on him keeping this one.

Chapter 13

Christmas Eve in Dead River was quiet and sadness hung heavily over the town. No one was on the street taking care of last-minute shopping. Snow fell from the sky and blanketed the streets. The town didn't have fuel to run snow plows or salt trucks, making the roads impassable.

The last count of the sick was over four hundred people. Four hundred people awaiting a cure.

Dr. Goodhue was sleeping in the doctor-and-nurse lounge. She had been awake for far too long and needed to rest. Perhaps sleep would help her find inspiration.

Rafe had the notes the government had provided. They were frustratingly bare. Buried in the document, one piece of information had been useful to them. Dr. Kayhill had noted that he'd had some success growing an antidote and he'd explained how he'd done it.

The antidote they'd created seemed to destroy the virus and Rafe was initially hopeful. Unfortunately, in the end, the antidote was beaten by the virus every time.

He'd had a burst of inspiration and had invited Theo, Ellie and Amelia to the clinic earlier that day. Theo and Amelia had been exposed to the virus, but they weren't sick. He'd taken some of Theo's blood and was looking for a natural antidote.

Rafe slipped the petri dish he was working with under his microscope. The virus mocked him. Using a syringe, he dropped potential antidote number eighty-nine into the dish. It had a small amount of Theo's blood in it.

Rafe watched in rapt attention as the antidote killed the virus. He had seen this pattern before. He waited for the virus to dwindle and then ultimately survive.

Within minutes, the entire dish had dead virus cells.

Dead virus cells could be used to make a vaccine, but in the more near term, his antidote had worked in this lab test.

He wouldn't get too excited and ring the bell of success. He needed to replicate his result several more times. And his antidote hadn't been tested on humans. It could have unintended side effects or it could be rendered entirely useless inside the human body.

Working to keep his calm, Rafe replicated his results. He needed Dr. Goodhue. She needed to see his tests.

Rafe exited the lab and froze when he saw the two policemen who'd been guarding the entrance to the clinic on the floor. Rafe rushed to them and felt for a pulse.

The men were dead.

Fear coursed over him. Dr. Rand was here. It had to be him, returning to finish whatever deranged plan he had hatched.

"Rand? If you're here, talk to me. Don't be a coward."

Dr. Rand stepped out of the patient triage area. He

was holding a gun and pressing a wad of gauze over his shoulder. The gauze was red with blood. Had the police officers shot Rand? Inside the lab in his suit, Rafe wouldn't have heard the gunfire.

"Are you happy, Rafe?" Dr. Rand asked. His voice shook with anger.

Rafe said nothing. "People I care about are sick. I am not happy about that."

Dr. Rand shook his head. "People can't be trusted. People will turn their backs on you the moment you need them."

"Is that how you felt about Mimi?" Rafe asked.

Dr. Rand twitched. His blinking was too fast and a nervous energy was taking over his body. "She was pregnant with another man's baby less than a year after our divorce. How do you think I felt about that?"

Rafe couldn't have guessed. She was Rand's ex-wife and Rafe knew nothing of their relationship. Rand should have moved on with his life. "I'm sorry about what happened with Mimi."

Dr. Rand winced and Rafe noted the rag he held to his shoulder was dripping blood. If it was a gun-shot wound, Dr. Rand would bleed out if he didn't get help. If Rafe could assist him, he could also move close enough to take the gun from him.

"Let me look at your shoulder. You know what can happen to an untreated GSW," Rafe said.

"I'm a doctor! Of course I know. I can fix this my-self."

Was he talking about his injury or the situation? "How are you planning to do that?"

Rafe needed a phone. He could reach Flint to call for help. "I'll clear out this clinic. I'll kill everyone in here. If I kill everyone with the virus, it can't spread any further."

Rand was feeling guilty and trying to clean up his mess. Granted, his plan was ridiculous and Rand had to know it. He couldn't kill four hundred people. "You don't need to kill anyone. We'll find a cure." Perhaps they already had, but Rafe wasn't telling Rand that. The man was unstable and Rafe didn't trust how he would respond.

Gemma was in the virus wing. Rafe had to protect her and his patients.

Dr. Rand lifted his gun. "I killed those cops in self-defense. I can kill you."

Rafe wouldn't give him the chance. He lunged at Dr. Rand and knocked him to the ground. He pressed his hand over Dr. Rand's shoulder and the man let out a cry of pain. Rafe twisted the gun from his hand.

He stood, holding the gun on Dr. Rand. "You made a mistake coming here. You should have run and not looked back."

"There is no escape from this town or from what I did," Dr. Rand said.

Rafe understood feeling as if there was no escape. He understood making a mistake that couldn't be undone. But now, Rafe had to make it right. He had never been more clear on what—and who—he wanted.

Rafe, Dr. Goodhue and Dr. Moore worked to make as much of the antidote as possible. They had to experiment carefully with the doses, but they saw almost immediate results with their patients.

As the antidote battled the virus, patients reported feeling better.

All patients except Gemma. She was still unconscious despite having been given the antidote hours before.

Rafe entered the virus wing for the first time without his suit. Family members and friends had joined their once-isolated loved ones in the virus wing.

Rafe saw Annabelle between her two parents, hugging them and laughing, each wearing a red Santa hat.

Tammy Flynn was opening a present her parents had brought for her.

Carter Saunders had left that morning with his wife, eager to be home with his family for Christmas.

Gemma's room was silent. Her brothers were at her bedside.

Rafe joined them. "Any change?" he asked, looking at the monitors.

Her brothers shook their heads.

Rafe moved close to her. "Please wake up. I love you, Gemma." He had spoken the same words to her ten times a day since she had fallen ill.

Theo and Flint seemed surprised by his words, but they said nothing as Rafe joined their vigil.

A slight movement from the bed. Just her leg, then her fingers and then Gemma opened her eyes.

"Water," she said, looking at her brothers and Rafe in confusion.

Rafe rushed to bring her a drink. Once she had taken a long drink she held her arms out to Rafe. He was happy to step into them.

"Tell me what happened and why you aren't wearing suits in here," Gemma said.

Rafe went for the simplest explanation. "Dr. Rand injected you with the Dead River virus."

Gemma touched her head. "Except for a vicious headache, I don't feel sick."

"I found an antidote."

Gemma's eyes widened. "You did? I knew you would!"

Her faith in him was unshakable. He loved that.

Flint cleared his throat. "Dr. Rand is in custody. I also arrested Felicia Martin as his accomplice. He admitted she had helped him try to cover up what he did to Mimi. This morning, I drove Danny out to be with Matt for Christmas. I hope that's okay with you."

Rafe nodded. "Of course it is."

"Molly went along for the ride," Flint said. "She and Matt seem to have a good thing going."

Gemma smiled. "I'm happy for her."

"Dr. Goodhue is submitting our test results and our patient information to the CDC. The quarantine should be lifted in a day or two, maybe three," Rafe said.

Gemma looked at Rafe, sadness in her eyes. "Can I have a moment alone with Rafe?" she asked.

"It's good to have you back," Theo said.

"Don't scare us like this again," Flint said.

Her brothers kissed her cheek before they left the room.

"You and I only have a couple more days together," Gemma said.

"I was thinking I would stay through the new year," Rafe said.

"Another week," Gemma said.

"Maybe for another year, at least," Rafe said.

Gemma inclined her head. "Another year? What are you talking about? What happened with your job?"

His job in New York was secondary to being with

Gemma. A job wouldn't make him happy, not the way Gemma could and did every day they were together. "I don't want to be without you. If that means living in Dead River, then great. If you're willing to move with me to New York, then I'm happy about that too."

"You would stay in Dead River for me?" she asked.

"I would go anywhere and do anything for you. When you were sick, I realized what should have been obvious. I'm in love with you. I love you. I need you in my life."

Gemma's eyes filled with tears and she covered her mouth. "You do? Because you know I love you too."

"I do now." Rafe pulled Gemma into his arms and held her. Dead River wasn't the purgatory he'd thought it to be, and with Gemma in his life, it was a little like heaven.

Epilogue

"A toast to the man of the hour," Nina said, lifting her champagne glass. "To Dr. Rafe Granger."

Everyone at the table lifted their glasses to him. Rafe didn't deserve their praise. He took Gemma's hand in his. "It was a team effort."

Molly, Danny and Matt were seated at the end of the table together. Theo and Ellie had baby Amelia in a high chair between them. She was banging her spoon against her tray and smiling a drooly, baby smile. Jessica and Tom were doting on Annabelle, who was wearing her princess Halloween costume.

Dr. Goodhue was working at the clinic, directing the researchers who had flown in to assist her. While the CDC weren't allowing anyone to leave the town yet, help had arrived to expedite the process and ensure every resident had been treated. Each patient who had been given the antidote was reporting it was a miracle cure.

Anand was seated at the table with Cathleen. She was holding up her wrist and showing off the bracelet Anand had given her for Christmas. Nina spoke to Cathleen and she laughed and turned to Anand. She kissed him and when they drew apart, their eyes lingered on each other for a long, heated moment. Rafe hadn't been aware they were dating, but apparently the clinic had more than one romance brewing.

Gram Dottie was seated at the head of the table. She was content watching her family as they gathered for a Christmas meal. She had recovered well, the color back in her cheeks and a sparkle in her eyes.

"I got a call from a doctor I know at Cheyenne Memorial," Gemma said. "Gabriella is in labor now. They think she and the baby will be fine. Trevor's a bit of a wreck, but only because he loves her so much."

With Lucas Rand in jail, Rafe had taken over as medical director of the Dead River clinic. Though the hospital in New York was disappointed he wasn't joining them, they had dozens of résumés from ER doctors vying for his vacated position. Rafe was satisfied in a way he hadn't been before. He looked at Gemma's smiling face and listened to the laughter surrounding him. He'd found the happiness he was looking for in the last place he'd have expected.

* * * * *

THE COLTONS: RETURN TO WYOMING
Don't miss a single story!

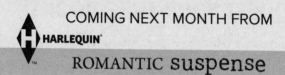

REQUEST YOUR FREE BOOKS!
2 FREE NOVELS PLUS 2 FREE GIFTS!

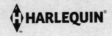

ROMANTIC suspense

Sparked by danger, fueled by passion

YES! Please send me 2 FREE Harlequin® Romantic Suspense novels and my 2 FREE gifts (gifts are worth about $10). After receiving them, if I don't wish to receive any more books, I can return the shipping statement marked "cancel." If I don't cancel, I will receive 4 brand-new novels every month and be billed just $4.74 per book in the U.S. or $5.24 per book in Canada. That's a savings of at least 14% off the cover price! It's quite a bargain! Shipping and handling is just 50¢ per book in the U.S. and 75¢ per book in Canada.* I understand that accepting the 2 free books and gifts places me under no obligation to buy anything. I can always return a shipment and cancel at any time. Even if I never buy another book, the two free books and gifts are mine to keep forever.

240/340 HDN F45N

Name _____ (PLEASE PRINT)

Address _____ Apt. #

City _____ State/Prov. _____ Zip/Postal Code

Signature (if under 18, a parent or guardian must sign)

Mail to the **Harlequin® Reader Service:**
IN U.S.A.: P.O. Box 1867, Buffalo, NY 14240-1867
IN CANADA: P.O. Box 609, Fort Erie, Ontario L2A 5X3

Want to try two free books from another line?
Call 1-800-873-8635 or visit www.ReaderService.com.

* Terms and prices subject to change without notice. Prices do not include applicable taxes. Sales tax applicable in N.Y. Canadian residents will be charged applicable taxes. Offer not valid in Quebec. This offer is limited to one order per household. Not valid for current subscribers to Harlequin Romantic Suspense books. All orders subject to credit approval. Credit or debit balances in a customer's account(s) may be offset by any other outstanding balance owed by or to the customer. Please allow 4 to 6 weeks for delivery. Offer available while quantities last.

Your Privacy—The Harlequin® Reader Service is committed to protecting your privacy. Our Privacy Policy is available online at www.ReaderService.com or upon request from the Harlequin Reader Service.

We make a portion of our mailing list available to reputable third parties that offer products we believe may interest you. If you prefer that we not exchange your name with third parties, or if you wish to clarify or modify your communication preferences, please visit us at www.ReaderService.com/consumerschoice or write to us at Harlequin Reader Service Preference Service, P.O. Box 9062, Buffalo, NY 14269. Include your complete name and address.

HRS13R

Calvin Sweet knew he was taking some big chances, but
taking risks always invigorated him. Coming back to his
home in Conard County was the first of the new risks. Five
years ago he'd left for the big city because the law was closing in on him.

Returning to the site where he had hung his trophies was
a huge risk, too, although he could claim he was out for a
hike in the spring mountains. There was nothing left, anyway. The law had taken it all, and the sight filled him with
both sorrow and bitterness. Anger, too. They had no right
to take away his hard work, his triumphs, his mementos.

But they had. After five years all that was left were some
remnants of cargo netting rotting in the tree limbs and the
remains of a few sawed-off nooses.

He could close his eyes and remember, and remembering
filled him with joy and a sense of his own huge power, the
power of life and death. The power to take it all away. The
power to enlighten those whose existence was so shallow.

They took it for granted. Calvin never did.

From earliest childhood he had been fascinated by spiders and their webs. He had spent hours watching as insect after insect fell victim to those silken strands, struggling mightily until they were stung and then wrapped up helplessly to await their fate. Each corpse on the web had been a trophy marking the spider's victory. No one ever escaped.

No one had escaped him, either.

He was chosen, just like a spider, to be exactly what he was.

Chosen. He liked that word. It fit both him and his victims. They were all chosen to perform the dance of death together, to plumb the reaches of human endurance. To sacrifice the ordinary for the extraordinary. So he quashed his growing need to act and focused his attention on another part of his life. He had a job now, one he needed to report to every evening. He was whistling now as he walked back down to his small ranch.

A spiderweb was beginning to take shape in his mind, one for his barn loft that no one would see, ever. It was enough that he could admire it and savor the gifts there. The impulse to hunt eased, and soon he was in control again. He liked control. He liked controlling himself and others, even as he fulfilled his purpose.

Like the spider, he was not hasty to act. It would have to be the right person at the right time, and the time was not yet right. First he had to build his web.

Don't miss UNDERCOVER HUNTER by *New York Times* bestselling author Rachel Lee, available January 2015 wherever Harlequin® Romantic Suspense books and ebooks are sold.

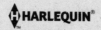

ROMANTIC suspense

Heart-racing romance, high-stakes suspense!

HIGH-STAKES PLAYBOY
by *New York Times* bestselling author
Cindy Dees

Available January 2015

Who will get this Prescott bachelor first— the girl or the killer?

To help his brothers, marine pilot Archer Prescott goes undercover to find out who's sabotaging their movie set. But the die-hard bachelor isn't ready for what he finds in the High Sierras: his doe-eyed girl-next-door camerawoman is the prime suspect.

Marley Stringer isn't as innocent as she seems. As Marley turns irresistible and the aerial "accidents" turn deadly, Archer begins to wonder who's more dangerous—the perfect woman who threatens his heart...or the desperate killer who threatens his life.

Don't miss the first exciting installment from Cindy Dees's *The Prescott Bachelors* series:

HIGH-STAKES BACHELOR

Available wherever Harlequin® Romantic Suspense books and ebooks are sold.

HRS27903